ALSO BY KARELIA STETZ-WATERS

Something True
For Good
Worth the Wait

Satisfaction Guaranteed

KARELIA STETZ-WATERS

FOREVER

New York   Boston

Forever
Hachette Book Group
1290 Avenue of the Americas, New York, NY 10104
read-forever.com
twitter.com/readforeverpub

First Edition: June 2021

Forever is an imprint of Grand Central Publishing. The Forever name and logo are trademarks of Hachette Book Group, Inc.

The publisher is not responsible for websites (or their content) that are not owned by the publisher.

The Hachette Speakers Bureau provides a wide range of authors for speaking events. To find out more, go to www.hachettespeakersbureau.com or call (866) 376-6591.

Print book interior design by Abby Reilly

Library of Congress Cataloging-in-Publication Data

Names: Stetz-Waters, Karelia, author.
Title: Satisfaction guaranteed / Karelia Stetz-Waters.
Description: First edition. | New York : Forever, [2021]
Identifiers: LCCN 2020053573 | ISBN 9781538735527 (trade paperback) |
    ISBN 9781538735503 (ebook)
Subjects: GSAFD: Love stories.
Classification: LCC PS3619.T47875 S28 2021 | DDC 813/.6—dc23
LC record available at https://lccn.loc.gov/2020053573

ISBNs: 978-1-5387-3552-7 (trade paperback), 978-1-5387-3550-3 (ebook)

Printed in the United States of America

LSC-C

Printing 1, 2021

For my wife, Fay.
You are my happily-ever-after.

acknowledgments

At this point in a career, there are more people to thank than could ever fit on an acknowledgments page. What a blessing to have been supported, educated, inspired, and entertained by so many wonderful people. But let me see if I can list just a few.

First, thank you to my readers. Thank you to those folks I will never meet and thank you to everyone who has joined my newsletter, hung out on social media, chatted at conferences, and written to me with your thoughts and comments. You are the reason I write, which means you have given me one of the great joys of my life. Thank you.

Thank you to my friends and colleagues at Linn-Benton Community College, especially Scott, Liz, and everyone in the English department. You have made my work life more joyful than anyone can reasonably expect.

Thank you to my writing partners, Alison Clement and Susan Rodgers, for your insights and support and for never being annoyed when I changed my main characters' names. And thanks to Bill at Interzone, the coolest coffee shop ever. May the shop serve coffee for decades to come.

Thank you to my editor, Madeleine Colavita. This book

would have been a train wreck without you. And thank you to everyone at Forever. Thank you also to my agent, Jane Dystel, who has been with me throughout my publishing career, and to everyone at Dystel, Goderich & Bourret.

Thank you to the folks at the sex toy stores She Bop and As You Like It. (Don't forget, folks: these fabulous stores ship!) Thank you to Jessie Fresh for talking to me about pleasure education and for giving the Mind Melting Erotic Spanking class that inspired my story at the Mystery Box Show. Thank you to Reba Sparrow and Eric Scheur of the Mystery Box Show for creating a place for sexual truth-telling. (Watch the Mystery Box Show at www.mysteryboxshow.com.) Thank you to my hairdresser at Dial H for Hair, Irene Gutierrez, for listening to me talk about my work and for always having insights and interesting videos. Also great haircuts. Thank you for the great haircuts.

Thank you to my students, especially my creative writing students in the Golden Crown Literary Society Writing Academy, for reminding me what a privilege it is to be a writer and how important it is to support each other.

Thank you to the queer community. I love your strength, your perseverance, your openheartedness, the way you approach challenge with joy.

And the biggest thank-yous of all…

Thank you to my parents for instilling in me the love of reading, for supporting my dreams, for modeling a loving marriage, and for so, so much more.

And thank you to my wife, Fay. Every day with you is proof that happily ever after really does exist and it is as glorious as all the romance novels promise.

chapter 1

Cade Elgin sat in the first pew at Whole Heart Departures Funeral Home feeling out of place because she was the only person in the room *not* wearing gold lamé. She wore a dark suit. Dry clean only. Expensive. Boring—at least to this crowd. Her father sat beside her in a gold-lined tweed coat and a gold bow tie. Her mother wore a gold dress. Around them, the crowd of friends and relatives passed flasks of whiskey. Cade recognized a few cousins. Before them, on a low dais, Aunt Ruth's urn sat on a pedestal surrounded by white lilies. Cade had ordered lilies because lilies were appropriate. She'd googled it.

A man in a gold bowler hat came by and shook her parents' hands. "Roger. Pepper. Such an honor to meet you."

Her parents greeted him like an old friend, which he would be by the end of the Elgins' stay. Her parents always made friends. A woman in the row behind them tapped Cade's mother on the shoulder and offered her a joint. Pepper accepted with a bow.

"Did you grow this yourself?" she asked as she exhaled.

The woman had.

Cade stared at the urn. She should have visited Ruth. She should have gotten over her I-don't-want-to-go-to-a-nude-beach-and-smoke-pot-with-you thing and just been a good niece and visited. How hard would that have been?

Okay, kind of hard.

The chapel organ rumbled to life. Cade recognized the melody: The Cure's "Lovesong." It was followed by Van Morrison's "Into the Mystic" and then Bruno Mars's "Uptown Funk," which did not want to be played on an electric organ. How many pop songs did the organist know? She waited.

"Be careful," Cade's mother whispered as a jar passed down their pew. "The edibles are powerful."

"I am not going to get high at my aunt's funeral," Cade said.

"Well if you do, start with one." Her mother shook a few jellies out of the jar.

"Thank you for the motherly advice," Cade said.

Her mother patted her on the knee. "It's okay to have a little fun, sweetie."

But not at my aunt's funeral.

Thankfully, "Uptown Funk" was the last song. The chaplain at Whole Heart Departures welcomed the guests. He'd known Ruth. She was the embodiment of love. After that, a woman lit incense and offered a call-and-response incantation to the Spirit of the Universe. Two drag queens wrapped a feather boa around the urn. Then there was a lull, as though something was supposed to happen and hadn't. The crowd murmured. On the other side of the aisle from Cade, a woman with short blue hair and a gold tailcoat nudged the friend sitting next to her.

"Selena, it's you now," Tailcoat said.

The friend clutched a sheet of paper.

Cade heard her whisper, "I can't."

"You can," her friend said. "This is for Ruth."

"I'll fuck it up."

"You won't."

"Come on." Tailcoat stood up and held her hand out to her friend. To the crowd, she said, "This is Selena Mathis, and she'd like to say a few words about Ruth, but she's nervous."

The crowd encouraged her.

"Speak from the heart, Selena."

"We love you, Selena."

Tailcoat led her friend to the dais and left her there. The woman, Selena, looked out at the crowd. She was gorgeous. Huge, dark eyes. Curly black hair was piled on top of her head and secured with jeweled pins. She had great curves too, the kind of curves a person shouldn't bring to a funeral, not in skintight pleather pants.

Everything about her outfit said, *Look at me.*

Everything else about her posture said, *I'm going to pass out.*

"There are no mistakes when you speak from the heart," someone called out.

"I remember," Selena began, her voice trembling, "when Ruth told me she'd named her clitoris Belinda."

There were eulogy mistakes. This was one of them.

"To Belinda!" someone said.

"I remember when Ruth decided to turn her backyard

into a bird habitat," Selena went on. "All those finches." Her hands were shaking. "Ruth was so many things." She looked at her notes. "She was a gardener, a mentor, a businesswoman. She taught people that nudism isn't about sex. It's about accepting the sunlight. And she was like a mother to me." Selena wiped her eyes, making smeared mascara look stylish.

It seemed like a good place to end the speech. Selena clearly wanted to be anywhere else, but she went on.

And on.

And on.

Ruth's theories on pruning wisteria. Teacups. Tampons versus the cup. Cade felt like Selena kept looking at her with a *help me* expression. Cade's mother believed in telepathy. Maybe it could work. *Stop now*, Cade willed. *Amen. You're done.* But the woman had started a eulogy with the deceased's clitoris, and telepathy didn't save her.

Finally, Tailcoat rose, stopped Selena midsentence, gave her friend a hug, and said, "Let's go get drunk."

The organist hit the first notes of "Total Eclipse of the Heart."

Cade's parents took their place at the front of the greeting line. Cade walked over to the urn. She wished there'd been a bit of solemnity, a moment of silence to gather her feelings. She looked at the urn wrapped in feathers. So small.

I know you're dead now.

That was a little obvious.

I'm sorry I wasn't the best niece.

A man sidled up to her.

"You're Roger Elgin's daughter," he whispered. "I know

this isn't the time, but I admire your father's gallery so much…If you're in Portland, I'd love to show you some paintings I've—"

"I'm at my aunt's funeral," Cade said.

Yes, she worked 24/7, but come on. Networking in front of the urn? Cade turned away.

I'm sorry, Ruth. I couldn't leave the gallery. If I took a vacation…my parents…they'd turn it into a commune. I know. You think that'd be cool. I should have come for a weekend.

A woman in a gold cape approached her.

"Ms. Elgin," she said in a way that would certainly lead to *I'd like to show you my granddaughter's work.*

"I'm praying," Cade said.

Not quite true but whatever.

I wish you hadn't had cancer. I know you would have liked to be struck by lightning or exploded in a volcano. Go out big. Like an Elgin.

She felt yet another person at her elbow and turned with a sigh. It was Selena, now wearing a purple fake-fur coat, still clutching the piece of paper that was too small to contain her epically inappropriate eulogy. Before Cade could say, *What do you want?* Selena said, "Do you mind if I stand over there?" She pointed to a place about ten feet away. "I want to talk to her, but I don't want to bother you."

That was sweet.

"You can stand here." Cade indicated a place beside her. Prime urn-talking real estate.

"You sure?"

Selena stepped forward, pressing the piece of paper between her hands and raising them to her chest in prayer.

"Even though I walk through the valley of the shadow of death"—Selena's voice was almost inaudible—"I will fear no evil, for you are with me; your rod and your staff, they comfort me."

She'd memorized more Bible than Cade had ever read. Surprising coming from a woman showing that much cleavage at a funeral. And where was this solemnity when Selena had been eulogizing? It was touching, though, that a woman wearing tight pleather knew that much scripture. People probably never guessed that about her.

Selena finished with the Lord's Prayer.

"Thank you," Cade said. "That was lovely."

Selena smiled at her shyly. "It's from the heart."

Then Selena walked up to the urn, tested the lid like she was trying to open a jar, wrapped her arms around it, and took it off the pedestal.

No. No. No. The urn stays there.

"When you're done…" Selena said, her voice full of prayerful reverence, "my friend Becket made pot brownies. We'd love it if you'd sit at our table and have one. We have absinthe too, but not the kind that makes you hallucinate. Sorry."

And that was an Elgin funeral.

chapter 2

Selena cradled Ruth's urn in her arms as she headed to Becket's table. She was glad nothing inside rattled. Rattling would be creepy. Nothing about this moment should be creepy. Ruth had wanted a joyful celebration of her life. No one should be thinking about bits of femur.

Selena's friends sat at a table beside a mossy shrine: her best friend Becket, Beautiful Adrien (who'd earned that nickname by looking like a cross between a runway model and Jesus), and Zenobious, distiller of the absinthe. Everyone was dressed in the finest outfits Becket's burlesque troupe, Fierce Lovely, could supply. Selena took her seat and set Ruth in the center of the table.

They all turned to her. Everyone liked Ruth, but Ruth was Selena's person.

"How you doing?" Becket put a hand on Selena's shoulder.

Heartbroken. Lost. Hopeless.

Ruth's last request had been that no one cry at the

funeral. *Don't act like this is the end.* It felt like the end. And Selena felt like she was going to fly into a million pieces. Burst into tears. Fuck a stranger against the wall of the nearest alley—provided they discussed consent and proper protection; Selena was still a sex educator, even if her life was a mess. She took another deep breath.

"Why did you let me give that speech?" Selena asked. It was easier to think about the speech than the fact that Ruth would never sunbathe in the backyard or snip another bouquet of wisteria.

"You went off on that eulogy." Becket looked like a sprite with her gold tailcoat and shock of blue hair. "You kicked that eulogy's ass."

"Dude, yeah," Zenobious said, his man-bun bouncing adamantly. "You were like, *Fuck you, high school speech class. I can talk for as long as I want!*"

"I don't even remember what I said."

"You said a lot," Becket said.

"And every word of it was gorgeous," Beautiful Adrien added.

"I remember when we picked names. She picked Belinda. I picked Artemisia. Was it okay to talk about Ruth's clit?"

She and Ruth had talked about everything, but maybe there was a time and place…

"Your speech was fuckin' beautiful," Becket said. "Ruth deserved more than some dearly-beloved-she-was-a-good-person bullshit. You felt like you needed to talk about her clit, and you talked about her clit."

"You don't think it was too much?"

Her friends looked at one another. It was too much.

"What am I going to do?" Selena said.

Someone had sprinkled foil hearts on the table. They stuck to everyone. Becket picked one off Selena's arm.

"God, there are so many casseroles at the house," Selena added. "I don't know what to do with them. It was so nice of everyone. Someone brought poke, but you don't want raw fish when someone's dying."

Her friends nodded sympathetically.

"I'll help you clean Ruth's house," Becket said.

They were quiet for a minute.

"I asked Cadence Elgin to sit with us." Selena scanned the room.

She hoped Cadence would come over. There was something comforting about Cadence's seriousness. Ruth had wanted gold, so they wore gold. But back in Selena's hometown everyone worn black to funerals, and it meant *this is serious and we care.*

"When were you talking to Cadence Elgin?" Becket took a sip from her Solo cup and passed it to Selena.

Zenobious's absinthe was terrible, but they all supported his dream.

"At the altar."

"Are you going to talk to her about your paintings?" Becket asked.

"When we were at McLaughlin, we would have killed to meet Roger Elgin," Beautiful Adrien added. "I still would, but I'm not going to push my portfolio at him at his sister's funeral, but I'd push yours."

"Me too," Becket said.

"I don't have a portfolio," Selena said.

"You could show him *Geoffrey in Cobalt Teal*," Becket said.

"If I showed Roger Elgin one painting, he'd say, *Where's the rest of the collection?*"

"You could show him the portrait of Ruth," Beautiful Adrien suggested.

Geoffrey in Cobalt Teal and *Can I Make You Laugh?* were the two paintings Selena hadn't burned, *Geoffrey in Cobalt Teal* because Becket had stolen it and *Can I Make You Laugh?* because Selena couldn't bear to let it go.

"That's two," Selena said.

"With you," Becket said, "two is enough."

The other friends nodded.

Selena shook her head. She could still smell the oil paints in the studio at McLaughlin Academy of Art. She remembered every person she'd painted. But painting— and her ex, Professor Alex Sarta—had nearly ruined her life. *Talent is worthless without discipline,* Alex used to say. Even if Roger Elgin liked Selena's work, he would ask for more; then she'd sit in front of a blank canvas for hours or, more likely, go to a bar and get drunk, because she couldn't paint under pressure...or when she was sad...or stressed...or in love...or not in love.

Her hand curled as if holding a brush. She shook it out. Ghosts and dreams. That was all painting was to her now.

"You were so good," Becket said.

Her friends were sweet. They were still convinced she could be a great painter. Optimists. It was annoying, and she loved them for it.

"Please don't talk to Cadence Elgin about me and art," Selena said. "I don't paint. And it's a funeral."

"Can I show her a picture on my phone?" Becket asked.

"I do not consent," Selena said.

"What's consent?" Becket drawled. "No one needed consent in the nineties."

"Becket!" Zenobious and Beautiful Adrien chided in unison.

Becket rolled her eyes. Of course, she understood consent.

"If you don't want us to talk about it, we won't." Becket put a hand over Selena's and squeezed gently. "I'm serious. But I still think you should."

"There she is," Beautiful Adrien said.

Selena turned around. Cadence was approaching their table looking like business school meets Megan Rapinoe in her suit with her blond hair swept off her face.

"May I?" Cadence touched the back of an empty chair.

"Of course." Beautiful Adrien nudged the chair out for her.

"Absinthe?" Zenobious offered her a Solo cup and an unmarked bottle. "Pot brownie?"

"I'm fine." Cadence glanced at the buffet. One end held a proliferation of bottles, the other a pony keg. "I wouldn't want you to run out." She held her hand out to Zenobious. "I'm Cade," she added.

Cade shook Selena's hand last. Her skin was warm and her grip firm.

"Cade Elgin. We know who you are," Becket said.

Selena shot her a look.

Don't.

"The Elgin daughter," Cade said with a half smile.

"We promise not to show you our amazing art," Beautiful Adrien said. "I bet you get that all the time."

"I do." Cade gave a self-deprecating shrug. "I get it. It's their ten seconds in the elevator with someone famous."

Zenobious poured Cade a Solo cup of absinthe.

"How about a toast to Ruth," he said.

"She was like a mother to me." Selena held up her cup and held back her tears.

"When she tried out for Fierce Lovely," Becket added, "I was like, *Damn. That's who I want to be when I grow up.*"

"To old ladies stripping." Beautiful Adrien picked up a cup.

They told more stories about Ruth. Cade nodded along.

"Do you have any memories of Ruth?" Selena asked Cade.

Cade looked surprised, like she hadn't expected anyone to care.

"When I was a kid, we used to visit her in the summer. I played in her backyard. She and my parents got massively high. She did have really nice wisteria." Cade didn't smile, but she looked at Selena, and her light blue eyes held something tender.

"Thanks," Selena said.

"Selena thinks she shouldn't have talked about Ruth's clit in her speech," Zenobious said.

"Unconventional. But…" Cade spread her hands in front of her. "But."

Apparently, that was all she had to say about it.

"I should go," Cade added. "I've got to settle things up with the mortuary." She didn't stand up. Her expression changed from sympathetic to *how is it that I have to ask this question?* "May I have the urn?"

"Oh." Selena wanted to keep Ruth. She hadn't thought about urn etiquette. People took the potted lilies. You couldn't take the urn. That seemed obvious now. "I'm sorry."

She picked Ruth up and held her out to Cade.

"Do you want to take her home with you?" Selena asked.

Cade looked pained. "I have a small apartment. I was thinking we would put her in a mausoleum with...the other dead people."

"She can't go in the mausoleum," Selena said. "She hated people who acted old. *Don't let me go to a nursing home where I have to sit around with a bunch of old people,* she said." Selena didn't want to scatter Ruth's ashes either. "I just thought she could go on the kitchen table. Someplace warm." *Don't cry.* "Someplace where she's not alone."

Cade exhaled heavily. But there was that flash of tenderness again.

"If you tell my parents the Spirit of the Universe told you to keep her, they'll probably go along with that." Cade rubbed the bridge of her nose. "Good luck. It was nice to meet you all."

And with that she was off. Selena wished Cade had stayed a little longer.

"She's sweet," Selena said, looking at the door through which Cade had disappeared. "She has kind eyes."

"You're not going to sleep with her," Becket said, a gentle warning in her voice.

"What? You think I'm going to say, *Thanks for the urn. Are you DTF?* How did you jump to that? I'm celibate. And even if I wasn't, I would not hook up with Ruth's niece at her funeral."

A year ago, she would totally have hooked up with Cade after the funeral.

"You asked me to remind you anytime I saw you looking at someone. You don't want to break your vow until you've got your shit together," Becket said. "Your words. Not mine. I never said you didn't have your shit together."

Selena did not have her shit together.

"But kind eyes isn't the worst reason to sleep with someone," Beautiful Adrien said.

Everyone knew about Selena's vow of celibacy.

"She let you keep Ruth's ashes," Zenobious said. "That's love."

"I am not going to sleep with Cade Elgin. I just thought she was nice. I mean, who *does* let you keep their relative's ashes?"

Selena stood up.

"I should go too."

She kissed Becket on the cheek, then made her way around the table, kissing Zenobious on his man-bun and Beautiful Adrien on the top of his glorious brown hair. Becket got up and followed her to the door, her brow furrowed.

"What?" Selena asked.

Becket put a hand on her arm.

"I didn't want to say this…You had so much going on with Ruth." Becket paused. "And I'm sure you've thought about it, so this is just me being obvious, but…"

"I said I'm not sleeping with her. I'm really not."

Becket pulled her into a full-body hug. Coming from tiny Becket it was kind of like being hugged by a bird, but Selena felt the love. Selena rested her head on top of Becket's blue hair.

"You do know that the Elgins are going to evict you, right?" Becket said, holding her tighter.

Selena hadn't thought about it.

"Of course," Selena said.

"And they'll shut down Ruth's shop."

The shop Selena worked at. The in-law apartment where she lived rent-free. Her home. Her job. Her life. She thought Ruth's death couldn't get any harder.

"You can crash with me for as long as you want," Becket said. "Tomorrow we'll see the lawyer, and then I'll help you pack."

"I've already started."

"No, you haven't."

She hadn't.

Selena hurried outside and walked to her motorcycle, parked on the sidewalk. She'd drunk too much to ride home. She'd gotten that far in her vow to get her life together. To-do list item one: Do not die in a motorcycle accident. She considered going back inside and asking Becket to call an Uber for her. Selena's phone still had a physical keyboard, and it didn't type reliably. The letters B, E, H, K, L, M, N, O, and Z were the most problematic, but sometimes it typed those and missed A, F, G, R, S, and T. She could get to numbered streets but not Wisteria Lane. That was okay. She needed a walk. She set off down the tree-lined street, pulling her fake-fur jacket up around her neck to keep off the rain.

An image of Cade Elgin flashed through her mind. Cade had looked sexy and elegant and powerful. Her short blond hair was cut perfectly to accentuate her high cheekbones. Her clothes hinted at strong shoulders and flat abs. She was athletic. Selena saw it in her lean jaw. But Cade was cute too. The way her blue eyes had widened at the idea of keeping Ruth on the kitchen table. She'd looked distressed and amused at the same time, her furrowed eyebrows saying, *Not this again.* All that straight-backed decorum made Selena want to ruffle Cade's perfectly cropped blond hair...and maybe kiss her.

But that was why she'd taken the vow of celibacy. Sadness made Selena horny. Stress made her horny. Worry made her horny. She was wired that way. The more upset she got, the more sex felt like an answer. Her body told her that if she could just fuck hard enough or come fast enough, her anxiety would melt away. It never worked. Afterward, she lay there, still stressed and sad and now worried that the man or woman in bed beside her would show up at her door with flowers. She'd have to tell them they weren't at the start of something beautiful; it was just that she owed a thousand dollars in parking tickets and that made her want cunnilingus. Trying to track Cade Elgin down after the funeral was not a life plan. Selena was twenty-nine. Almost thirty! And it was time to get her shit together on her own.

chapter 3

It was raining, and Selena's coat was wet by the time she arrived at the cottage at the back of Ruth's property. Her home. Except it wouldn't be in a few days. She tossed her coat on a chair, stripped out of her funeral attire, and lay down. She didn't realize she'd fallen asleep until she woke up to dark windows. She rose slowly and turned on the water for a cup of instant coffee. No one drank instant in Portland; it was like drinking Keystone Light. But Selena had grown up in the middle of nowhere where Folgers crystals and light beer were comfort foods.

She sat on the floor and leaned against her bed. She'd drink her coffee and then do something with those casseroles. She pulled out her phone and checked her voice mail. At least that still worked. There were a lot of condolence messages. So many people loved Ruth, and so many people cared about Selena.

Selena was holding back her tears as she listened to a message from one of the customers at Ruth's boutique when the phone rang. She didn't recognize the number.

For a moment, she thought *Cade*. With her serious outfit and her kind eyes (which were not a reason to sleep with her), Cade was the type of person to call after a funeral. And it'd be nice to hear Cade's voice. Maybe Cade had more stories about Ruth, or maybe Cade would like to hear how Ruth loved Cade and understood why Cade couldn't get away from her work.

"Hello," Selena said hopefully.

"Hi, Selena."

She leaped up. *No!* It wasn't Cade. It wasn't anyone reassuring.

"Selena. It's me."

How long had it been since she talked to her ex? Forever. She shouldn't even recognize Alex's voice. She pulled the phone away from her ear and stared at it.

"I heard the woman you were renting from passed. I'm sorry."

How was that any of her business?

"What... do you want?"

"To say I'm sorry for your loss." Alex made it sound obvious. How could Selena mind a sympathy call?

Selena paced across the room. Ruth's urn sat on a table by the window. (The Elgins had agreed that one should always heed the Spirit of the Universe.) Selena looked out the window. Was Alex there? Alex used to do that. Just pop in at the Aviary art co-op where Selena painted, catch Selena shooting the shit with Becket, and pull Selena aside. *Hanging out with your friends? Really? Have you finished your painting?*

"How did she die?" Alex asked.

None of your fucking business. Selena's heart pounded.

"Cancer."

"That's hard."

"Yeah."

"I know we haven't talked for a while," Alex said.

We broke up. We don't talk. Why had Selena kept the same number? Fuck that. Why did she have a phone?

"My mother died of cancer," Alex said. "It was terrible."

Alex described some of the side effects of her mother's chemotherapy. It made Selena's stomach turn.

"I…I don't really want to think about that." Selena scanned the dark yard for a sign of movement. "But it was nice of you to call."

Not.

"The last days of my mom's life were really gruesome. I just want you to know I've been there too." That was Alex. Saying something to make Selena feel bad and then making it sound like Alex should get a gold star for being considerate. "Was she sick for a long time?"

"No."

"Well, I'm glad for you."

Selena put her hand on Ruth's urn. *Can you believe her?* Neither Selena nor Ruth said anything.

"Are you there?" Alex asked.

I don't need this.

Selena tried a power posture. Feet wide apart. Shoulders back. Head up. Alex wasn't her professor anymore. Alex didn't have power over her. Selena wasn't the trembling art student. Selena had given up painting. She worked at Ruth's shop…she had worked at Ruth's shop. And she'd been good at it. She was a woman who was getting her shit together, even if she didn't know what to do with all those casseroles.

Hang up. A shit-together person would hang up. Selena couldn't. Her shoulders dropped. She crossed her arms over her chest, squeezing herself. *Hold it together.* So much for power postures.

"I'm here."

"I know you're not in the loop at the McLaughlin Academy anymore," Alex said, "so you probably didn't hear. Derrick and I split up." She paused. "I broke up with him because of you."

Selena spun around. She felt trapped. Alex's words reverberated through her body. She'd begged Alex to leave her husband, and Alex hadn't, and Selena had dropped out of school and burned her paintings, and Alex had gone on teaching her classes and drinking tea in her nineteenth-century, polished-wood-and-brass office. Selena took a few steps across her room, but there was nowhere to go.

"You were really special, Selena."

Selena could hear Alex's smile.

"I tried to tell myself you were my midlife crisis," Alex went on. "You weren't. You aren't. I kept thinking about you. You and I had something Derrick and I didn't. And I know what you're going to say. You knew that years ago. You told me we should be together, and I didn't hear you. But I hear you now."

Selena felt sick. The twinkle lights that crisscrossed her room danced in front of her eyes.

"It's taken me this long to realize it," Alex said, "but I have. I want you. We'll take it slow. I know this is a surprise, and your friend just died, but hopefully it's a happy surprise."

No. It wasn't. But Alex's feelings were always the right feelings. Selena's were always wrong.

"We'll start with coffee," Alex said.

"I'm busy." Selena paced the length of her room.

"If you call hanging out with your friends busy. Just coffee. We don't have to rush into anything."

The right thing to say would be, *I'm not comfortable with this call, and I'm not interested in reconnecting.* Selena had coached customers at Ruth's boutique on having these kinds of conversations. *You need to respect my boundaries.*

I don't want to! Selena clutched her phone. She'd never been able to stand up to Alex. Not once. *I'm going to go back to her.* The thought hit her like a gunshot. She wouldn't want to. She'd hate it. Her friends would try to stop her. But Alex would bring out her professor voice, and every argument Selena could think of would fail. *Don't be childish, Selena. You were never good at making decisions.*

Selena crossed her room again. She'd lost every argument she'd ever had with Alex. Alex always got what she wanted. What could Selena say that would make it totally, absolutely, one hundred percent clear that Alex could not get back in her life?

"I'm dating Cade Elgin," Selena blurted out. "Cade Elgin. From the Elgin Gallery. And I love her, and it's perfect, and she makes me feel safe, and she makes me laugh, and she's a great lover, which you weren't."

What the fuck was she thinking? *Cade Elgin?*

"Selena," Alex said, calm-professor voice shifting into disappointed-professor voice. "That's a little far-fetched, isn't it?"

Selena sat down on her bed and pulled her knees up to her chest.

"No, it's not."

There were plenty of reasons why Cade Elgin would date…a soon-to-be-homeless art school dropout with no bank account. Okay. There were no reasons except that Selena was hot. She knew that. That also wasn't a life plan.

"Selena, you don't have to make up a girlfriend," Alex said. "And the Elgin daughter? Really? I'm someone who loves you who is asking you out for coffee. You don't have to lie to me."

"I'm getting married."

Selena pressed her face to her knees. She knew what would happen. Alex would come by the store, probably as the Elgins were shutting it down. Cade would be long gone, or she'd be appalled at Selena's lie. Alex would chastise Selena, then demand that they get coffee. And Selena would go because that's the kind of person she was.

"I said we're getting married!"

Why was she still talking? Saying they were dating was ridiculous; saying they were engaged was worse. So, of course, Selena kept going. She raised her face, and in her strongest voice said, "She's Ruth's niece, and she loves me. I've bought my dress. She's going to wear a tux. We're having it at the Aviary, and you can't come because she'll kick your ass."

At least Selena followed through with her bad choices. *Go big or go home.* If she was going to fuck up, she was going to fuck all the way up.

chapter 4

Cade checked her phone as she walked to her hotel room. Her friend Josiah had texted.

Don't want to do this to you but... He'd sent a picture of a delicate piece of glasswork.

Josiah bought art for rich people who wanted art without the hassle of choosing it themselves. Cade was a gallery manager. It was a symbiotic relationship, but they had a friendly competition going to see who could discover the next unknown genius.

Below the picture he'd texted, *Seriously. How are you?*

Cade had booked her room and her parents' room on the opposite sides of the hotel. The smell of marijuana wafting out of her room told her she had not put enough space between them. A piece of hotel art—a painfully clichéd oceanscape—hung in the hall by the door. She texted it to Josiah. *Like this.* She considered walking away and booking a room across town, but she needed her laptops. She had two, one for work and one for personal business, except work always bled into personal, and her personal life was basically working on the weekends. She ought to dump one, but that felt like defeat. Better to lug around a heavy briefcase than admit work was her whole life and it always would be. She pushed the door open.

Her parents were sitting on her bed. On the other bed sat an old woman with wild, gray curls and a couple about Cade's age.

"Cadence!" her mother exclaimed, as though seeing Cade was a delightful surprise.

"How did you get in my room?" Cade hadn't even told them her room number. "And why are you in my room?"

"The hotel manager didn't understand that tonight is Bacchanalia," her father said, "the night of fauns and centaurs."

Fuck the Bacchanalia.

"Who let you in?"

"We just explained that we'd lost our keycards. Our name is on the reservation," her mother said, "so they made us up some new ones. So kind. The young fellow at the desk didn't know that…" Cade's mother fluttered her fingers.

"That you got kicked out of your room?" Cade said.

"The neighbors complained." Her father waved his joint. "Edibles are practical, but tonight calls for the rush of fire."

"And now they'll kick us out of mine," Cade said.

"Ruth's soul hovers over us," her father said.

Cade couldn't imagine Ruth's soul hanging out at the Extended Stay Deluxe Motel. Portland was full of boutique hotels that were probably haunted by interesting ghosts. The Extended Stay Deluxe was probably haunted by the souls of alcoholic salesmen, but it was cheap.

"Ruth will protect us," Cade's father added.

"From getting kicked out of my hotel room for smoking pot? Why didn't she protect you from getting kicked out of your own hotel room?"

"Oh, don't worry. We'll head out soon," her father said.

"This is Calendria. We met at the funeral," Cade's mother clarified. To the couple she said, "And darlings, tell me your names again?"

The couple didn't seem to mind that they were smoking pot with people who did not know their names.

"Forest." The man pressed his palm to his chest.

"Maple," the woman said.

"Maple! Of course, the tree of sweetness," Cade's mother exclaimed. To her new friends Cade's mother said, "This is my daughter. My Athena. My jewel. Cadence, sit down. We were just talking to Calendria about raising alpacas. I think we should get some."

"Where will you put them?"

Why was Cade entertaining this conversation?

"We could stable them upstate," her father said. "Or maybe keep them in the gallery."

"No."

"Cade's so responsible," her mother said. "She's the only real adult in our family. We think she was switched at birth." Cade's mother winked at Calendria. "She's actually the daughter of accountants, but we'll keep her. She's ours now."

"Alpacas have soft feet," her father said.

"Lions have soft feet." Cade's voice rose.

"You could walk them," her mother added.

Cade ran her hands through her hair, looking around for her laptops. Hopefully they weren't sitting under a bong.

"I will not walk anything."

"And, Cade, honey," her mother said, as though Cade hadn't spoken, "don't worry about the room. Calendria has invited us to her houseboat. We're going to dance on water under the stars and make garlands of river grass."

Calendria and the young couple nodded.

"The waters are sacred," Calendria said.

"Before I forget." Her father reached into the pocket of his tweed coat. "Here's the key to Ruth's house. The lawyer said there are some papers there you should pick up for tomorrow. Life is so burdened with paperwork."

Someone had written the address on the keychain—because *that* was a good idea. Cade grabbed her laptops off the table and picked up her suitcase. She never unpacked when she stayed at hotels.

"Do not get arrested," she said. "I will see you tomorrow." *If you're not tied up in river grass.*

"We're releasing lanterns at dawn," her mother said.

"Goodbye," Cade said wearily. "Have fun."

She hurried until she was out of the building and away from the marijuana smoke. Then she slowed and stopped. She set down her suitcase and looked up at the sky. It wasn't raining for the first time since she'd landed in Portland. The low clouds looked muddy with city light.

She didn't want to go to Calendria's houseboat and weave river grass, but just for once, it would have been nice to be asked.

Honey, would you like to dance under the stars on a house-boat? It just wouldn't be the same without you.

Thanks, Mom. I thought you'd just want to be with your interesting friends.

No one is as interesting as you, Cadence. We don't really think you're so boring you must have been switched at birth.

She sighed. Taxes and accounts payable. That's what she was good for.

A few minutes later Cade got out of her Uber. Ruth's house was on a wide street with large, old houses set deep in their lots. Vines shrouded Ruth's porch. Everything was dark except for a little cottage on the property directly behind Ruth's house. Cade rattled the key in the lock, pushed open the door, and fumbled for the light.

Then she gasped. Ruth's ghost wasn't at a boutique hotel. It was here.

A painting of Ruth hung on the other side of the living room. She was topless, although only her shoulders showed in the painting. Her head was tilted back in laughter. The painting radiated joy. Cade dropped her suitcase and crossed the room. The brushwork was amazing. Oil. She could almost feel the warmth of her aunt's skin. She checked for the artist's signature, but the name had been scraped off.

"Wow," Cade said out loud.

The work was amazing. She would have to ask Ruth's friends for the name of the painter. Forget online portal submissions. She'd show this work at the Elgin Gallery. The painting could be at the center of an exhibit dedicated to her aunt.

She texted a picture to Josiah.

It's oil, Cade texted.

It's all right, Josiah texted, which meant he was jealous.

Cade smiled and texted a close-up of the brushwork. Then she looked around. Her smile faded. The painting was the only bright spot in the room. The rest of the space was sad. Wads of tissue, pill bottles, and junk mail covered everything. Cade lifted up a catalog featuring a woman in a bondage chair (Of course. This was her family. Aunt Ruth couldn't get old-lady clothing catalogs) to find a desiccated lasagna.

Her phone vibrated in her coat pocket. Her best friend, Amy.

How was it?

It was my family.

I love your family.

You can have them.

You okay?

Was she? Cade didn't even know. Her parents were annoying. Nothing new. She'd had to arrange for the cremation and mausoleum (not that Ruth was going there), call the lawyer, get the hotel, buy the airline tickets. Her mother had offered to help, but her parents would have booked a Cessna and burned Ruth's body on the river.

Tired, Cade texted.

Want to talk?

Tomorrow?

I'm here if you need me.

Cade returned a heart emoji.

* * *

It took Cade an hour and a half to find the paperwork she thought her father might be talking about. In a spare room full of crafting supplies, she found a file cabinet. The drawers held yarn. A basket on top held folders bulging with papers. The labels were descriptive but not helpful. *Death stuff. Life stuff. House Stuff. Throw away when I die.* (That one contained the title to a car.) *Things for Friends. Bills.* A true Elgin filing system. Cade gathered everything up and put it with her suitcase by the front door.

She should find another hotel. There was something creepy about sleeping in her dead aunt's house. What if Ruth had lovers who came in and were shocked to find her there? She wandered over to the TV. For once, she didn't have the energy to be proactive. She'd stay there. She turned on the TV. A naked woman lay on a large bed receiving cunnilingus. Cade tried to change the channel. Nope. She pressed the remote harder. Still nope. She knelt down in front of the TV console. A DVD was stuck on play. She pressed stop and then eject, but neither worked.

Of course.

The woman moaned in ecstasy. Cade turned the TV off. She did not feel like watching porn in her dead aunt's house. That left one thing, the thing she always had energy for: a good, hard workout.

She got shorts and a tank top out of her suitcase and changed in the bathroom. The house was too cluttered to work out in, but there was a patio in the backyard. She switched on the outdoor light, stretched briefly, and started in with burpees.

Fifty burpees.

Fifty squats.

A hundred high-five crunches.

Nothing made her feel free and relaxed like exercise. She'd learned that when she'd joined the Boston University crew team. Pulling against the current, listening for the coxswain's calls, there'd been no room for thought.

It was just her, the air in her lungs, the strain in her abs, and...

Two muddy bare feet.

Standing in front of her.

One of Ruth's lovers? Pissed that a stranger was doing ab work in the backyard? Cade jumped to her feet, an apology on her lips. *I'm sorry. I'm her niece.*

Words died on her lips when she saw the person in front of her: Selena, in a short, cream-colored robe as thin as moonlight. It fell off one shoulder. The robe barely covered the top of her thigh. She'd released her hair from its messy knot, and it spilled around her shoulders in a tangle of black curls. She'd been unreasonably pretty at the funeral. Now she was breathtaking...and unexplainably wearing a robe and holding a towel and bottle of shampoo in Ruth's yard. Of course, Cade was doing high-five crunches in Ruth's yard, so she didn't really get to complain. But how was Selena here?

Cade gaped. Selena looked mildly surprised.

"What are you doing?" Selena asked.

"X-Caliber Cardio Core Bodyweight Training."

"I'm going to take a shower in the house," Selena said.

They looked at each other, and both gave a little laugh at the same moment.

"Okay," Cade said.

"I live in the in-law apartment." Selena nodded toward the cottage at the back of the lot. "But it doesn't have a shower or a kitchen, so Ruth and I shared the house."

That's right. Cade had forgotten. Ruth had mentioned something about a tenant, an artist Ruth had met somewhere.

Cade wiped the sweat off her face. "I was supposed to pick up some papers. I felt like getting a workout in. I'll go."

"Stay." Selena looked at the house behind Cade, a faraway look in her eyes. "It's your house now. And your parents'."

"Unless Ruth willed it to bulldog rescue or something like that."

"She liked finches," Selena said. "I'm sorry about the casseroles. I know I should have cleaned up, but I'm not good at cleaning. You have to find places for things, and...it's just so sad in there." She pulled her robe back onto her shoulder, shivering. "Thanks for sitting with us at the reception. I'm guessing the funeral wasn't what you wanted."

"It was a little extra." Cade stuck her hands in the pockets of her shorts, found an old receipt, and looked at it like it mattered that she had bought a $2.95 coffee at Marco's Bakery. It felt wrong to look at Selena in her moonlight robe. Selena hadn't meant to be seen by anyone...except maybe the neighbors on both sides. "But it's my family. I'm used to it. At least no one brought an alpaca. My parents want to buy one."

"Alpacas are nice. They have soft feet," Selena said with gentle optimism.

"How does everyone know that?"

"I was a farm girl. Well, not a farm girl, but a crap-trailer-on-a-whole-bunch-of-rangeland girl." For a second Selena looked shy. "It's not as bad as it sounds."

"It doesn't sound bad," Cade said. It sounded like a version of normal; maybe not her version but someone's version. "My parents are probably falling off a houseboat by now. I'll take the trailer."

"Alpacas are only about a hundred and twenty pounds," Selena offered. "I could almost pick one up." Selena cocked her head. "You could pick one up. I like a girl who can pick up an alpaca."

The compliment glowed in Cade's heart. She worked out every day. She was proud of her body. She *could* pick up an alpaca. No one appreciated that about her. The only thing women appreciated about her was her parents. Maybe in Portland she was sexy. But…no. Selena was kidding. Cade made that mistake sometimes, mistaking a joke for a compliment. Mistaking a compliment for flirtation. It'd be nice if a woman occasionally looked at her and saw more than a tax consultant and their chance to give an elevator speech. Cade settled her face into a look of mild amusement.

"Is there a dropdown menu for that on OkCupid?" Cade asked.

"Maybe on Craigslist." Selena laughed.

Cade wasn't sure what to say next. *Enjoy your shower?* Selena shivered harder, wrapping her arms around herself. The smile faded from her face. She didn't make a move to leave.

"We'd have been serious if that's what Ruth wanted,"

uching and her whole body melting into Cade's.
eping. Nothing like it.

sorry. I'm supposed to be self-actualized." Selena
ot to sniffle the words. "I'm supposed to be happy
n and her new adventure."

just held her.

text you my exercise routine. It's very self-
ed. And fuck Ruth's new adventure," Cade mur-
"What if Ruth went to France, but you could
rite or Zoom or anything? You'd be sad, but you'd
ieve in France. It wouldn't mean you thought she
xist anymore."

a stopped trying not to cry and sobbed against
chest.

's gone…and the casseroles…and cancer." It
ven make sense to Selena. "And my ex called
d I didn't eat the poke, and the tuna died…and
as going to hang Christmas tree ornaments…and
e." *And you're going to evict me.* "And the urn…it's
…how can it be so small?"

nestled Selena's head against her shoulder. She
ay, *shh* or *don't cry* or *my mother died of cancer, let me*
he gory details.

ly, Selena's sobs subsided. She could feel hard
against her cheek. She could feel her breath match
and fall of Cade's. In and out. And she wanted to
ething like, *I feel like we met in a past life* or *please*
e to me with the biggest dildo we can find so that I can
there's no room to think.

appropriate either way.

believe in France," Selena said.

Selena said, "but she said throw a party. She said death would be a wonderful adventure. She said, *Don't you dare be sad.* But I am sad."

A spatter of rain hit them, then burst, like the sky was thinking, *Oh, shit. It's Oregon. I forgot I was supposed to rain forever.* The wind kicked up. A violent shiver shook Selena's body.

"You should go in." Cade wished she had a jacket to wrap around Selena. "It's cold."

Selena clutched her towel and her shampoo to her chest.

"And that means I don't believe her, doesn't it? If I cry it means I don't think death is a wonderful adventure. I loved her." Selena's voice broke. "Love her. Why does it get past tense so fast?"

If Cade had been at the gallery dealing with a crying artist—they weren't a rare occurrence—she would have taken them in hand with calm, measured compassion. *It's going to be all right. I'll get you a sparkling water.* But this beautiful woman who dressed like a hot Instagram influencer and recited the Bible was crying because she'd lost a friend who was like a mother to her. Sparkling water didn't fix that.

"English grammar can be difficult." *Not helpful. Not consoling.* Cade kicked herself. Why didn't she have a nice poem memorized?

"I was always good at grammar in school." Selena wiped at her eyes.

"I just meant…" Cade stumbled over her words. "…is the past tense attached to the love or to the person? The person is past but the love isn't."

"But you can't fix it." A tear streaked silently down

Selena's cheek. "Once they're dead, you can never say the sentence right, but I'm not going to cry." And with that, she started to cry. "I can't. If I cry, she's really gone."

"It's okay to cry," Cade said. Selena's tears made tears well up in her own eyes. She reached out and touched Selena's arm gently. "It really is. Ruth went on a wonderful adventure without you. You get to be sad."

chapte

Rain hit Selena's back. She was freezing. She knew th go inside. Shower. Go to bed. T a résumé. *Do not sleep on Becket not throw yourself at Cade.* But th much more attractive than the Selena's arm, her fingertips war was all it took. Selena fell ag surprised step backward, but Selena nonetheless.

It felt so good. Cade's body at the same time and warm lik Selena's robe and Cade's exerc lot of clothing. And, oh, the fe comforted Selena even though when she slept with people: eith picked all of Portland.

I'm not sleeping with her. She w with this beautiful woman's ar

skin to
Not sl
"I'm
tried n
for Ru
Cad
"I'll
actuali
mured
never v
still be
didn't
Sele
Cade's
"Ru
didn't
me…a
Ruth w
her sto
so sma
Cad
didn't
tell you
Slow
muscle
the rise
say sor
make lo
be so fu
Not
"I do

Cade stroked a piece of hair off Selena's cheek. "See? You get to be sad because Ruth died," she said. "You just do. And it's sweet that everyone threw a party if that's what she wanted."

Reluctantly Selena pulled away. "Thank you."

Cade looked down at the ground. She was wet from rain and her workout, and her clothes stuck to her.

"Would you like to go inside?" Cade asked. "I could make you a cup of tea."

Inside, Cade took a blanket off Ruth's sofa and handed it to Selena. Cade was dripping rain too, but she didn't seem to notice the chill as she busied about the kitchen.

"There're so many teacups, but I don't see any tea," Cade said.

Cute. Ruth's teacups were all for whiskey drinking.

"I guess maybe a coffee?" Cade said.

Selena held up a bottle of Sadfire Whiskey to stop her.

"It's like tea," she said.

Cade sat down across from her. Selena poured herself a teacup full of whiskey. Cade poured a tiny bit into her own cup.

"You remind me of Becket," Selena said. "Becket's good in a crisis."

"Paperwork, yes. I don't know how good I'd be in an earthquake," Cade said ruefully.

"I guess it's not a crisis anymore," Selena said. "Everything was a crisis before Ruth died. I was here." That was one thing Selena knew. She'd been with Ruth until the end, even if she hadn't cleaned the house or paid for the funeral. Who knew it was so expensive to die? "Now, nothing is."

"How'd you meet Ruth?" Cade asked.

Selena pulled Ruth's blanket around her.

"She was friends with Becket. My ex broke up with me, and I didn't have any place to live. Beck was probably sick of me sleeping on her couch, so she said, *Ruth, I've got this great person who could live in your in-law.* Ruth and I...I'd never had a mother really, and she'd never had a daughter. I live here and work at Ruth's boutique."

Lived. Worked.

"My aunt said you were a painter."

"No."

Cade took a sip of her whiskey and raised her eyebrows approvingly. It was Sadfire. Even if you drank Boones Country Kwencher—which Cade surely didn't—you had to admit Sadfire was good.

"Do you want to do anything?" Cade asked. "To memorialize Ruth...a toast or a moment of silence?"

Selena wiped some rainwater off her face with the edge of the blanket.

"Photo albums?" she suggested.

"Of course."

"I'll get them," Selena said.

"I'm going to change real quick." Cade indicated her own damp tank, then looked away. "Do you want, um, clothing?"

Cade's shy chivalry made Selena smile.

"I *am* wearing clothing."

"More clothing?"

"I'll run back to my place and grab something."

Selena said, "but she said throw a party. She said death would be a wonderful adventure. She said, *Don't you dare be sad*. But I am sad."

A spatter of rain hit them, then burst, like the sky was thinking, *Oh, shit. It's Oregon. I forgot I was supposed to rain forever*. The wind kicked up. A violent shiver shook Selena's body.

"You should go in." Cade wished she had a jacket to wrap around Selena. "It's cold."

Selena clutched her towel and her shampoo to her chest.

"And that means I don't believe her, doesn't it? If I cry it means I don't think death is a wonderful adventure. I loved her." Selena's voice broke. "Love her. Why does it get past tense so fast?"

If Cade had been at the gallery dealing with a crying artist—they weren't a rare occurrence—she would have taken them in hand with calm, measured compassion. *It's going to be all right. I'll get you a sparkling water*. But this beautiful woman who dressed like a hot Instagram influencer and recited the Bible was crying because she'd lost a friend who was like a mother to her. Sparkling water didn't fix that.

"English grammar can be difficult." *Not helpful. Not consoling*. Cade kicked herself. Why didn't she have a nice poem memorized?

"I was always good at grammar in school." Selena wiped at her eyes.

"I just meant…" Cade stumbled over her words. "…is the past tense attached to the love or to the person? The person is past but the love isn't."

"But you can't fix it." A tear streaked silently down

Selena's cheek. "Once they're dead, you can never say the sentence right, but I'm not going to cry." And with that, she started to cry. "I can't. If I cry, she's really gone."

"It's okay to cry," Cade said. Selena's tears made tears well up in her own eyes. She reached out and touched Selena's arm gently. "It really is. Ruth went on a wonderful adventure without you. You get to be sad."

skin touching and her whole body melting into Cade's. Not sleeping. Nothing like it.

"I'm sorry. I'm supposed to be self-actualized." Selena tried not to sniffle the words. "I'm supposed to be happy for Ruth and her new adventure."

Cade just held her.

"I'll text you my exercise routine. It's very self-actualized. And fuck Ruth's new adventure," Cade murmured. "What if Ruth went to France, but you could never write or Zoom or anything? You'd be sad, but you'd still believe in France. It wouldn't mean you thought she didn't exist anymore."

Selena stopped trying not to cry and sobbed against Cade's chest.

"Ruth's gone…and the casseroles…and cancer." It didn't even make sense to Selena. "And my ex called me…and I didn't eat the poke, and the tuna died…and Ruth was going to hang Christmas tree ornaments…and her store." *And you're going to evict me.* "And the urn…it's so small…how can it be so small?"

Cade nestled Selena's head against her shoulder. She didn't say, *shh* or *don't cry* or *my mother died of cancer, let me tell you the gory details.*

Slowly, Selena's sobs subsided. She could feel hard muscle against her cheek. She could feel her breath match the rise and fall of Cade's. In and out. And she wanted to say something like, *I feel like we met in a past life* or *please make love to me with the biggest dildo we can find so that I can be so full there's no room to think.*

Not appropriate either way.

"I do believe in France," Selena said.

chapter 5

≋

Rain hit Selena's back. Tears burned her eyes. She was freezing. She knew the right thing to do was go inside. Shower. Go to bed. Take up meditating. Write a résumé. *Do not sleep on Becket's couch for six months. Do not throw yourself at Cade.* But the wrong choices were so much more attractive than the right ones. Cade touched Selena's arm, her fingertips warm on Selena's skin. That was all it took. Selena fell against Cade. Cade took a surprised step backward, but her arms closed around Selena nonetheless.

It felt so good. Cade's body was soft and muscular at the same time and warm like life itself. And between Selena's robe and Cade's exercise outfit, there wasn't a lot of clothing. And, oh, the feeling of skin on skin. It comforted Selena even though she knew what happened when she slept with people: either she picked Alex or she picked all of Portland.

I'm not sleeping with her. She was just standing in the rain with this beautiful woman's arms around her and their

Cade stroked a piece of hair off Selena's cheek. "See? You get to be sad because Ruth died," she said. "You just do. And it's sweet that everyone threw a party if that's what she wanted."

Reluctantly Selena pulled away. "Thank you."

Cade looked down at the ground. She was wet from rain and her workout, and her clothes stuck to her.

"Would you like to go inside?" Cade asked. "I could make you a cup of tea."

Inside, Cade took a blanket off Ruth's sofa and handed it to Selena. Cade was dripping rain too, but she didn't seem to notice the chill as she busied about the kitchen.

"There're so many teacups, but I don't see any tea," Cade said.

Cute. Ruth's teacups were all for whiskey drinking.

"I guess maybe a coffee?" Cade said.

Selena held up a bottle of Sadfire Whiskey to stop her.

"It's like tea," she said.

Cade sat down across from her. Selena poured herself a teacup full of whiskey. Cade poured a tiny bit into her own cup.

"You remind me of Becket," Selena said. "Becket's good in a crisis."

"Paperwork, yes. I don't know how good I'd be in an earthquake," Cade said ruefully.

"I guess it's not a crisis anymore," Selena said. "Every-thing was a crisis before Ruth died. I was here." That was one thing Selena knew. She'd been with Ruth until the end, even if she hadn't cleaned the house or paid for the funeral. Who knew it was so expensive to die? "Now, nothing is."

"How'd you meet Ruth?" Cade asked.

Selena pulled Ruth's blanket around her.

"She was friends with Becket. My ex broke up with me, and I didn't have any place to live. Beck was probably sick of me sleeping on her couch, so she said, *Ruth, I've got this great person who could live in your in-law.* Ruth and I...I'd never had a mother really, and she'd never had a daughter. I live here and work at Ruth's boutique."

Lived. Worked.

"My aunt said you were a painter."

"No."

Cade took a sip of her whiskey and raised her eyebrows approvingly. It was Sadfire. Even if you drank Boones Country Kwencher—which Cade surely didn't—you had to admit Sadfire was good.

"Do you want to do anything?" Cade asked. "To memorialize Ruth...a toast or a moment of silence?"

Selena wiped some rainwater off her face with the edge of the blanket.

"Photo albums?" she suggested.

"Of course."

"I'll get them," Selena said.

"I'm going to change real quick." Cade indicated her own damp tank, then looked away. "Do you want, um, clothing?"

Cade's shy chivalry made Selena smile.

"I *am* wearing clothing."

"More clothing?"

"I'll run back to my place and grab something."

"I can loan you a sweatshirt."

A moment later, Selena returned with one of Ruth's overpacked photo albums, and Cade returned wearing slacks and a gray sweater. She held out a pair of sweatpants and a sweatshirt to Selena. Neatly folded.

Her clothes.

If it had been Ruth, Selena would have stripped right there, but Cade seemed to have trouble looking at her when she wasn't wearing a blanket, so Selena trailed the blanket into the living room to change. Cade's clothing was incredibly soft. It smelled faintly of expensive cologne. Selena pressed her face to the sweatshirt. It smelled the way forests really smelled, clean without being soapy, not the piney imitation you got in candles.

"I got this one because it might have pictures of you," Selena said. "As an adorable little kid."

She set it on the table and sat next to Cade. She thought Cade stiffened at her closeness, but when she looked over, Cade was smiling.

"I was never an adorable little kid," Cade said.

"I'm sure you were adorable."

Selena opened the album. She and Ruth had sat at this table looking at albums like this. So many nights. So much laughter. Selena turned the first page. There was a picture of Ruth and her brother when they were young.

"Your dad," Selena said.

Cade groaned. "That mustache makes him look like a pirate."

Selena flipped through a few more pages. There was

Ruth's house before the wisteria grew in. There was Ruth sunbathing naked.

Cade covered the picture with her hand. "No one should see their aunt naked."

"It's okay. She was a nudist."

Cade scrunched up her nose. "That doesn't make it better. That just means there's going to be more pictures."

The next photograph was a child with a boyish haircut and a girl's swimsuit running through a sprinkler in Ruth's yard. The girl's mouth was open wide, her arms and legs going in every direction, pom-poms in each hand. Selena waited for Cade to recognize herself. Cade's expression remained neutral.

"Yard looked nice back then," Cade said.

"And?" Selena said.

"What?" Cade looked at her innocently.

"It's you."

Cade pretended to study the picture closely.

"That must be some child my aunt picked up off the street. I have *never* had pom-poms," Cade said with mock indignation. Then a shadow passed across her face. "I played banker."

Ruth had always said her niece worked too hard.

"Where are the pictures of you?" Cade asked. "Did you know my aunt long enough to do something embarrassing with pom-poms?"

Selena leaned her shoulder against Cade's for just a second. "What day don't I do something embarrassing with pom-poms?" Selena turned the page.

They looked through three more albums. Selena could tell Cade was tired, but Cade didn't leave the table until

Selena said she'd better get back to the in-law apartment. They both rose. Cade held out her hand to shake Selena's, then they both laughed at the formality, and Cade hugged her, politely this time. Just an acquaintance-friend shoulder-hug.

"How long are you staying for?" Selena asked.

"I fly out on a redeye tomorrow."

"You want to get lunch? Do shots at a dive bar?"

Cade shook her head.

"I've got so much I have to sort out before I go. Ruth's papers are…the papers of a true Elgin. And I have to see her lawyer tomorrow and make sure nothing goes to probate."

Becket would have told Selena that now was a good time to ask Cade when Selena was getting evicted and whether she'd get her last paycheck from Ruth's shop. Selena didn't. The night felt like a time outside of time. Like the only things that existed were them, the lamplight, the teacups, the photos, and Ruth's memory.

Cade swept her hair off her face, revealing a sharp undercut. Selena longed to caress that flash of rebel beneath Cade's buttoned-down look. Old Selena would have said, *Come back to my place.* But that was a mistake. Backslide now and she'd be back to picking up people at clubs and waking up hungover. And there was something about Cade that told her breaking her vow with Cade would be more dangerous than breaking it with one of Becket's art scene friends. Cade was all alpha female on the outside, but beneath that exterior Selena sensed a shyness or a sadness that Selena wanted to coax and comfort. And yes, she wanted to have sticky, toy-filled sex with her, but for the first time in a long time that was *a* thought, not her only thought.

"Good night then, Cade Elgin," Selena said. "If you change your mind about the shots, you know where to find me."

chapter 6

"I'm sleeping." Selena answered Becket's fourth knock and pulled the covers over her head.

"I have a key. I'm just being polite," Becket said. To prove it, she let herself in and hopped onto the bed, her petite frame barely springing the mattress.

Selena pulled the covers down. Becket held her motorcycle helmet under one arm. She had stickers for all the flags in the LGBTQIA+ continuum on the helmet. The blue of the bisexuality flag complemented the blue of her hair, and as her hair dye faded, she'd match the lighter blue of the trans pride flag and eventually fade to the pale green of the agender flag. It was very egalitarian.

"You ready to go see the lawyer?" Becket asked.

Selena vaguely remembered Ruth's lawyer making an appointment with her. At the time, she hadn't been thinking about leaving her apartment and closing down the store. She'd thought maybe Ruth wanted to give her something special, an heirloom necklace or her snow globe collection. Maybe Ruth wanted it to be a surprise.

Would she get to keep any of Ruth's things now? Would they let her take Ruth's portrait? She'd given it to Ruth; did that make it the Elgins' property? She tightened her grip on the covers. Cade had been so sweet, and Roger and Pepper Elgin had seemed so fun and free-spirited—just like Ruth—and now they were all going back to New York and leaving Selena with eviction papers.

"Why do I need to?" Selena said. "They can just call and tell me to get out."

Becket patted her shoulder.

"I'll be there with you. You can ask for more time to move out. Maybe it'll be okay. Closure."

"I don't want closure."

"The lawyer says you need to be there."

"What if he says I need to leave the apartment *today*?"

"You'll crash with me," Becket said. "It'll be okay. When haven't I had your back?"

Becket had had her back since they arrived at the McLaughlin Academy freshman orientation, the only two students who'd ridden in on junkyard motorcycles, the only two who weren't eighteen.

"Never," Selena said.

"Right. Now get dressed."

Becket's brow furrowed. Selena was still wearing Cade's clothes.

"What's this?" Becket tugged on the cuff of Cade's sweatshirt.

"A sweatshirt."

"When did you start wearing…is this Adidas fleece?"

"Cade loaned it to me."

It occurred to Selena she needed to give the clothing back. It was just so cozy.

"You didn't," Becket said.

"We just talked."

"And how do you define *talked*?"

"Like someone who would not sleep with Ruth's niece the night of her funeral."

Becket shook her head. "Let's go see the lawyer."

They rode together on Becket's bike, as easy together as one body, like they'd been riding since college. The lawyer's house was in a bungalow off busy Hawthorne Street, and Selena suggested they park on the sidewalk. Becket said something about ordinances and circled the block for ten minutes.

Inside, a secretary greeted them and indicated the double doors to the lawyer's office. Selena pushed them open and stopped. Inside was a stately room, lined with bookshelves and dominated by a heavy conference table. But it wasn't the conference table that dominated Selena's vision. It was Cade, her parents, and Ruth's attorney sitting at the table.

"They're here?" she whispered to Becket.

You should be able to evict someone and take away their job—basically take away everything—without making a conference out of it. And she didn't want to see Cade here. It ruined the whole *time out of time* feeling she'd had the night before. Couldn't ruining her life be an anonymous transaction?

Cade sat with her hands folded, looking posh in a gray sweater and subtle tartan scarf, not one strand of silky blond hair out of place. She looked over when she heard Selena.

Hey, she mouthed.

The lawyer stood up and shook Selena's hand and then Becket's. "Delmar Thompson," he said. "I was a friend of Ruth's. She was an amazing woman. I'm so sorry for your loss."

Selena and Becket took the remaining seats. Selena got the one next to Cade.

"I don't know what this is about," Cade said.

Becket snorted.

Selena wished it were true.

"Cadence, Selena, I know you're wondering why you're here." Delmar sat down at the head of the table. "I'll get right to it. Ruth changed her will."

"She was always so spontaneous," Roger Elgin said.

"Roger and Pepper and I have talked about this," Delmar said, "but Ruth wanted Cadence and Selena to hear the details of the will together. And she wanted it to be after her death. She didn't tell you herself—especially you, Selena—because it's bad news."

Becket would help her pack. The Elgins would sell the house. Someone would cut down the wisteria. Selena began to tear up.

"Ruth left a letter and instructions to be read today," Delmar said. "Are you ready?"

No.

"A missive from the beyond," Roger Elgin said. "Read on!"

Delmar put on reading glasses, took a sheet of pink paper out of an envelope, and unfolded it.

"*Dear ones, this is my final will and testament or whatever they say in the movies. Cadence, I know we haven't seen each other much these last years, but you're still my girl. And Selena, you're the daughter I never had. Working at Satisfaction Guaranteed and having you in the guest house: those were some of the happiest times of my life.*

But Satisfaction Guaranteed isn't doing well. I'm an Elgin. I've done business like an Elgin. We're not good at business, except Cade. Delmar will fill you in on the details. But the store isn't doing too well."

"Satisfaction Guaranteed is fine." Selena leaned forward. "It's beautiful. People love it."

"It's not doing well," Delmar said apologetically.

"How bad is it?" Cade tapped a tablet in front of her and poised the stylus over the screen.

"Here's the deal," Delmar said. "Ruth bought her stock from three distributors." He checked his notes. "Adult Playground, Palace Perfect, and Swing Set. They're big distributors. It's a small store. So she flew under the radar for a long time, but they finally noticed that she hadn't made the minimum payments on her accounts for... years. I think. Her records aren't the best. It looks like she owes close to a hundred thousand."

A hundred thousand dollars in debt? Ruth had said everything was fine. They were doing better than ever.

"Swing Set is willing to work with you, but the other two aren't," Delmar went on. "They know Ruth passed away, and they are collecting on their debts. The house is also double mortgaged, so you can't take out a home equity loan."

"When are they collecting?" Cade asked.

"Probate gives you about a month. But there's more."

Delmar adjusted his reading glasses. "Ruth writes, *But that's just an old woman letting things slide. Cadence, you've always been good at business. Don't roll your eyes, sweetie. I remember how you used to do that when you were a girl. So serious. None of us know where you came from, our little accountant, but if anyone can save Satisfaction Guaranteed, it's you. Take care of my Selena. She needs an accountant in her life.*"

"Everyone does," Cade said wearily.

"*It's on you two,*" Delmar read on. "*I know death is the next great journey, but even if it's just lights-out, I know my love is going to float around in the universe forever. I'm sure there's some law of physics that explains it. Or God. Or maybe we're all just part of the same beautiful dream. I'll be looking down on you in one way or another. I know you can do this. Your loving friend and aunt, Ruth.*"

The letter sounded so like Ruth. Selena held her breath to hold back her tears. Becket squeezed her hand.

"What does it mean?" Cade twirled her stylus around in her long fingers.

"She's splitting her property between you," Delmar said. "Her shop, her house, and her little cabin in the woods. The conditions are that you have to live in the house. Selena stays in the in-law apartment. You both have to work at the shop, and if you can get it back in the black everything is yours. Fifty-fifty."

Ruth had left everything to her and Cade? *Everything?*

"We get the house?" Selena couldn't believe it. "And the store?"

Ruth loved surprises, but this? It was like one of the movies Ruth watched where a sad, lonely woman inherited money or won the lottery or got sent to Italy for work and she blossomed. (That was the word Ruth used.) She kissed a sexy lifeguard, and became a novelist, and when she went back to Ohio she was a new woman. Ruth was giving that to Selena. Not an apartment she lived in rent-free, her own home. Not a job, a business.

"Why didn't she tell us?" Selena's mind reeled. "I could have thanked her. I could have told her…this is…it's everything. Cade, can you believe it?"

"Yes, why didn't she tell us?" Cade asked Delmar.

Delmar shrugged. "She said she was ashamed she'd let it all slide. She got sick and she didn't want Selena to worry."

"So, we have a month to get over a hundred thousand dollars?" Cade asked. "That does make a person worry."

"Swing Set is a woman-owned company. They knew Ruth," Delmar said. "They liked what she was trying to do. They said if you could prove the store was financially viable, they'd work on a payment plan."

"So, we work with one company and then what?" Cade said. "We owe the other two suppliers and mortgages on the house. You're basically saying my aunt willed us bankruptcy."

"A challenge!" Roger Elgin smiled encouragingly at his daughter.

"Why did she do this?" Cade leaned her forehead on the tips of her fingers.

"The Spirit of the Universe moved her," Roger Elgin said.

"This is Ruth's dream," Pepper Elgin added, "and we honor that."

"Joyfully," Roger Elgin added.

"No. We don't honor it joyfully." Cade looked back and

forth between her parents. "*You* move to Portland and run a boutique. *I'm* not moving to Portland to run Ruth's gift shop. I run your gallery."

"Our gallery," her parents said in unison.

"Can we just do a short sale?" Cade asked.

"Hell no." Becket placed her palms on the table. "You can't do that to Selena."

Selena loved that Becket knew what a short sale was and was defending her against it...whatever it was.

"Is the store profitable?" Cade asked. "Could we get it out of debt fast?"

"Not even close." Delmar shook his head. "The store loses money every month, but Ruth believed in you. She said you have the know-how, and Selena had the passion."

Cade looked at Selena.

"I didn't expect this," Selena said quickly. "I'm not one of those people who comes in and tries to change someone's will right as they're dying. I wanted her erotic coffee table books, maybe some teacups, or her snow globes. That's all. But you probably want the snow globes. I didn't scam her. I swear."

"Selena would never do that," Becket said.

Cade's shoulders slumped. "I don't think you scammed her. I think this is my family." She glared at her parents. "This is what they do."

"This will be a wonderful adventure for you, honey," Pepper Elgin said.

"I have a life in New York," Cade said.

"Not much of a life." Pepper Elgin reached across the table and patted her daughter's arm.

"Thanks, Mom. I'm not moving to Portland." Cade said it with disgust.

"What's wrong with Portland?" Selena asked.

How could Cade not want to move to Portland? Portland was lovely. It was February, but soon the city would bloom with roses and rhododendrons. And Cade had held Selena in the rain. And it was the sweetest, safest thing she'd felt in so long. How could Cade not want to…drop everything to move across the country to live with a stranger she'd hugged once? Okay. Yes. Selena could imagine why Cade didn't want to do that.

Cade leaned back in her chair, looking up at the ceiling and running a hand through her blond hair.

"Everything," Cade said. "It's wet. It's full of nature. I don't *live* here!"

"You love being on the river," Roger Elgin said.

"Rowing crew is not *nature*. And I am not going to drop everything because my aunt had a whim."

"Thou must embark," Roger Elgin declared. "Forward, Odysseus."

"I am not embarking," Cade protested. "Are those the accounts?" Cade gestured to a stack of papers on the table in front of Delmar.

He passed them over. Cade examined them. She looked sexy reading them, like a CEO who'd been called away from her weekend at the lodge to handle a crisis at work. She also looked tired, although the shadows under her eyes only enhanced her good looks. Circles under Selena's eyes said, *I shouldn't have done that last night.* The circles under Cade's eyes said, *I could be a soulful Norwegian model.*

"This is bad." Cade turned a page. "How do you even…"

She looked up. "Did she pay taxes? This has to be a short sale."

What was a short sale? Selena didn't know, but it meant selling. And that meant losing Ruth again. Selena had just started thinking about the possibilities: living in Ruth's house, with Ruth's memories, pruning the wisteria, watching the garden flower in the spring. She couldn't lose it already.

"It's a wonderful shop!" Selena said. Cade had to understand. "You'll love it."

"What kind of store is it?" Cade asked warily.

"A feminist sex toy store."

That alone should make Cade want to work there. Who wouldn't want to teach vulva owners about their bodies and empower everyone to enjoy healthy sexuality?

Apparently, Cade.

Cade closed her eyes and rubbed her face.

"Of course it is," she said.

"We sell cookware too," Selena coaxed. *Come on. Smile. We'll have fun. We can do this.* "And candles. Christmas stuff."

"Why do you sell Christmas stuff at a sex toy store?" Cade asked. "No. I don't care. Because it's my aunt. Of course she sells sex toys and Christmas stuff."

"And cookware."

Obviously that didn't make it better.

Cade leaned back, staring up at the ceiling.

"And we teach classes," Selena said.

"On cooking?"

"On sex."

"Right."

"Do you want to add cooking classes? We could teach cooking. Well, I can't. I don't cook, but someone does. We could even make it sexy cooking, maybe make a whole meal where everything is in the shape of a vulva. Although there's no kitchen. It would have to be…plates of cheese or something." Selena should stop talking now, but she didn't. "Or fruit. We could do melon carving." *Please say yes. Please stay.* "Or maybe we could—"

"The store is a hundred thousand dollars in debt," Cade said. "I don't want to make a vagina cheese plate."

"Vulva," Selena corrected.

Cade ran her hands through her hair again.

For a moment, Selena thought Cade was going to stand up and walk out.

"Ruth said you were a genius at business," Delmar offered.

"I am," Cade said.

Cade looked like she'd been awake for days. Ruth had told Selena how much Cade did for her parents. She'd shown Selena pictures from Cade's Instagram. *She works too hard*, Ruth always said. Cade probably needed to lie down. She needed someone to rub her shoulders and make her cereal and play ASMR videos for her until she fell asleep. Selena would do all of that if Cade would just agree to stay and save Ruth's store and her beautiful house.

"What happens if Selena wants to stay, and I go back to New York?" Cade looked at Selena, her blue eyes kind but determined. "I could give you some advice or find a good tax preparer."

"It has to be a joint effort," Delmar said. "Honestly, I

don't think Ruth really considered that you'd say no. But if you do, it just goes into probate and then you collect whatever's left over, which is probably nothing."

"I'm sorry, Selena," Cade said. "The debt load on the store...a second mortgage. There's no way."

chapter 7

Suddenly, everyone was talking at once, all of them looking at Cade. Cade opened her mouth to speak, but there was no way she was getting a word in edgewise, even if she knew what to say.

"We can watch ASMR videos," Selena said. "There's one where a woman brushes her cat."

What?

"You really do need more friends," Cade's mother said. "Selena would make a nice friend."

"We switched you at birth so we could have an accountant in the family," her father said.

"You should get out more," her mother went on. "You're twenty-nine. Portland would be good for you. You're so responsible. You could get old before your time. They say that's happening to millennials. They aren't drinking or having sex."

"Pepper, she doesn't want to get drunk and have sex," her father said. "This is her raison d'être. To do business." He waved his hands as though performing a magic trick.

"There's too much debt," Cade said.

"Something will work out. It always does," her mother said.

But it didn't. People got run over by buses. People found terrible things in their fast food. Right now, a gallery was showing an installation of selfies people took right before stepping backward off cliffs or getting eaten by hippopotamuses.

"I'll help," Selena added. "I know the store. Isn't it at least worth a try? It's an opportunity. It's one month. You're a businesswoman. Ruth said that's what you were good at."

"It's what you do," Pepper Elgin agreed.

"If you've kept your parents out of trouble all these years, you could give Ruth's shop a chance," Delmar said.

"Please," Selena said.

"We all have one great calling, and this is yours," her father added, "to do the books!"

Cade did so much more for the gallery. She chose the shows. She coaxed shy artists out of attic studios. She tracked down graffiti artists no one knew by name. She had no social life because she was always at events and openings courting buyers. And all anyone saw was her parents, and all her parents saw was a free accountant.

"You don't get to have it both ways." Cade stood up, pushing her chair back with a clatter. "Either I know how to do this and you trust me, or I don't and you can do whatever you like with the property. But you can't say I'm the goddess of accounting, and then say I'm accounting wrong. This business has tanked. The ship sailed. The train wrecked. I'm telling you because I *know*."

"Isn't it worth at least trying?" Selena's dark eyes pleaded. She leaned forward, hands clasped on the table. She was bowing before Cade. For a moment, Cade imagined Selena was begging *her* to stay: *please stay, Cade, so we can embark on this adventure together.* Cade almost relented.

Then Cade's mother said, "You're so good at this stuff, honey. It's who you are."

And Selena said, "I've fucked up half my life. This is my chance to get my shit together. I want to own a business."

And Cade swept the papers off the table and walked out.

Cade didn't wait for an Uber. The fastest Uber arrival would still give her family and Selena, Delmar, and Selena's friend Becket, who'd spent the whole time glaring at her like a vicious elf, time to rush out of Delmar's office and keep telling her how she was the patron saint of TurboTax.

It's who you are.

What if I want to be someone else?

Instead, she ducked down an alley (which might have been someone's backyard) then turned left, then right, then left again, walking as quickly as she could without jogging. Rain seeped into her gray suede Cole Haans.

No. No. No. I don't want this.

It didn't take her long to emerge on a busy street lined entirely with brew pubs.

Which one would Selena and her parents never go to?

Rookies Beers and Balls fit the bill. A neon football and basketball flashed below the sign. She escaped inside.

Televisions lined every wall. She ordered a grilled chicken breast salad and found the quietest corner, deep in the bar where she could probably escape to the bathroom if, by some miracle, the entourage found her. She called Amy.

Amy picked up on the second ring. Cade could hear the sounds of Amy's vegan food truck in the background.

"Hi, baby doll. How's it going?" Amy asked.

There was a scrabble of sound as Amy put her earbuds in. The sound of sizzling told Cade Amy was at the grill. She could picture Amy's round, rosy face smiling into the steam of frying bok choy.

"You won't believe this," Cade said. "No. You totally will. It's my family."

"Your mom didn't buy that alpaca, did she?" Amy said cheerfully. "I love your mom."

Cade's parents visited Amy's food truck at least once a week. It was disturbing that they'd mentioned the alpaca to her. The alpaca could not go from passing-whim to plan-you-tell-friends.

"My aunt willed me a sex toy store," Cade said.

"What?" Amy called over the noise of the grill.

"A bankrupt sex toy store," Cade projected over the sound of Guns N' Roses.

A bro at another table grinned at her.

"Aw! Hell yeah!" Amy said. "Classic Elgin! God, I wish I had your family."

Amy had been raised by matching CFOs who worked until midnight and lived in a house entirely furnished in white linen. Maybe she and Cade had been switched at birth.

"I'm supposed to stay here and run it for a month until

it goes completely under," Cade said. "I mean the idea is that I wrestle it back from death and then as punishment for that, I get half of it. And I have to run it with her friend. She gets the other half."

"I'm taking ten," Amy said to someone in the truck. When she was away from the sound of frying, Amy said, "Okay, tell me again. Everything."

Cade described the meeting with Delmar. She left out the moment of panic she'd felt as she cut across someone's side yard. *Is this really who I am? For the rest of my life?*

"Are you sure it's not worth staying in Portland to see if you can make it work?" Amy asked. "It's just a month."

"Of course it's worth staying in Portland for a month." Cade took a napkin and rubbed at a sticky spot on the table. "I'd be crazy not to. If there's a chance in hell…Portland real estate is hot. That house is worth half a million at least. I'll have to talk Selena into selling. I think she'd want to keep the store and the house. We'll figure something out if hell freezes over and we don't lose everything."

"Selena?" Amy asked with interest.

"Ruth's friend."

"Is she nice?"

Yes.

"A little all over the place."

"Old?" Amy asked.

"About our age."

Cade knew what was coming next.

"Cute?"

"I don't know."

"Which means yes."

"Okay. Yes."

"And you need a vacation," Amy said.

"I love working at the gallery, and this isn't a vacation."

"'Portland: where young people go to retire,'" Amy quoted from *Portlandia*. "A change of scene."

The bartender delivered Cade's salad. At least, he delivered a pile of iceberg lettuce and a pale, thin chicken breast. Basically, the plate said, *Fuck you for ordering healthy at a sports bar.* Cade poked the chicken with her fork. It had the consistency of leather.

"I'm not going to point out the obvious," Amy said, which meant Amy was going to point out the obvious. "Maybe this is what you need. You know. To get there."

To have an orgasm.

When Cade had told Amy, when they were nineteen, that she'd never had an orgasm, it wasn't that big a deal. Nineteen. They were still kids. But at twenty-nine...Amy had been checking in to see if Cade had *gotten there* for ten years, and the answer was always the same. *It really isn't that big a deal to me.*

Of course it was.

The blogs called it "pre-orgasmic" as though "post-orgasmic" was a guarantee. Cade didn't think so.

"You could try one of everything at the store," Amy said. "Maybe it'll help. Like those desensitization therapies they do if you're afraid of flying."

"I'm not afraid of sex toys."

"Maybe you could date a little bit in Portland. Maybe this Selena woman."

Cade could have dated a little bit in New York if she thought anything good would come of it. The last woman she'd slept with had literally kicked her out of bed for poor performance, then called a week later to ask if Cade's parents would look at some of her work. Most of the women Cade met wanted her parents to look at their work.

It was part of why Cade hadn't had a lot of sex. It was better to think of it that way—not a lot of sex—than to actually count. Six times. She'd been shy at nineteen and too busy with school and the gallery to meet someone. Then suddenly she was twenty-five, then twenty-nine. It was like being out of the job market for too long. Eventually you couldn't get back in.

"It's not that it's so bad to stay in Portland for a month. I'll live. It's just that they all expected me to do this," Cade said. "This was my aunt's crazy idea, and no one asked me, and I'm just supposed to say, *Sure, Ruth. I'll put my whole life on hold, so that you can* not *know that I did this because, obviously, you're dead.*"

"Maybe your aunt picked you because she thought this would be good for you."

"Please don't tell me that she secretly guessed about..." Cade ate a piece of sad lettuce.

"Your sexual dysfunction?"

Cade could see Amy's brow furrowed with concern.

"Ugh. Don't say it like that. It sounds like I need Viagra."

"There is nothing to be ashamed of."

Cade didn't bother lying and saying she wasn't ashamed. That would just prolong the conversation.

"Selena gave the worst eulogy ever."

Cade described it. Amy laughed her big, full-bodied laugh.

"I love her already," Amy said. "She works at the sex

toy store. She talked about your aunt's clit. She could definitely help you. Give you advice. Like a mentor."

"No," Cade said, loud enough to break through "Sweet Child O' Mine." "I am not going to tell her anything," Cade said at a lower volume.

She hadn't thought about actually being at the sex toy store with Selena. They would have to talk to people about sex toys. Selena would have opinions. She'd ask Cade her opinions. Selena had probably had sex with dozens—hundreds?—of gorgeous people. She was probably the kind of person who had sex with someone once and ruined them forever. After Selena, no one else would be good enough.

"Fuck me." Cade leaned her head on her palm.

"That is the idea," Amy said.

Reluctantly, Cade called an Uber and waited outside Rookies Beers and Balls. Her parents were right. She was the responsible one, and the responsible choice was to stay and do what she could to salvage Ruth's assets. She wandered around Ruth's house when she got back. It looked a little cheerier in the day. It was possible that Selena had tried to clean up. Someone had picked up the old tissues and cleaned up the casseroles...well, not exactly. When Cade looked out the back door, she saw them piled on the little sidewalk that ran the perimeter of the house. A really responsible person would bring them back in and clean the pans. A really, really responsible person would try to return the pans to their owners. Cade wasn't that good. She walked outside and dumped them in the trash.

chapter 8

Then, since she was outside already, Cade squished across the lawn to the in-law apartment where Selena lived. Selena's lights were on although her curtains were closed. Cade hesitated at the door. She hoped Selena would just say thank you. Not *I told you so. Of course you have to stay. You owe this to your aunt.*

She knocked.

"Go away!" It sounded like Selena was standing right against the door. "You don't get to just show up. I don't want you here."

That was the opposite of thank you. Cade rubbed her hands over her face.

"I just came to talk about the shop."

Cade turned to go. The door flew open. Selena stood in her moonlight-white robe, a phone pressed to her ear. A voice on the other end of the phone crackled. Cade made out, "Why would I have called you if I was at your house?"

"I have to go," Selena said to the caller.

"I want..." the person on the other end said. "...you owe me...running away..."

Cade couldn't make out all of the caller's words, but she made out enough to know she didn't like her.

"You don't get to." Selena's large, dark eyes looked troubled, and her voice trembled.

You okay? Cade mouthed.

"Cade's here." Selena said, her voice gaining a little strength. "And don't tell me I'm making it up because she's right here."

That would be a strange thing to make up.

The caller began to say something, but Selena said, "No, no, no," moving the phone away from her ear as she spoke. Then she closed her...flip phone. A motion Cade hadn't seen since she was in high school when the popular girls snapped their phones closed aggressively, a sign that the caller had been thoroughly scolded. Had flip phones come back, like vinyl and Polaroids? Cade had missed it.

"I'm here," Cade said.

Cade glanced at Selena's space. The studio apartment looked like a vintage clothing store at Christmas. Twinkling lights hung from the ceiling. A feather boa slithered across the floor. The furniture was strewn with velvet capes and piles of lace. Selena's perfume hung in the air, musky and floral, like jasmine vines mating at night. It was lovely and the exact opposite of Cade's apartment.

"That was my ex." Selena tossed her phone on her bed. "She's awful." She tugged at the hem of her robe, took a shaky breath, and straightened her shoulders. "You want your sweatshirt back."

"I'm staying," Cade said.

The smile that lit Selena's face was almost worth the thought of spending a month working in a bankrupt sex toy store while her parents filled the gallery they co-owned with live alpacas.

"It's a long shot," Cade added. "Some cities have grants to help small businesses. Maybe because Ruth was sick...we could work out something with the other vendors. But please don't hope too much."

"If you're staying, I know it will work out."

It would have been nice if the delight in Selena's voice was for Cade, not for Cade's ability to salvage her inheritance, but whatever. That was the story of Cade's life.

"What made you change your mind?" Selena asked.

"You were right," Cade said. "It's too big an opportunity not to try."

"Really?"

"Yeah. I don't really want to be here," Cade said, "but I wasn't being reasonable. You were."

"Come in. Sit down." Selena hurriedly picked up an armload of clothing, revealing an easy chair beneath.

"I should go," Cade said. "Tomorrow you can show me the store."

"You'll love it." Selena clasped her hands to her chest. "It's gorgeous. You're going to be speechless."

Unfortunately, Selena was right.

The next morning, Cade's Uber dropped her off on a street lined with boutiques and restaurants. A place called Portland Lumbersexual sported a neon beard in the window. The smell of burnt sugar wafted out of an ice cream shop. The letterboard outside a store called

Suck Me Succulents read *Find eternal peace in a pot.* A big promise.

At the far corner of the courtyard, a large neon sign read *Satisfaction Guaranteed.* Cade approached warily. A sign on the door said this was a safe space.

She pushed the door open. Selena was already there, wearing black jeans, a corset, and a fake-fur stole. Of course she looked fabulous, her dark curls piled on top of her head except for one tendril that caressed her cheek. Cade was wearing a gray cashmere sweater and gray trousers and gray oxfords. They were different shades of gray. She'd gone crazy.

"Satisfaction Guaranteed." Selena spread her arms wide, her face radiating eager pride.

Cade took another step in. From a marketing perspective...or maybe from any perspective...the store was horrifying.

If Selena's cottage looked like a vintage thrift store at Christmas, this looked like a thrift shop had a three-way with a Hallmark store and a bag of sex toys. There was a rack of clothing in Day-Glo 1960s paisley. Some cookware. Way too many pillows emblazoned with *YOLO.* There was a shelf of lifelike cat dolls...sculptures...their sides rising and falling as if they were breathing. Above them dangled Christmas tree ornaments in the shape of mermen. One had a BDSM flag draped over his shoulders. Another one held a martini. And tucked in around the kitsch were sex toys. Vibrators. A crop. A box labeled *Twist Clit & Nipple Triple Sucker.* And there were dildos everywhere: Wedged between plush teddy bears. Hanging from ribbons above the counter. Dildos marching in a line across the windowsill...The window which was not frosted and gave passersby a clear view of the store's contents.

Above the counter was a large neon art piece. Five wings or prongs spread out from a central core. One curved forward like a neck. The others flared out like the petals of a stylized orchid, swan, or butterfly. It also looked kind of like a fat penguin. The neon was very pink and very bright.

"I can feel Ruth's spirit here." Selena hugged herself. "What do you think? Isn't it amazing?"

Amy was a big proponent of if-you-can't-say-anything-nice-don't-say-anything-at-all. And Cade let artists down gently when they showed her terrible work.

"I like..." She couldn't finish that sentence.

"I've been thinking about what we can do to sell more stuff." Selena released her arms and put her hands on her hips in a kind of I-can-do-this power pose. "I thought a midnight sidewalk sale. Becket could get her burlesque troupe to perform outside the shop. She does an amazing act where she climbs out of a balloon and strips at the same time. We could do live demonstrations, or we could do a storytelling session about our experiences. You and me, talking about why sex toys are important. We could do a mini *Vagina Monologues*."

Cade did not blurt out *I will die first*.

"Oh! And even better," Selena said. "The sex industry Sexpo is happening in two weeks. We can flyer there, talk to people, get the word out."

It was a good idea, but the idea of flyering a sex toy expo made Cade's stomach churn.

"Right," Cade said. She pressed a button on a rubber fish attached to a plaque. It flapped its tail and began singing "Take Me to the River."

"I'll show you around." Selena made a sweeping gesture that encompassed the store.

It wasn't a large space, but the clutter made it hard to take in.

"First we've got dildos," Selena said. "Ruth loved dildos." *I didn't need to know that.*

Selena's voice got a little teary. "This was our favorite." She picked up a butter-yellow dildo complete with balls and veins. It was very large.

"I think of this as the all-purpose dildo. If I could only take one in my carry-on, it'd be this one."

Selena looked down at the dildo. It was the size of Cade's wrist. A perfect, movie-star tear slipped down Selena's cheek. Cade half expected Selena to clasp the thing to her breast. It was the kind of bizarre, awkward moment Cade's family thrust her into. If she were a real Elgin, maybe she'd know what to say.

"I like the girth." Selena ran her hand up and down the dildo.

Cade looked away.

"Sorry. TMI?" Selena asked. "You want to feel?" She held the dildo out to Cade.

Cade did not want to feel, but she took the dildo and slapped it against her palm.

"Sturdy." Cade felt herself blush. She hoped Selena didn't notice. "Big."

Cade had tried a few dildos. They hurt. She handed the dildo back.

"The only thing I don't like about it is the name: the Titan." Selena wiped the tear off her cheek. "It's very heteronormative. I mean why can't something this size be the Helena or the Camilla? Although maybe Titans could be women. I don't know. It was modeled after a real porn star, and we sell Clone-a-Willy kits. If you have someone back home and you want to have a dildo made in the shape of his penis. Unless you've already done that."

"I'm gay," Cade said quickly. At least she could get out of the Clone-a-Willy conversation.

"Lucky for the girls." Selena smiled, as though flirting was her natural inclination, even when she was sad.

It wasn't personal.

"You could make one from a friend's penis," Selena said, "but that could be weird…or not. Depends on the friend."

Cade would have passed out from embarrassment if she had to ask Josiah to clone his penis for her.

Selena picked up another dildo.

"Sticky," she said.

Why was it sticky?

Selena held it out for Cade to feel.

"I believe you." Cade clasped her hands behind her back.

"People come in here after eating Ruby Jewel waffle cones." Selena picked up another one. "Yep. Sticky. Then over here are condoms, garter belts, crotchless panties, vases, cards, Ben Wa balls, and bondage and kink." Selena motioned to the neon orchid-penguin over the counter. "Ruth's friend made it." She smiled sadly. "For her sixty-fifth birthday. It's the clitoris. Obviously. But a lot of people don't know it looks like that, so it's a great demo.

My clit is named Artemisia. And here we've got bakeware, butt plugs, butt plugs with tails…"

Cade walked toward a shelf and perused the contents.

"Why couldn't my aunt sell succulents?" She hadn't really meant to say it out loud. "Or ink cartridges."

"Because this is more fun," Selena said. "Don't you think so?"

Maybe it would have been if Cade could find one sex toy that worked for her. All they'd done was make her feel like a failure. She'd googled *lesbian porn* and watched women with long nails suck on dildos. She'd tried. It was as erotic as sucking on a toothbrush.

"We'll need to get a portal for online sales," Cade said. "I looked at the website and it says, *If you want to order by mail, call Ruth.*"

Selena took a step closer. Cade caught a whiff of her perfume. She touched Cade's arm, and Cade jumped. Selena pulled her hand back quickly.

"I know you didn't want to do this," Selena said. Then, tenderly, like she was holding Cade's heart in the palm of her hand, she said. "We could sell succulents if you'd like, but we have to be really careful to tell people not to put them in the anus."

Cade looked at Selena.

"People make that mistake all the time," Selena said apologetically.

Please tell me that's not true.

There were a dozen things Cade needed to do to triage Ruth's finances, but Selena wanted to open the store, and it seemed unfriendly not to work one shift beside her.

"I'm glad we're doing this together." Selena sat on the counter. She took a penis-shaped chocolate pop out of a display box, unwrapped it, and popped it in her mouth. "Thank you."

Cade stood beside her, leaning against the counter a few feet away.

"I read about that exhibit the Elgin Gallery did: *Male Fragility*. The one with all the dildos melted into welding hoods," Selena said.

That had been Cade's mother's idea.

"It was cool."

"Thanks," Cade said.

"Although I thought it was a little too conceptual," Selena said.

Cade was surprised that Selena thought anything about *Male Fragility*, but Selena was right. It was too conceptual. Cade would never have picked a show that wasn't great art on its own, with or without a sociopolitical message.

"But what do I know," Selena added.

They fell silent for a moment. They'd yet to see a customer.

"So what do you do in New York?" Selena offered Cade a chocolate penis.

Cade shook her head. "I don't do sugar."

Why was she so boring? She could have eaten one chocolate penis to be polite.

"I'm the gallery manager and curator...and accountant. Basically all of it."

"Do you love it?"

"Mostly. I started doing the gallery taxes when I was sixteen."

"I did my taxes once."

Cade wasn't sure if she was joking.

"I started tattooing when I was sixteen," Selena added. "Helping my dad out with shading and some flash. And don't judge. I'm from Tristess, Oregon. It's the Wild West." Selena sucked on her chocolate penis for a moment. "Your parents are über cool."

Everyone loved Roger and Pepper.

"My friend Becket's in an art co-op called the Aviary," Selena said. "Everyone there's heard of them. We had to tell people *you cannot come to the funeral just to meet the Elgins*. But what about when you're not at the gallery? What do you do?"

What did she do? Go to galas for work and pretend she was there for fun. Cade's phone buzzed in her pocket. She glanced at it. Josiah had texted a picture of a remarkable piece of marble work. *Piss off*, Cade texted with a heart emoji.

"That's my friend Josiah. He's a buyer. He buys a ton of our stuff for his clients, but we're always fighting over who's found the next Maya Hayuk." She showed Selena the marble sculpture. "It's good, but I won't tell him."

"So what else? Dating?" Selena tapped her heels against the counter. "Pets? I had a snake once, but Becket said I couldn't let him be loose in my apartment because he'd eventually kill me."

"There's a feral cat that lives on my fire escape. Sociopath. I guess he's mine. I feed him. He hates me."

"I'm sorry."

"He hates everyone," Cade said. "In the apartment, we

say if he shows up on your fire escape something bad is going to happen to you. We call him the Harbinger. But he doesn't do that to me."

Unless getting stuck with a dying sex toy store in a city where it rained twenty-three and a half hours a day was her calamity. She'd thought it was. Chatting with Selena and watching the rain fall outside the store, it didn't seem quite so bad.

"I had to ask four people before I found someone who'd feed him while I was away," Cade said.

"You take care of things."

"That's me."

"That's important. I bet people love that about you. And how about dating? Girlfriend? Wife?"

"Not right now."

Not ever.

"Crazy-ass hookups?"

"Do I look like a crazy-ass-hookups person?" Cade gestured to her gray sweater.

"You never know." The corner of Selena's mouth quirked up in a smile. "It's the serious ones who are really kinky. Or maybe you answer fucked-up Craigslist ads and then go to the park just to see what kind of person shows up," Selena mused. "Then you go sit on the bench where you're supposed to meet but when they give you the secret word, you're just, like, *I don't know what you mean.*" Selena cocked her head to one side. "Heartbreaker."

"I've never answered a weird Craigslist ad."

"That's what they all say. Or do you write them?"

Maybe she should. *Want to have an orgasm before I turn thirty. Am probably a bad lover.*

"Are you looking for someone?" Selena asked. "A type?"

Apparently she skipped small talk and went right to inner longings.

"I don't know." *Someone who likes me. A friend. Maybe another pre-orgasmic.* "Someone I can count on," Cade said. "Someone who is not like my parents. Maybe an accountant. But what about you? What do *you* do for fun?"

"Besides waiting for you on the park bench?"

Cade hid her smile. She met women like Selena at art openings, women who flirted with everyone because they were beautiful and playful and they knew no one would mind. It didn't mean anything, but it was fun to pretend.

"I do too much." Selena ate the last bite of chocolate off her penis pop and set the stick down. "Or at least I used to. Too many parties. Too much absinthe. Too many people."

She took another chocolate out of the display and unwrapped it.

"What can I say?" Selena said. "There's a lot of sexy people out there. You just walk down the street and there they are." Selena tapped her chest. "Hence, celibate."

Cade looked over.

Celibate?

"I don't mind talking about it," Selena said, although Cade had not asked. "All my friends know."

"You don't have to tell me," Cade said quickly.

Selena started telling her.

"It's all about the sexual excitation system," Selena said. "You know how most people, when they're stressed out, they don't want to have sex? Kind of like if you're camping in bear country and you hear something outside your tent, you lose your boner?"

Not an experience Cade had had.

Selena went on. "But me, if the bear's outside the tent, I'm like, *I can fuck this bear away*! Anyway, after my ex and I broke up, I kind of fell apart. I was stressed, and I just went at it. One hookup at a time. Like I tried to cover all of Portland. It's not that I made bad health choices. But everything else was a mess. I was crashing on Becket's sofa. I didn't have a job. Some of the people I slept with liked me."

That wasn't hard to believe.

"I hurt some people. They thought we were going somewhere, but I was just spinning in circles. So I made my vow. Get my shit one hundred percent together. Then think about dating and sex." Selena cocked her head to the side. "I think that's why Ruth willed me half her shop." She gestured to the room. "*This* is getting my shit together."

If a bankrupt shop full of YOLO pillows, muffin trays, and dildos was getting her shit together, Selena was in trouble.

"But I'm not saying there is anything wrong with having all the sex you want," Selena added quickly, as though she might have offended Cade, as though Cade had lines of lovers going into her apartment and thought Selena was criticizing her lifestyle. "I just wasn't enjoying it emotionally. Physically I'm dying for it." Selena exhaled heavily. "When I break my vow, I'm going to explode."

The thought sent a startling pulse through Cade's body. *None of my business.*

Selena hopped off the counter.

"This vibrator"—she picked a seashell-shaped thing off one of the shelves where it was hidden between two fluffy teddy bears—"is my go-to. Love it. What's your fave?"

Cade coughed.

"Ah, shit!" Selena said. "I'm sorry! I'm used to talking about sex, and Ruth and I were always like, *Have you tried this? Have you tried that?* But I made you uncomfortable. That was inappropriate."

"Not at all. Totally cool." Cade scanned the shelves for an answer that wasn't *I'm a twenty-nine-year-old almost-virgin and none of this stuff works for me.* Luckily Cade sold art at a high-end gallery, and a lot of selling art was standing beside people, nodding thoughtfully, while they deliberated over their purchase.

"That kind," Cade said, nodding thoughtfully toward one shelf.

Selena walked over to the shelf and picked up a vibrator that looked like a turtle mounted on top of a dolphin mounted on top of...a banana with jellyfish-like tentacles? And there were also straps like maybe you wore it underneath your clothes.

"This one?" she asked.

"Yes." *Say it with confidence.*

"Wow." Selena raised her eyebrows. "I don't know anyone who knows how to use that one. We've never sold one. You're a real pro."

chapter 9

Selena stirred beneath her black satin sheets and the quilt Becket had sewn for her out of Crown Royal bags. Ruth would be calling soon to tell her to get up and come to the house and make coffee. Then they'd walk down to the shop, admiring the gardens they passed, Ruth nipping off sprigs of hydrangea and clematis to root and grow in her garden.

Selena opened her eyes and remembered. She would never have coffee with Ruth. They would never walk to the store or peruse sex toy distributors' websites. A lump formed in her throat. Ruth was gone. But Selena would be working with Cade. That was a consolation.

Cade had looked confident leaning against the counter, her hands in her pockets. Nothing could go wrong with a woman like that in charge. And the fact that Cade was handsome and her blond hair looked like heavy silk and she had an adorable way of pursing her lips and widening her eyes when she was thinking...there was no harm in appreciating an attractive woman. Selena wasn't going to do anything about it, and Cade wouldn't be interested if Selena tried. There were beautiful accountants in New York with 401(k)s—whatever those were—who would lure Cade into their beds. But that made it safe to have a little, tiny crush. Just for fun.

On the way to the store, Selena stopped at Out in Portland Coffee and bought two double caramel mochas from the rainbow-tattooed barista. She and Cade could start with chocolate and whipped cream. Then maybe they could talk about a sidewalk sale or some new class offerings. Then they could have lunch at the Thai place that served crickets. The crickets weren't that good, but Selena had felt very worldly the two times she'd had them. *Yes, I eat all the way to the bottom of the food chain to save the world.* Cade would be impressed.

When Selena arrived at Satisfaction Guaranteed, Cade was kneeling on the floor surrounded by boxes. Her gray, ribbed sweater hugged her body just enough to hint at muscular shoulders and soft breasts. She looked like an old-money New Englander—or what Selena imagined wealthy New Englanders looked like—mixed with a genderqueer boi. It looked good on her.

Selena handed her a coffee.

Cade looked at the tower of whipped cream.

"That's a meal," she said.

"You don't take it black, do you?" Selena asked. "Why would you have black coffee when you can have joy?"

"I take it black, but thank you." Cade took a sip.

Selena sat down next to her.

Cade's blond hair was perfect, her skin dewy. She looked

freshly washed, maybe freshly dry-cleaned. But she had soulful-Norwegian-actor shadows under her eyes.

"Tired?" Selena asked.

"I was up late." Cade reached onto a low shelf, removed a merman Christmas tree ornament, and put it in one of the boxes.

Each merman was a kind of gay man—a bear with his leather vest, a boy with a martini glass, a man wearing the BDSM flag. They did rely on stereotypes, but they captured the stereotypes perfectly. And they were mermen. Who didn't love that?

"Did you go out?" Selena asked.

Cade gave a little laugh. "Working on Ruth's accounts. They are epically screwed up."

"No one should be up that late thinking about accounts," Selena said. "You should have come over to my place and drunk absinthe."

"Somebody has to think about accounts." There was an edge to Cade's voice.

She was probably just tired.

"Sorry," Cade added. "There's just a lot to do. We've got a month until her creditors can claim her assets, if we can't find a way to get that money and get the store looking like the kind of place Swing Set wants to give a break to." Her face wrinkled in a frown. "I don't know how we're going to pull this off."

They were sitting close together on the floor, and Selena wanted to put her hand on Cade's knee. *Thank you for staying.*

"But you're tired. You want to go get tots?"

"Tots?"

"Tater tots."

They were always an answer.

"We need to open the store."

Selena pulled her phone out of her pocket and flipped it open. "In an hour. You can eat a lot of tots in an hour."

Cade pulled a protein bar out of her pants pocket. "Breakfast."

"People eat protein bars to punish themselves." Selena hoped Cade would smile. "We'll go to lunch today. How about that? Thai Lotus has amazing noodles and they have crickets."

"Crickets?" Cade's brow furrowed. "We've got to get this place in shape. I've drafted a marketing plan. Let me get my laptop."

Cade retrieved her laptop from the counter and sat back down on the floor beside Selena. Cade took another sip of her coffee.

"Enough empty calories to kill someone, but it is good." Cade opened her laptop to a spreadsheet. "These are the financials." She flipped through several tabs of numbers. "I'll handle that part. And this is the physical marketing plan. I was hoping you could do that part."

The slide showed two columns. Each featured a list of products and a percentage, some struck through.

Sex toys—75%
Sexual accessories—11%
Sexual costuming—10%
~~Other clothing—< 1%~~
Books—4%
~~Home décor—< 1%~~

~~Cards and stationery—< 1%~~
~~Cookware—< 1%~~

"These are product categories based on percentage of total sales," Cade said. "We're lucky that sales correlate to a consistent brand image."

"What do you mean?"

"About three-quarters of the inventory is off-brand and wasting shelf space."

Suddenly Selena saw what Cade was doing. Cade was boxing things up. She was clearing the shelves. She was getting rid of things Ruth loved.

"I'm going to try to find a discount store that'll take this stuff," Cade said. "We'll lose money on it, but it's better than nothing." Cade put another merman Christmas tree ornament and put it in a box.

"That's Jonathan." Ruth had named the mermen after the Fab Five. "We can't get rid of him."

Selena took Jonathan out of the box.

"Next year, we were going to get a Christmas tree and do it all in gay pride stuff," she said. "Ruth didn't give up. Even when the doctors said it was over, she talked about next year. Right up until the last day, when she told us not to cry at the funeral. No. We have to keep everything. This is *her*."

Cade looked distressed.

"We have to rebrand."

Cade had already filled several boxes. Now she took a basket of sand dollars off a shelf and added it to a box.

"But people love Satisfaction Guaranteed." Selena looked at Jonathan's smiling face.

"They don't buy anything." Cade pushed her laptop toward Selena. "Look."

"You can't pack this stuff up. This is what we sell." Selena took a sand dollar out of the box. Perfect. No one found perfect sand dollars on the Oregon coast except Ruth. "You can't get rid of these." She felt tears rising.

Cade picked up her coffee and stood. Selena stood with her.

"You can take them home." Cade sipped her coffee.

This time she grimaced, which was ridiculous because the human body was biologically programmed to like caramel mochas. They were at the bottom of Maslow's pyramid.

"Making a profit means maximizing shelf space and having a clear brand image. You can't have these"—Cade tapped the shelf in front of the Twist Clit & Nipple Triple Sucker set—"and also sell those." She waved her coffee in the direction of the breathing cats, the air bladders inside their chests rising and falling. "What are they anyways?"

"Cats," Selena said.

"They're kind of creepy."

Ruth usually switched the cats off at night, but they'd been breathing for weeks now. Two of them had run out of batteries. It made Selena want to cry.

"People like them," Selena said.

They didn't. Only Ruth thought they were cute. She patted one. It wasn't that bad. It didn't feel like those creepy rabbit's-foot keychains…not too much like that. Selena snatched it up and clutched it to her chest to show Cade how cuddly it was. (It wasn't.)

Cade rubbed her forehead. "They look like taxidermy that's not quite dead."

"But what do you want this place to look like?" Selena asked. "This is Ruth's vision."

Cade shrugged. "A gallery. Clear shelves. A few high-end products. Brighter lighting. Like Target."

"Ruth hated Target."

"How can you hate Target?"

"Big box stores are a capitalist conspiracy."

Selena didn't like the way Cade sighed. Alex had sighed like that. *How can you be so impractical, Selena? Some of us live in the real world. You're not a child.*

"This stuff is *not* what I want when I'm thinking about..." Cade shrugged.

"Sex?" Selena filled in.

"Yes, sex." Cade ran her hand through her hair. "Can you imagine"—she pointed to one of the sleeping cats—"being with someone with this breathing next to you on the dresser or something?"

Selena would not admit that Cade had a point. She would certainly not tell her that Becket had been urging Ruth to clean up the store for years. Ruth was dead. She and Ruth would never gather sand dollars again. The Fab Five belonged on the shelves until Christmas, when she would buy a tree from Ruth's favorite tree farm and string it with lights and cute gay mermen.

"Running a business isn't just about profits," Selena said.

Selena felt like an avalanche had started. Ruth was dead. Cade would pack up all these beautiful things that were Ruth's. The store would be blank, Ruth erased. Then Cade would do it to the house. And if Cade was right, they'd lose the house and the store anyway. And there'd be no reason to walk down Wisteria Lane. And everything would be over. Really, really over. There wouldn't even be a place to put her memories.

"It actually is about profits. Right now it has to be." Cade's face said, *I don't want to fight with you about this.* "I'm really sorry. I know this is fast, but we don't have time to be sentimental."

Selena set the breathing cat on a shelf and stomped across the store, although there wasn't really anywhere to go. She settled for taking a stand behind the counter.

"You can't change Satisfaction Guaranteed," Selena said. "This is Ruth's place."

"Ruth was a good person." Cade looked around. "But this doesn't work."

"You don't know about Satisfaction Guaranteed," Selena said.

It was a good thing Selena had taken a vow of celibacy, because she was stressed, sad, and overwhelmed, and Cade was pissing her off, and Cade was hot. Before Selena's vow that was exactly when she would have slept with someone. Probably Cade.

"Everybody wanted me to help." Cade set her coffee on the counter in a way that said *I'm not drinking the rest of this stuff.*

They stared at each other from opposite sides of the counter.

"I know how to run a business," Cade said. "People won't shop here because they don't feel comfortable. Men, masc women, trans men...they won't feel comfortable. Everything here says cis, white female Red Hat Society,

YOLO. Literally everything says YOLO. All this stuff says *one kind of person belongs here.*"

"Ruth loved everyone!" Selena shot back. "And people don't feel uncomfortable here. *You* feel uncomfortable. It's 2021. You're picking up dildos like they're going to bite you. They're not fucking sea cucumbers."

Selena didn't mean it. Cade hadn't picked up the Titan in any particular way. It was just the kind of dumb thing Selena said when she was mad. But as soon as the words left her mouth, she saw Cade's face fall. She stuck her hands in her pockets and hunched her shoulders protectively.

"I do not feel uncomfortable," Cade said.

Selena knew that look on their customers. The shy ones. The scared ones. She was extra careful with them. She didn't know what people had been through or how much it took for them to walk through the door. If Cade was nervous, she deserved that care too. Selena should slow down. *If you've had experiences that make this a challenging place for you…*

But Selena had a gift for fucking things up, so instead she said, "You come in here for two hot seconds and think you know what to do with the store, but you don't." She put her hands on her hips. "This is more my shop than it will ever be yours."

"Thank god," Cade said.

"And I know what Satisfaction Guaranteed needs. We need events. We need music and burlesque and *Vagina Monologues.* I'm going to teach a paint-your-vulva class, and this place is going to be packed."

"No one is painting their vagina in this store."

"They're not painting their vaginas; they're painting their vulvas."

"I don't care. They're not painting anything here."

"They will, and it will be awesome, and if I say we're not getting rid of anything, we're not getting rid of anything," Selena went on. "You don't have Ruth's vision. You swept in looking all hot, uptight, genderqueer prep-school boi in your gray sweaters." She hadn't actually meant to say that either. "This place has a soul. Ruth had a soul. *You* are a soulless capitalist." No. It was wrong to identify the whole person with one trait or disability. "You're *acting* like a soulless capitalist. We're not going to save Satisfaction Guaranteed by turning it into Target. We're going to save it by letting it be what it was meant to be."

Selena sounded authoritative. That was a surprise. She'd never won an argument with Alex, and Cade's cool efficiency reminded her of Alex. But unlike Alex, Cade didn't answer Selena's outburst with a cutting remark.

Cade yanked her hands out of the pockets of her perfectly pressed, subtly pinstriped trousers.

"Fine. I'll get new batteries for the cats. They'll look less creepy if they aren't dead." She whirled around. Then, as though she decided she wanted to get the last word in, she turned back.

"Sea cucumbers," she said, "do not bite. Everyone knows that."

With that, she pulled her gray overcoat off the rack by the door, swung it around her like a cloak, and stomped out. If Selena hadn't been mad at her, she would have been half in love with the fabulous exit.

chapter 10

That evening, Selena stomped up the metal staircase to the Aviary artists' co-op like it had personally offended her. The staircase had once been a fire escape. Rainwater shook off the steps as they rattled. Inside, a few painters were working at their stations, their projects illuminated by lamps. The high windows were dark. It had been a warehouse once, back when warehouses needed natural light. The space smelled of turpentine and clay. Familiar smells. She could almost feel a brush in her hand.

"What's up?" Becket emerged from behind a rack of costumes. She was wearing a bra with a beaded fringe that hung down to her waist.

The center of the warehouse floor was full of ornate, mismatched furniture and Turkish rugs. Selena threw herself down on a gold settee.

Becket hurried over.

"You look pissed. What happened?"

"Fucking Cade Elgin," Selena said.

"You didn't?"

"Of course not."

Really, there was no *of course* about it.

"Take ten," Becket called to the members of the Fierce Lovely burlesque troupe who were waiting for her direction. She sat on a brocade sofa across from Selena and picked up a crystal decanter from one of the many liquor-laden carts. The Aviary was always ready for a party.

"Zenobious's latest." Becket poured her a shot.

Selena took a sip. It tasted like Everclear and cilantro.

"There's a learning curve." Selena puckered her lips. "He'll get it sometime."

"What happened?" Becket asked again.

"I can't work with Cade. She's going to ruin the store. She wants to change everything." Selena draped her legs over the arm of the settee and staired at the high ceiling. "She wants to take out all of Ruth's stuff, like the breathing kittens. Just throw them away like trash."

Becket cleared her throat. "You know those kittens are creepy as fuck, right?"

"Ruth loved them." They were creepy. "I just want Cade to save the store without ruining everything, and I could help her, but she won't listen to any of my ideas. She's just like, *We need to streamline.* Get rid of everything." Selena sat back up. "She wants to make it look like Target."

"I'd go to that Target," Becket said.

"Don't laugh."

"I'm sorry."

"She hates everything Satisfaction Guaranteed stands for."

"It stands for those taxidermized cats?"

"They're real fake fur."

"Doesn't help."

"She thinks we should just sell sex toys. Nothing else."

"And that's a bad thing because?"

"It wouldn't be Ruth."

"I know." Becket's face gentled. "If you really think Cade's wrong, put your foot down. Say, *We're doing this. Period.*"

"I did."

"That's great. See? You got this."

"I called her a soulless capitalist," Selena said.

Becket suppressed a smile. "That's kind of what you need right now. Your passion, her soulless capitalism."

Selena sat up and poured herself another shot of Zenobious's creation.

"What if Cade's right? What if it's not enough and we lose everything?"

The thought swirled through her mind like a black cloud.

"You'll be back where you expected to be three days ago. On my couch. Embraced by the love of your friends and looking for a job. But that's why you have to work together, so you don't end up on my couch."

Selena swirled the flecks of green in her drink.

"You're thinking," Becket said.

"I thought this was going to be fun," Selena said. "I liked her. She seemed nice." Selena paused. "She held me in the rain."

It sounded like a Hallmark movie.

"What?" Becket drew out the word.

"The night after the funeral. I was going to take a shower. She was exercising. I was sad."

Becket would never let up about her vow now.

"She just held me and told me it was okay to cry. It wasn't a big deal." It had felt like a big deal. At least it had felt special. That made Cade's cold efficiency harder to take. "We fought about sea cucumbers."

"You what?"

"Do they bite or not?"

"You fought about *cucumbers*?"

"Sea cucumbers."

"An important distinction?"

Becket's next thought was interrupted by one of the artists stopping by their settees on his way to the bank of sinks on the other side of the floor.

"Beautiful Adrien needs your help," he said to Selena. "He says he's deep in alizarin crimson, and he knows it's wrong, but he's lost his vision."

Selena knew the feeling. She shook her head.

Becket stood up. "You should help him."

"Okay," Selena said reluctantly, "but I don't know what I can do."

Becket snorted.

They got up and headed for Beautiful Adrien's station. Selena hugged him and gave him a chaste peck on the lips. He was the last person she'd slept with before taking her vow. Neither of them planned on doing it again, but it had moved their friendship from long-and-amiable to something deeper.

"Selena, my savior," he said. "What am I doing wrong?"

It was easy to see the problem. A teenage girl posed for him in a sweatshirt and jeans. He'd painted her in shades of red. They screamed like writing in all caps.

"Alizarin crimson's hard," Selena said. "You get in and you can't get out. It's the Hotel California."

"I know. I only meant to use a tiny bit."

Selena took a brush from Beautiful Adrien's collection and mixed the right shade on his palette. She missed the feel of oil paint gliding beneath a brush. She missed the way time disappeared. She missed working so late she fell asleep beside her easel, dreaming in colors that didn't exist yet. She looked back and forth between the canvas and the girl. If it were her painting, she'd darken the background to black, so the girl's face shone like a Caravaggio painting by moonlight. If it were her painting, she would...freak out, decide it was worthless, cry, fuck someone, strip the canvas, regret doing it, cry, and gorge on tater tots. But it was easy to fix other people's paintings.

"Her soul is light blue," Selena said without taking her eyes off the girl. "It's in her eyes. Red locks her into who she is now. But she's still becoming the person she's going to be."

A smile of agreement flickered on the girl's lips.

"You needed the red to get the light here, but it's only for the gradient, not for the color." She eased a palette knife along the canvas, loving the way it scraped gently like a lover's teeth on a bare shoulder. "And here." She dabbed a dark blue into the background. "You'll mix it like this." She chose a brush and showed Beautiful Adrien how to do it, then stepped back.

"You're amazing," he said.

They all studied the painting.

"You know, we've always got a painting station for you," Beautiful Adrien said.

"Nah," Selena said. "I was never any good."

"Come on," Becket and Beautiful Adrien said together.

Becket put an arm around Selena, still looking at the painting. "You were the best," she said, squeezing Selena's shoulders.

Were.

"So," Beautiful Adrien said, his perfectly sculpted lips opening in a teasing smile, "I heard you were having trouble with the roommate. Lovers' quarrel?"

"Adrien," Becket scolded.

"I like her for Selena," Beautiful Adrien said. "I talked to her a bit outside the funeral. She's cool."

"Are you betting on when I'll break my vow?" Selena asked. "Do you know how #metoo that is?"

"No one is betting, we're conjecturing," Beautiful Adrien said. "Becket wants to put you in a little bubble and keep you safe forever. I think the answer to too much isn't nothing, it's balance."

"You're so spiritual." Becket smiled at Beautiful Adrien and shook her head.

Beautiful Adrien grinned. "And she's hot. I'd swipe right."

"Don't listen to Adrien," Becket said, "but maybe you should give Cade a chance with the store. Self-preservation. You need her. Don't give her a hard time."

And maybe she doesn't deserve it, Selena thought as she headed back down the clattering staircase. Selena remembered Cade's arms around her. Then she flashed back to Cade's hunched shoulders. *You're picking up dildos like they're going to bite you.* Selena was a sex educator. She didn't shame people about their sexuality. She worked at a sex toy store. Her job was telling people they were okay. Everyone had anxieties. There was no normal to strive for, just consensual and happy. And there was Cade, looking so pulled together in her genderqueer, boardroom outfits and doing push-ups like a marine, and Selena hadn't stopped to think what Cade might be feeling underneath all that. Before her vow, Selena would have tried to seduce her; at least now she could have said something kind.

Selena got on her motorcycle and pulled her riding gloves out of her bag, but before she put them on her phone rang. Alex. She let it go to voice mail. When she played the voice mail, it was nothing new. Alex wanted to see her. Just a coffee date. Blah. Blah. Blah. But every word made Selena's stomach clench. She hit delete.

How could she have gotten herself into a relationship like that? Alex had never been gentle with her. It was always, *You're a genius* or *You're wasting your talent.* She'd never said, *It doesn't matter if you're a good painter; I love you.* She'd never even given Selena her old paints, even though Selena had worked three jobs to pay for supplies. And Alex's staticky voice mail still made her sweat. Ridiculous. Selena was a feminist. She was going to be a business owner. She was empowered. But none of that seemed to matter when it came to Alex, so even if she had, for just a second, felt a little love-hate attraction to Cade, Selena was celibate. Shit-together goal number one.

chapter 11

The next few days were no better. Selena was charming to the customers and icily polite to Cade. Cade texted a litany of complaints to Amy even though Amy was totally unsympathetic. *Cute!* Amy texted back to a picture of the mermen ornaments. *She's just sad*, Amy texted when Cade complained about Selena's petulant behavior.

At five o'clock on day four, Cade stood behind the counter ringing up a leather thong and bubblegum-scented candle. The third sale of the day. She ran the customer's card for the fifth time, then gave up and typed the number into the system. At the Elgin Gallery, they had a metal disc on which customers set their Visa Platinum cards. The receipt was a contract of authenticity signed by Cade, the customer, and the gallery's attorney. The Satisfaction Guaranteed register began spitting out yards of register tape.

It was going to be a long month.

Amy called a few minutes later.

"Just checking up on you," Amy said. "How's the store? How's everything?"

Pots and pans clattered on Amy's end. Cade could almost smell the tofu roasting. In the background, she heard the Doomsday Man. He walked by the cart every day proclaiming that the world would end at midnight.

"I wish I was back in New York," Cade said.

"But you're having an adventure."

"You sound like my parents."

"Thank you. So how is it?"

"I was looking for grants last night. I found this grant from something called the Gentrification Abatement Coalition. They've got a Small Business Revival Grant. Long fucking shot but maybe."

"How's the co-owner?" If it was possible to waggle eyebrows across the phone, Amy did it. Every eligible woman that crossed Cade's path was a potential romance in Amy's mind. "I googled her. She is Instagram-influencer hot. Is she single?"

"She's celibate."

"And you know that." Amy sounded delighted. "You guys have been talking."

They had talked before the whole thing with streamlining inventory. For a moment, Cade had thought this month might be fun, but then they'd gotten down to business and Cade had become the bad guy.

"She's the kind of person who tells everyone anything," Cade said.

"Open. Talkative. Not repressed. I like her for you."

"Amy, please."

"I'm serious."

"She's celibate."

"That doesn't mean she's not interested in a relationship. You're pretty celibate too."

"We're in business. No one is thinking about that except you."

"So you work together and you get close. You talk about not having sex…"

"She's not even here," Cade grumbled.

That wasn't fair. Selena had told Cade she wanted to help her friend Beautiful Adrien build a stage for some artists' co-op auction. Cade had said it was fine. She could handle the store. How hard could it be to wait on three people in eight hours? Now she resented Selena's absence. As always, Cade had to do everything.

"She's the one who cares about the store," Cade said. "She wants me to do everything." Cade sighed. "I mean, she did say she'd teach a class where you paint your vulva."

Please let that have been a joke.

"Fun," Amy said.

"You're supposed to be on my side."

"Okay. Fine. Can you run the store without this woman?"

Cade sat down on the stool behind the counter. "I can run it better without her. I mean, if she was embezzling, this place would still be in better shape. At least an embezzler would try to make it look like things were okay. But this…I don't know how you could mess a store up this bad and still be in business. And Selena's just like my parents with these crazy ideas. She wants to plan a party, not run a shop."

There was a crash of pans on Amy's end. Someone yelled, "The quinoa is on fire!"

"You have to go," Cade said.

"On my way," Amy called to her crew. "I love you. You can do this," she added. "You never fail."

Cade ended the call and set her phone down. Twenty-six more days. They'd salvage what they could, then they'd sell.

"I would never steal from the store."

Cade spun around. Selena had come in through the back room. The door to the back room opened onto the space behind the counter, so they were close, Selena standing with her feet planted wide, Cade wishing she could spin the stool around three times, make a wish, and be back in New York.

"And we've done paint your vulva before and everyone loved it." Selena's voice was ice cold.

Now she showed up to work. Cade sighed. Selena looked beautiful and fierce in a leather skirt and thigh-high fake-fur boots, but she looked hurt too. Cade wanted to say, *Don't sneak up on people if you don't want to hear what they're saying.*

The image of Selena delivering her terrible eulogy flashed through Cade's mind. Selena dressed like a dominatrix. Shaking with nerves. Her little page of notes clutched in one hand. So wrong and trying so hard. Suddenly, Cade felt a deep desire to put her arms around Selena the way she had on Ruth's back patio. *I'm sorry. I didn't mean it. Let me hold you.*

"You weren't supposed to hear that," Cade said.

"I would never embezzle from Ruth," Selena said.

"I don't think you did." Cade ran her hand through her hair. "I said the store would be in better shape if someone had."

Selena was holding two coffees. Now she slammed them down on the counter. She'd brought one for Cade. Cade felt bad. Selena had been thinking about her. She'd brought a peace offering.

Selena pulled her dark hair back and wrapped it in a messy knot on top of her head. She flexed her hands.

You are not going to try to girl-fight me.

"You are not open to a diversity of viewpoints." Selena glared at Cade.

"We are not talking politics. We're running a business." Cade motioned to the back room. "There is a box full of unopened bills labeled *Chardonnay, Clitorises etc.* It should be labeled *We're Fucked.* But I'm sorry. I didn't mean what I said. I'm just…" *Tired. Frustrated. Lonely.* "I'm an asshole."

Selena removed the lid on her coffee and managed to suck the whipped cream top aggressively.

Cade lifted the other coffee. "For me?"

"Yes," Selena said sullenly.

Cade took a sip. Selena had remembered that she took it black. No whipped cream. It was strong as swallowing a mouthful of coffee beans.

"Thank you," Cade said.

They stood in silence, Cade wishing things hadn't gone wrong. Selena was supposed to be glad she was there. And Cade had even thought they might have fun together. That had been a dream.

"You don't even want my help," Selena said.

Because selling dildos at a midnight sidewalk sale is not helpful... and probably not legal.

"The Chamber of Commerce is putting on a presentation on small business inventory management." Maybe if Selena understood what Cade was doing. "Let's go together."

As soon as she said it, Cade realized how much she needed Selena to say yes. *I want a team.* She hadn't felt that since she rowed crew. Now she was just rowing frantically for everyone else. By herself. With no one to say, *Take a break,* or *Let me take over.*

Please.

Selena put her hands on her hips. "If you go to the Sex Industry Expo with me."

"Okay."

"And hand out flyers."

Why was this her life? Cade wished she could think of a reason why advertising a sex toy store at a sex expo was a bad idea, but it wasn't. Obviously.

"Yes," Cade said reluctantly. "I will go to the expo and hand out flyers."

"We'll have fun."

Not Cade's idea of fun.

"Okay," Cade said.

Selena rewarded her with a genuinely warm smile.

"I love the Sexpo," she said. "Now I've got to run. I'm just stopping by for a sec to grab a few vibrators. Are you still good by yourself here?"

"I'm good," Cade said. "Good luck with your..."

Just stopping by to grab a few vibrators. Of course. Everyone stopped by work to grab a few vibrators. Selena was supposed to be building a stage. What were the vibrators for? Cade had a vision of Selena in her tight skirt, with a vibrator, on a stage… That thought did not belong in her mind. She felt heat rise in her cheeks. She hoped Selena didn't notice, but the twinkle in Selena's eyes said she probably did. Of course Cade noticed her. Surely everyone noticed Selena. Cade felt like a little sister caught admiring a big sister's boyfriend.

"Well, go," Cade said. "Your vibrator stage isn't going to build itself."

Cade stayed late working on creating an online sales portal. Finally, she closed her laptop. She was almost out the door when she stopped. Maybe Amy was right. It had been a while since she'd tried any sex toys. There'd been the long wand that looked like a medical device from the fifties that had left her feeling bruised, and there was the vibrator with the porn star on the box and the warning label saying it caused cancer in California. Satisfaction Guaranteed did seem to have better stuff. And if she was going to work at a sex toy store, she'd better give the merchandise another shot. She picked up a Satisfaction Guaranteed shopping bag. She went into the back room and selected the Titan, the Ella, the Womanizer, and the Petit Lapin in her bag. Her hand hovered over the Twist Clit & Nipple Triple Sucker set, but it looked like something researchers attached to human subjects before there were ethics laws.

When she got home, she retreated to her room, locked the door, and listened to make sure Selena wasn't in the house. She opened the bag from Satisfaction Guaranteed and took out the Titan. Then she took off her pants and crawled under the covers. Maybe the Titan would open a new world. She'd plunge it into her body. Fireworks would go off. Her body was beautiful. She deserved pleasure. The next time she looked in the mirror, she'd see something different. Someone irresistible. A woman who'd had an orgasm.

She positioned the Titan at her opening, took a deep breath, and pushed it in. It hurt like hell. She tried to pull it out, but it stuck, like her vagina was made of the sticky pads people used to hold cell phones to dashboards. And the Titan's plunge had pulled her labia in with it. Maybe she should have gotten a mirror. Maybe it would have given her a better idea of how to insert the thing. But she'd rowed crew in college, the most painful sport, and if she could do that, she could do anything. She closed her eyes and pushed the thing in and out. In and out. In and out. She tried to breathe into the discomfort, but that didn't help.

Finally she stopped. Rowing crew taught her endurance. It also meant knowing when the stroke was off and it was time to go back to the dock. She pulled the Titan out, wincing, and set it on the bedside table. It stood there, reminding her just a little bit of Sociopath, staring in through her kitchen window. *Things are not going to work out for you,* the dildo seemed to say. *Twenty-nine is too late.*

chapter 12

The next day, Cade stood at the counter watching Selena charm a couple who'd come in to buy a pair of handcuffs. Selena was good with their customers—all ten or twelve of them—approaching the shy ones with care and joking with the bold ones. Earlier, Cade and Selena had made small talk about the rain, and they'd talked about movies. Cade never had time to watch them. Selena watched vintage sexploitation films on Becket's reel-to-reel projector. Not much in common there. And they were no closer to profitability, but at least Selena didn't seem to be actively mad at her.

The couple bought their cuffs. After they left, Selena wandered to the door and pushed it open, leaning against the frame. She turned to look back at Cade.

"It's not raining," she said. "Take a look."

A city where people stopped to look at clouds that weren't raining. Cade sighed, but she walked over to Selena. Selena held the door open, and they stepped outside. It was four o'clock and the street was quiet.

"Sunshine." Selena pointed. Light gray clouds had pushed aside the dark gray ones.

"Optimist," Cade said.

"I wish I still smoked," Selena said wistfully.

"On the list of wishes that could come true, that's near the top," Cade said. She should make an effort. She should try to get along. "Why do you wish you smoked?"

"I smoked in high school. You can go outside when you smoke. If you're at a party and you're drunk and you've had way too much weed, and you want to be alone, you go out for a smoke, and no one thinks anything about it. You know?"

"No."

Selena wrapped her arms around herself, goose bumps puckering on her bare arms. She was wearing a corset that looked like it belonged on a burlesque stage.

"No?" Selena said.

"I don't get drunk, and I don't smoke weed. My parents do enough of that for the family."

God, she was boring.

"Sorry." Selena looked down at her feet. "Of course you don't. That's on me."

They were silent. Cade talked to people all the time. Part of her job. She didn't know why she couldn't think of something to say now. Their first day together Selena had told Cade more about herself than Cade should learn in a month, and she'd asked Cade about her life, and listened to the answer…which was rare. Now Cade couldn't tell if Selena was giving her the cold shoulder or just lost in her own thoughts or maybe Selena was just legit cold because she'd worn lingerie to work in the winter.

Finally Cade said, "I get what you mean about parties. I can network the hell out of a party, but sometimes I'm standing there and I just want to go sit on the roof instead."

Selena looked up as though Cade had given her a gift.

"Totally," she said.

"When I was a kid, I used to wish that I could freeze time for everyone but me," Cade said. "Everyone else would be, like, statues, and I could walk around in the world."

She'd never told anyone that. She didn't know why she was telling a woman who thought she was a soulless capitalist, but something about the empty street and bright gray sky made the moment feel like time had indeed frozen. Cade looked at Selena. *Truce?*

"Was it so you could see what they had in their drawers?" Selena asked. "Could you open drawers, or were you more like a ghost who could move around but not touch anything? That might be more useful, because you could walk through walls. You could see more. Catch criminals. See people having sex. That's what I'd do. And I'd love to see Ruth again. But you have to be careful. If you got to be a ghost for a little while, do you come back like Lazarus, all half-dead and shit?" Selena cocked her head. "But it's your freeze-time fantasy. What do you want to do?"

"When I was a kid, I wanted more time to do my homework." She rolled her eyes at herself so Selena wouldn't have to.

Selena said, "Because you cared about doing a good job."

"Thanks."

"For what?"

"For not saying how dull that is. I didn't even think about catching criminals."

"I worked hard in school too," Selena said. "I was valedictorian for Tristess High."

Cade was surprised and felt bad about being surprised all in the same moment. Just because Selena had a full wardrobe of fake fur and wanted to paint her vulva didn't mean she wasn't scholastic.

"Of course, that only meant I studied harder than eighteen other kids," Selena added.

"Valedictorian is valedictorian," Cade said.

"So why would you watch people have sex if you were a ghost?" Not a question Cade would usually ask, but Selena had told her about her celibacy vow and her favorite dildo, and Cade was making nice.

"I want to see that moment when you can't hide who you really are," Selena said.

Cade had never reached that moment. That was her problem.

"Dance like no one's watching." Selena leaned against the doorframe and smiled at Cade.

"We have that pillow," Cade said.

"And you love it."

"I do not."

"I'm going to get you a shirt that says YOLO." Selena reached out and gave Cade's arm a little shove.

Cade noticed the touch like Portlanders noticed a light gray sky, like it was special when it really wasn't.

"I never dance like no one's watching," Cade said.

"Sure you do. I've seen it," Selena said.

"When?"

"When you're working," Selena said. "On your computer. At night, when I come in for cereal and you don't even hear me."

That's when she showed her true self. Sad.

"It's cool," Selena said. "You're doing something you're good at."

The sky faded back to dark gray. A few drops of rain hit the pavement. Selena shivered again.

"I'm sorry I called you a soulless capitalist," she said. "There's nothing wrong with being a businesswoman. You're a feminist. You're like Ruth Bader Ginsburg."

"I don't know if I get to be in RBG's class, but I'll take it."

Selena looked at Cade very seriously.

"Did I hurt your feelings?"

Yes? No? I don't talk about feelings?

"I'm fine," Cade said. "I probably am a soulless capitalist."

"You're not."

Cade looked away from the intensity in Selena's dark eyes. She probably looked at lots of people like that.

"You stayed in Portland to help," Selena said. "You have a life in New York, your job, your friends, your cat, your weird Craigslist ads—I'm not judging—and your houseplants are probably dying, unless someone's looking in on them for you, but that's a weird favor because it's a pain in the ass to watch other people's plants, so you don't want to ask, but then if you don't they die, and you come home to dead spider plants." Selena said it all in one breath, like the eulogy. "I really appreciate that you stayed."

Selena was close enough that Cade could see the flecks of green in her dark eyes. A few freckles on her nose. She wasn't as magazine-perfect as Cade had thought.

Someone might say her nose was big. Her lips weren't symmetrical, and it gave her a mischievous look even though her face was serious. The imperfections made her prettier.

"I didn't mean what I said on the phone," Cade said. "You helped Ruth run the shop the way she wanted to run it. She didn't tell you that unpaid bills are in a box labeled *Chardonnay and Clitorises*."

Selena looked around. "But if the bills are in *Chardonnay and Clitorises*, where are the clitorises and Chardonnay?"

Cade laughed.

"We'll have to look for them," Selena said, a hint of coquettishness in her voice.

She was charming. It was obvious why everyone at the funeral had cheered her on. She was so real, so open.

"I think they're in a box labeled *Life Stuff*," Cade said.

"What more is there?" Selena grinned.

Banks. Mortgages. Contracts.

Selena bounced on her toes and rubbed her arms.

Cade slipped out of her blazer and was about to settle it over Selena's shoulders when she realized what she was doing. Cade did not drape jackets on beautiful women. She stumbled over her words around beautiful women, then invented conference calls so she could run away from them. But Selena turned her back, and it was obvious she expected Cade to help her into the jacket. As Cade laid the jacket over her shoulders, Selena pressed her hand to Cade's for a second.

"You're a gentleman...woman...person." Selena ran her hands down the front of Cade's blazer. "And you've got great style. I always liked preppy girls."

That meant nothing, small talk. But Cade still had to swallow a smile.

At closing, Selena retrieved her fake-fur jacket from the back room.

"I'll take you home on my bike." Selena gestured to her motorcycle parked on the sidewalk outside.

They stepped out. Up close, the motorcycle was huge and looked like something out of a steampunk anime, with a telescopic headlight and unexplainable gears. Cade eyed it.

"Have you ridden one?" Selena asked.

Cade wished she could say, *Yes, of course.* What self-respecting twenty-nine-year-old lesbian hadn't ridden a motorcycle? Probably to Provincetown, zipping in and out of the weekend traffic with a rainbow flag flying off the back. Cade shook her head.

"Are you scared?" It sounded like an honest question, not a taunt.

"That's like a car without any of the things that make cars safe," Cade said.

"I'll make sure your first time is everything you want," Selena said, with a stagey wink. More seriously, she added, "I fuck a lot of things up, but I ride beautifully. And my dad built the bike. He knows what he's doing."

It was the shy pride in Selena's voice that persuaded Cade. She took the helmet from Selena and stared at her reflection in the shiny, black dome. It wasn't too late to be the kind of woman who rode a motorcycle.

Selena swung one gorgeous, pleather-clad leg over the bike.

"Where's your helmet?" Cade asked.

"I've only got that one. You wear it."

"You can't ride without a helmet."

"I'll be fine." Selena did something, and the bike roared to life. "It's not far. Two miles. Side streets."

What self-respecting twenty-nine-year-old lesbian didn't want to ride a motorcycle with a beautiful woman's dark hair flying in her face?

"You *have* to wear a helmet," Cade said. "It's the law, and head injuries are a huge risk."

God, she was boring, but she was right too. Selena couldn't ride unprotected, side streets or not. Cade opened the Uber app.

"All right, Mom," Selena said, putting on her helmet and snapping the visor down.

"You have to wear a helmet," Cade said. "Always."

The motorcycle belched smoke. The muffler backfired. Over the noise Selena yelled, "You're sweet, Cade Elgin. You know that?"

And she sped off, her hair flying out from beneath her helmet, her purple fake-fur jacket flying out behind her. Despite all the artists Cade had discovered, all the openings she'd been to, all the museums, all the galas, Cade had never seen something so magical.

chapter 13

Selena stood at the door to Satisfaction Guaranteed, looking out at the pouring rain. Not sex toy buying
weather, even for Portlanders. Selena wished the store
were busier. A day like this made it hard to convince Cade
that Satisfaction Guaranteed was doing just fine without
any of Cade's Target-style interventions.

Cade sat behind the counter with her laptop.

"I've signed you up for the inventory management
class," she said.

"You're going too, right?" Selena asked.

"I'm pretty good with inventory management already,"
Cade said, still staring at her computer.

"Oh."

Selena felt a pang of disappointment, not that she
wanted to spend more time with Cade. They spent enough
time making stilted conversation in the store and passing
each other politely in Ruth's kitchen. But it'd be interesting to see Cade in a different setting. Selena liked to watch
her. Cade was a handsome woman, and Selena had been

celibate for quite a while, so obviously…it was hard not to look. But Cade was a bit of a mystery too. She was uptight, so professional. But standing at the door the other day, Selena had glimpsed sparks of humor and a touch of shyness that made her wonder what Cade was really thinking. She wanted to know.

"It wouldn't be the same without you," Selena said.

Cade looked up. "It will be exactly the same without me."

"You have to suffer with me."

"I can get work done at the house."

"It's going to be so boring I will pull my hair out, and I'll leave if you're not there to inspire me."

"Really?" Cade rolled her eyes. "It's three hours."

"That I will never get back."

Selena tossed her hair over her shoulder. She had gorgeous hair. That was not a life plan, but it was a nice asset. She thought she caught Cade's eyes lingering.

"Fine." Cade typed something into her laptop. "There. I'm registered."

"Fabulous." Selena went back to wandering the store, straightening the shelves as much as she could when they were packed tight.

"Hey," Cade said. "I'm working on an online portal. For sales. I need product descriptions. You want to look at mine and see if they work?"

"You're going to let me be useful?"

Cade looked confused. "You are useful."

Selena walked over to the counter. Cade turned her laptop around.

The Vilo comes in turquoise, black, and ivory. Six vibration speeds. Waterproof up to a depth of seven feet.

That'd be adventuresome, even for Selena.

Product packaging contains forty percent recycled materials. Heavy charging cord gives a lower voltage drop. Average charging time for a full charge = ninety-five minutes for 110 volt grids, sixty-two minutes for 220 volt grids.

"I've…" Selena began. *Read sexier descriptions of motor oil.*

She remembered Cade's hunched shoulders when she'd barked at her: *You're picking up dildos like they're going to bite you.*

I'm sorry, Cade.

Selena pretended to read a few more descriptions. They'd be great if Cade were describing printers.

"This is a good start," Selena said, "and maybe because I've worked here for a while, I could add a bit here and there."

Cade looked relieved.

"You did a good job with the cables. Our toys do charge fast."

Selena took Cade's place behind the counter. She caught a whiff of Cade's cologne as they passed each other in the tight space, and she breathed in deeply. Just because it was a nice cologne. It was hard to find foresty colognes that didn't smell like Pine-Sol. That was all. *Just interested in your perfume.*

It was fun thinking of ways to describe the toys. How was the Sundance different from the Titan? What were the best features of the Dolphin? Selena was engrossed in her work when the door chimed. On the other side of the store, Cade was staring out the window at the rain. She'd been talking about frosting the glass, but it hadn't happened yet. Cade turned to the new-comer.

"Let me know if you have questions," Cade said, in a tone that said, *For the love of God don't have questions.*

Selena looked up to see if the customer needed help. Then she froze.

"I'm here to see Selena," Alex said to Cade.

Selena could leave through the back. She'd be on her bike before Alex followed her out.

"Don't hide in the back," Alex said, reading her mind. "I'm not armed, and you're not a child."

She looked just like she did the day Alex told Selena it was over. Her navy suit accentuated her tiny figure. Her fine, straight, black hair fell to her waist. She had the same long nails—her own, not acrylic. No one who slept with women should have nails like that, but Alex had been a pillow princess, so it hadn't mattered.

Selena gripped the counter.

"Don't look so surprised. I left you a dozen messages."

"How did you find me?"

Selena had started working at the store about six months after Alex dumped her. Satisfaction Guaranteed had felt like a safe place, a place Alex wouldn't think to look.

"You're listed on the website: sexual education consul-tant. I like it," Alex said. "You were good at sex."

The compliment made her feel dirty. Selena crossed her arms and wished she wasn't wearing a bustier. She could face Alex in one of Cade's turtleneck sweaters.

"You look beautiful as always." Alex eyed the store with the same look Cade had given it on her first day.

"Why are you here?" Selena asked.

"I want to see you, and that's not too much to ask, after what I put on the line for you."

"*You* put on the line?"

Selena had lost everything. She'd dropped out of school. She'd destroyed her work. She'd stopped painting.

"I was your professor." Alex walked to the counter. "I could have lost my job. I left my husband for you. And you won't even have coffee with me."

"I don't have time," Selena said. It was hard to hold on to that argument with the store empty.

"I'd hate to see slow." Alex looked around. "We'll just get a drink. Half an hour."

"I don't…want to." Selena wished she sounded confident.

Cade came behind the counter and stood next to Selena. She was a comforting presence, all that cashmere and cool, New York confidence. Cade had probably never been in a bad relationship. When she told women to leave her alone, they left. Maybe some of that would rub off on Selena.

Alex flicked a rainbow feather boa hanging from a shelf near the counter.

"You don't mind if I steal her away, do you?" she said to Cade. "It doesn't look like there's going to be a rush."

"I can't." Selena resisted the urge to wrap her arms around herself. She stood up straight and clamped her hands to her sides.

"Don't tell me you're still intimidated by me," Alex said.

Alex had always loved to point that out. *Selena has been my advisee for three years, and she's still intimidated by me.* As though that was Selena's fault, not hers.

"Or are you worried about what your fiancée will think?" Alex said in a mocking tone.

Shit! Her lie. *I'm engaged to Cade Elgin of the Elgin Gallery.* Cade was standing right next to her. Most definitely not her fiancée. Not any part of anything that involved a wedding dress. Selena had set herself up for this embarrassment…unless she could get Alex away from Cade.

"I will get a drink," Selena said quickly.

Beneath the counter, out of Alex's sight, Cade touched Selena's wrist.

Cade turned away from Alex, leaned toward Selena, and whispered, "Are you sure?"

Selena felt Cade's breath against her cheek and Cade's fingertips still lightly resting on her wrist.

When Selena glanced at Cade, there was concern in Cade's blue eyes. That was all. No long-suffering *why do I have to deal with this* look. That didn't mean Selena wanted to explain how Cade had become Selena's pretend future wife.

"Definitely," Selena said. "I'd love a drink. How's the McLaughlin Academy? You're probably a full professor now. That's a thing, right? Let's go."

She had to get Alex out of the store before Alex said anything else.

"Good," Alex said.

"I'm ready." Selena rummaged under the counter for her jacket.

"Are you going to tell me all about your engagement?" Alex asked. "You're a little old for a pretend girlfriend."

"I didn't make it up." Selena tried to put on her fake-fur

jacket, but it was upside down. The damn thing looked the same from every angle. She shoved it under her arm instead. "I'll tell you all about it."

"And Cadence Elgin," Alex drawled.

"What?" Cade asked

If only Alex was talking to Cade, not about Cade.

"Your lies are fantastic," Alex said.

Selena never lied. It wasn't a virtue. She just spoke thoughts exactly as they crossed her mind and then regretted them. Except this one time, by accident, because her friend had died, and Alex was the last person she'd expected on the phone, she'd told a lie that made up for all her regrettable honesty. Maybe getting her shit together involved learning how to tell the right lies.

"You could have just said you met some girl. Did you really think I'd believe you were engaged to Cadence Elgin of the Elgin Gallery?"

Fuck.

Humiliation washed over Selena. She clutched her coat, staring at the counter. She just had to make it through the next few seconds, get Alex out of the store, take Alex's mocking, then maybe run back to Tristess and never set foot in Portland again. It was just the next few seconds— in which Cade would say, *What the hell? I'm not engaged to you*—that were going to be incredibly painful. Selena took a deep breath.

"Selena?" Cade said.

Selena made herself look at Cade. *Sorry*, she mouthed.

Cade raised an eyebrow.

Selena was pathetic. Immature, just like Alex said. Creepy too. Who lied about something like that? She squeezed her eyes closed. It would be so nice if a meteor struck her or a sinkhole opened under her feet or—

She felt Cade's arm around her waist.

"She hasn't told you about our wedding?" Cade said.

What?

Cade pulled Selena a little closer, her touch as tender as it had been the night on the patio.

"It's going to be beautiful." Cade held out her hand to Alex, keeping her other arm around Selena's waist. "Cade Elgin. Nice to meet you."

"You are not Cadence Elgin." Alex looked back and forth between them. "Is she?"

Even if Cade wasn't the daughter of the Elgin Gallery, she and Selena would make an odd couple. Cade in her trim gray sweater and spotless tan suede loafers. Selena in a Fierce Lovely hand-me-down, a bustier that would, if you knew which panel to pull, come off in one quick rip. That was the beauty of burlesque costumes.

"Last time I checked I was," Cade said.

Alex squinted, as if trying to place Cade's face.

"My parents are Roger and Pepper Elgin," Cade went on, "as far as I know. I might have been switched at birth, but no DNA test. I know last month we showed Kathryn Von Holt, but we were missing her self-portrait because she'd already sold it." Cade rattled off a New York address and phone number, presumably the gallery. "And you are?"

"Professor Alex Sarta. McLaughlin Academy of Art." Alex shook Cade's hand vigorously.

Selena sank against Cade's side. Cade pulled Selena closer. Cade was doing this. For her. This fabulous save. Alex's face fell and then rose in an obsequious smile.

"It's an honor," Alex said. "We'd love to host you at the school. Do you think your parents will be in Portland any time soon?"

"We're busy," Cade said.

"Selena…how did you meet her?" Alex asked.

Cade looked at Selena, eyebrows raised.

At my friend's funeral a few days ago was not a good story.

"How did we meet?" Cade repeated. "It was very romantic."

Selena had come up with the first lie, but now her mind went blank.

"Yes?" Alex prompted.

Cade gave Selena a bemused smile, cuddling her with both arms.

"Skydiving," Selena blurted.

Cade's eyebrows rose. Her face said, *We're going to do it like this?*

"Selena saved me when my parachute didn't open," Cade said.

"You skydive now?" Alex asked.

"All the time," Cade answered for Selena.

"And you're getting married." Alex focused in on Cade. "If it's in Portland I could help with arrangements. I know a lot of people who—"

"We've got everything settled," Cade said casually.

"Maybe I could take you both out for a drink," Alex said.

Who at the McLaughlin Academy wouldn't throw themselves at a chance to do drinks with Cade Elgin?

"I don't get jealous of Selena's exes," Cade said. "You are her ex, right? You don't get jealous when you have what we have. But I don't think there's any reason why you need to see her when she told you she doesn't want to." Cade's face tightened as she said the last words.

She released Selena the second the door closed behind Alex. Selena realized she'd been gazing at Cade adoringly, like a puppy. She tore her gaze away and rested her arms on the counter and her forehead on her hands.

"It's not as weird as it seems." Yes, it was. "I just…Alex called the night of Ruth's funeral. I hadn't talked to her in forever. She said she'd left her husband." Selena raised her head. "I'd wanted that when we were together, but I don't want it now. And I know it was so dumb, but she wouldn't give up about seeing me, and I just told her I had a girl-friend. Fiancée. And you were at the funeral and…first words out of my mouth. Agh."

She rubbed her face. Cade already thought she was a flake. She *was* a flake. She'd never convince Cade she knew what to do with Satisfaction Guaranteed. She clearly didn't know what she was doing in her personal life. *Go ahead. Tell me how fucked-up that was.*

Cade put her hand on Selena's back, a steady, comfort-ing touch.

"It all happened so fast. There you were falling out of the airplane…" Cade said.

"I know it's stupid."

"Skydiving. That was taking it to the next level." Cade's eyes were a bright, sky blue, with a ring of darker blue around the edge. Mesmerizing. And full of laughter, but not laughter at Selena, just at the world. *The things we get ourselves into*, she seemed to be saying. "Go big or go home. You should have been an Elgin."

chapter 14

Cade wanted to hold Selena again. Selena looked shaken, twisting her hands in front of her, her face pale. And the ex was an asshole, sucking up to Cade, after she'd just picked on Selena. Like Cade wouldn't notice. Like Cade was supposed to be impressed by the McLaughlin Academy.

"You okay?" Cade asked.

"Fine. Yes. Thank you." Selena released her hands. "Totally. I'm heading out. You want a ride home?"

Selena's face said she wanted to get away, as fast as possible, by herself.

"I'm going to work a little longer," Cade said.

Cade wished Selena hadn't looked relieved. Cade could still feel the shape of Selena's body against hers, the way Selena sank against her, Selena's head on her shoulder, her hand on Selena's soft waist. Like they belonged together. They fit. Something inside Cade ached.

But it wasn't for Selena. Surely. Cade shook her head. People needed to be touched. Cade had just had many long nights and no girlfriends. She was like one of those dogs no one played with at the pound. They got clingy or they bit people. Still it would have been nice to share a drink after their little performance. Congratulate themselves. Laugh. But that wasn't fair. Selena's bad ex wasn't Cade's entertainment.

Cade brought her thoughts back to the work she needed to do that night. Look at Ruth's taxes (or lack of taxes). Finalize the web platform for online sales. Figure out how to sell Selena on the idea that they could not sell whips and aprons that said *Grandma's Kitchen, Grandma's Rules* on the same shelf.

Back at the house, Cade boiled chicken breast for dinner. Selena was out. Cade checked her phone while she watched the chicken breast float around in the pot. Amy had sent her an encouraging quote. She replied with an emoji heart.

Josiah had texted her, *Any word on that oil? Artist?*

No, she texted back.

I'll find them first.

Hell no!

Watch me.

She sent him an emoji skull. Then she took her laptops, a box of Ruth's files, and her chicken to the dining room table and sat down. Her phone rang before she could open the first laptop. It was her mother. Unfortunately. She would have preferred a scammer trying to get her bank account number. Cade put her mother on speaker.

"My jewel!" her mother said.

"Hi, Mom."

"How is your wonderful adventure, darling?" her mother asked. "You work too hard. Your father and I want you to be free, unburdened."

The box of bank statements stuck together with lube (please let it be lube and nothing else) did not say free and unburdened.

"You know who else is having an adventure?" Cade's mother asked.

"Everyone you know?"

Cade's mother laughed.

"You didn't buy an alpaca?" Cade asked.

"No, sweetie. Boric Savana is going on an adventure."

Boric Savana was showing next month.

"Does he need anything?" This didn't sound good. "I'll be back in time for the installation."

"He's moved to Costa Rica."

"How does he want to handle the opening?"

"We were showing him around the gallery," her mother said, "talking about the lighting, and he just sat down on the floor and told us he couldn't take the pressure of showing his work. The push to sell. All this emphasis on provenance and not on the art."

"We don't worry about provenance," Cade said.

Half the people they showed had never shown outside their local coffee shop. That was what made the Elgin Gallery the Elgin Gallery. Cade found brilliant unknowns, and then her parents took credit for them and made them stars.

"He's not pulling the show, is he?" Cade leaned her head in her hand. She felt a headache coming on.

"Your father and I told him to be free. We said, *Go on*

an adventure. Like you, sweetie. We know so many ex-pats in Costa Rica, so we hooked him up with a friend."

"The opening!" Cade demanded.

"Oh, he sold his collection. He needed money for the house he wants to build."

It was February. They didn't have a March show. She was stuck running Portland's tackiest sex toy store, and the gallery didn't have a March show.

"When was someone going to tell me?"

"It has a green roof."

"I don't care if it has a green roof. We've got less than a month!" Cade said.

"Something will work out. It always does."

"Because *I* work it out!" Cade said.

"You're so good at that."

"I've got to go."

"I love you, my jewel," her mother said.

Cade hung up without saying it back.

"Fuck me." She opened one of her laptops. The Wi-Fi was terrible. The fact that the network was called TheGuntherFamily told her they were stealing it. Ruth's portrait smiled down at her, her face full of joy and free-spiritedness.

"You did this to me."

Cade opened the Elgin Gallery submission portal. The new March artist had to be in New York. There was no time to ship a collection. She'd like something strikingly different from the last two exhibits, but she'd take any-thing good. She clicked through the portfolios, trying to intuit their qualities from the small screen. Maybe she could do a multi-artist show. One piece from each portfolio. But that was a lot of artists to manage. A lot of people who might move to Costa Rica.

By midnight, she knew she should go to bed. She kept flipping back and forth between the portfolios, but she didn't know what she was looking at.

"Hey." It was Selena in the doorway to the living room. She was wearing a ripped T-shirt and stained skinny jeans and eating cereal out of a box. Cade could still feel the way Selena had leaned against her in the store. She couldn't quite believe that she had touched this woman. Selena looked like something out of a movie or a famous actor's wife.

"Hey there," Cade said as casually as she could.

"I was with Becket, at the Aviary," Selena said, although Cade hadn't asked.

"How's Becket?"

"Freaking out over Fierce Lovely's next show. They're always amazing, and Beck always get scared the show's not going to say what she wants it to say. You know...that the sociopolitical commentary won't come through because there's too much emphasis on the stripping and the eating fire."

"I can't see how that would be distracting."

Selena came over and pulled up a chair.

"And she talked me down about Alex." Selena looked into the cereal box and picked out some choice kernels of corn and corn syrup. "Thanks for being my fiancée. Becket says you're kind of a rock star. And look at you. Super boss. Wearing a suit at midnight."

It was just slacks and a sweater.

Selena looked Cade up and down. "You're all, *hedge-fund and what glass ceiling, bitches! I'm rocking the world.*"

"It's not as glamorous as it looks." Cade motioned to her half-eaten chicken breast and cold coffee.

"Oh! You have to eat something." Selena held out her cereal.

"The dinner of champions?"

"I usually eat it with cream," Selena said.

Selena's curves confirmed that. Cade looked away quickly. Selena looked as gorgeous in a T-shirt as she did in a corset, maybe more so because she wasn't wearing a bra. Not that Cade looked. Of course.

They both hesitated. Cade tried to think of something to say. Portlanders like to talk about the rain. But what did you say about the rain? *Wow it's raining...again?* She should get back to work. The March show. Costa Rica. Her face must have registered her distress.

"How's your work?" Selena asked.

"Our March artist pulled his show." Cade propped her cheek in her hand. "My mother convinced him to leave the country and he sold his collection."

"People kill to be in the Elgin Gallery."

"Not Boric Savana. Now I have to find someone to fill in."

"You pick them?"

"Usually."

"I thought it was your parents."

"Everyone does. I'm not on-brand. They're the face of the gallery. Who wants this?" She tugged at the cuff of her sweater. "I'm boring."

"You're not," Selena blurted so quickly it seemed like she really meant it.

No? If Selena didn't think she was boring…

Work. That was what Cade had to focus on. She *had* to be boring. Boring was how she single-handedly kept everything from going to hell.

Cade touched the laptop's touchpad to bring it back to life. "But I don't know what I'm looking at anymore." She zoomed in on one of the thumbnails. "Is this genius or does it look like a squished lizard? Or both? I've been looking at these too long. Which one should I pick?"

Cade expected Selena to glance at the paintings and declare them *pretty* or *weird*, but she stared at them for so long, Cade worried that Selena actually thought she expected her to make a decision.

"I know," Cade said. "Nothing comes through on that screen."

Selena took another handful of cereal without looking away from the laptop. Cade waited. The minutes stretched. The only sound was the sound of Selena reaching into the cereal box, crunching, and tapping her finger on the right-arrow key.

Selena finally spoke through a mouthful of cereal. "This one has a complex color story, but the structure of the images is too exaggerated. It's like he's trying on different ideas. You believe the first one, but not the second. It's trying too hard. But this one…this is a landscape painter experimenting with nudes, and it works. I'd pick him if I had to pick someone for the show. Then this one, it's romantic but not sentimental, but his portfolio doesn't hold together."

"Wait," Cade said.

Selena swallowed. "Anyway, there's a lot here. I can see why it's hard to pick."

"How did you see that?" Cade asked.

"What?"

"He *is* a landscape painter. These are his first nudes. You saw that. That's genius."

Selena shrugged, a short, sharp movement, like she was dodging a blow. "I went to art school for two hot seconds."

"Well you were right about the landscapes. I'll call him tomorrow."

"You're not going to take my advice!"

"Yeah, I will."

The distress that had flited across Selena's face vanished, replaced by a smile. She must have known it was dazzling because she hid it behind her hand.

"You're crazy," she said, but she was glowing.

"Say," Cade said, glancing at Ruth's portrait, "you don't know who painted that, do you?"

"No clue," Selena said quickly. "One of Ruth's friends. They only painted that one."

chapter 15

Three days later, Selena and Cade sat side by side on padded folding chairs in the Beaverton Capital Center, waiting for the start of the class on small business inventory management. The gray-on-gray pattern on the chairs matched the carpet. Selena sat up straight, trying to look eager. She'd bought a gray sweater at Goodwill so she could match Cade's professional style. She matched the carpet and chairs too, so that was a bonus.

Cade checked her email on a tablet.

"So you know all this stuff already," Selena said.

Cade wrinkled her nose. "I don't really," she confessed. "This is inventory management for small retail. The Elgin Gallery sells four or five pieces a month, and at the end of the month we return the unsold pieces to the artist."

"So it's different from selling chocolate penis pops," Selena said.

One of the men in front of them turned and shot Selena a hungry glance. Selena put her arm around the back of Cade's chair. *Not today, buddy.*

"No one is going to take back stale penis pops." Cade leaned toward Selena. "If we wanted returnable inventory, we could sell plastic houseplants," Cade whispered, "that people don't put in their anuses."

Selena laughed louder than she meant to. That comment. Coming from Cade! She would never have suspected.

"No such thing," Selena whispered back.

Cade rolled her eyes. "God, why?"

"Do you really want me to tell you?"

"No." Cade bugged her eyes, in a look that said, *You are too much.* But Selena could tell she was amused.

A man approached the podium and cleared his throat in a screech of feedback. "Our speaker today..." he began.

The introduction went on for a long time, but finally the presenter took his place. He was a small man with round glasses and high-waisted slacks. He adjusted his glasses and clicked a button on the podium, and a screen lowered behind him. A PowerPoint slide read "The Ten Principles of Small Business Inventory Management."

"The first principle is economic order quantity." He spoke in a monotone as dull as the room around him.

Selena tried to pay attention. This was adulting. Getting her shit together. Impressing Cade with her seriousness. She had found a notepad—already a triumph—and she'd remembered to bring it with her. But the presenter's voice short-circuited something in her brain. It was like a bad sensory deprivation experience. Instead of feeling at one with the universe, she was becoming one with a box of defunct fax machines.

"Now principle two," the presenter continued.

How long had it been? Selena checked her phone.

Only fifteen minutes. She tried to do the math. If one principle took fifteen minutes, ten would take two and a half hours.

Selena nudged Cade. "Are there really ten principles?"

Cade frowned, but her eyes were smiling.

"Take notes." She held up her tablet to demonstrate.

"I am." Selena showed Cade her notepad. "But ten is a lot."

The speaker continued. Selena wrote down a few key words. Principles three and four were blessedly short, but principle five was broken down into six subsections.

"Five-a, five-b, five-c, five-d, five-e…" the presenter said slowly.

"And, surprise, five-f," Selena whispered in Cade's ear. She smelled Cade's subtle cologne.

Cade looked down at her tablet.

Selena could see the corner of her smile behind the sweep of her perfect blond hair.

"It's really interesting," Selena whispered.

It wasn't.

"Five-a is further divided into subsections a-one, a-two, a-three…" the presenter said. "The most important principle of five-a is don't sit on your inventory. If you have back inventory that does not sell or you are not selling, don't hold on to it. The cost of keeping back inventory is greater than most business owners understand."

The presenter moved on to 5b. Selena straightened again, trying to look interested. What did interested look like? Selena nodded each time the presenter paused, but finally boredom broke her. She tapped Cade's arm.

"What do you think he's like in bed?" Selena whispered.

"I can't unsee that," Cade said, keeping her eyes focused on the screen.

"Don't judge. Maybe he's a beast."

"This is very important stuff."

Selena leaned over and wrote on Cade's tablet. *I'm staying for you.* It was only after she put the period on the sentence that she realized she was in Cade's space, her arm resting on Cade's leg, the way she and Becket would get in each other's space without even thinking about it. Selena jumped back. Cade cocked her head with a look that said, *You started it.*

Never mind. As you were.

But she had almost made Cade laugh and she wanted to do it again.

Cade turned toward Selena, moving close enough that Selena could feel Cade's breath on her ear. It sent a shiver through her.

"Okay, this is the most boring thing I've ever been to," Cade said without parting her lips.

Are you learning a lot? Selena wrote on her own notebook.

Cade took the notebook and pen from her and wrote, *Maybe if I could stay awake.*

Now this was a business problem Selena was ready to solve.

"I'm going to go to the bathroom," she whispered against Cade's cheek. "You follow me in five minutes. Then we run."

"Principle six has eight subsections," the presenter said.

Selena slipped out the back door. Cade only waited a minute before following her out.

"Let's go before they catch us and bring us back," Cade said.

"Run!"

Selena only meant to run a few feet down the hall as a joke, but Cade charged along beside her, and suddenly they were sprinting. At the end of the windowless hall, they burst through the doors, into the five o'clock darkness, laughing.

"I'm sorry," Selena said through her laughter. "I tried to pay attention."

"It was really bad," Cade said. "I'm not selling you on these lectures, am I?"

"Don't sit on your inventory," Selena said. "I got that part. What's a FIFO?"

"Do you want me to tell you?" Cade stretched her arms behind her head. "I could divide it into subsections."

"You wouldn't."

"Punishment for something you did in your past life."

Selena stopped, suddenly noticing the rain on her face.

"If I'd known this stuff, the store wouldn't be bankrupt. I'd...I'd have helped Ruth in a way that mattered."

Cade's face melted into the kindest expression Selena had ever seen.

"Selena." Cade put a hand on her arm. "You were there with her when she was dying. There is no profit or business or subsection that means anything close to what that means."

And then Cade hugged her. The rain pelted them both, but Selena didn't feel it anymore. She just felt Cade's warmth. After a quick moment that Selena wished would last longer, Cade released her. Still holding Selena's shoulders, Cade looked into her eyes.

"I'm serious," Cade said. "You don't think that you let her down, do you? You didn't."

"Okay," Selena said.

"I'm right," Cade said. "You don't like my fabulous business lectures and my Target vision, but I am right about this. She was so lucky to have you."

Cade's words warmed her as much as Cade's embrace.

"Okay," Selena said with more certainty.

"Good." Cade dropped her hands. "Let me buy you dinner. An apology for the minutes you will never get back." She nodded ruefully toward the building behind them. "Want to see if we can find anything healthy around here?"

This part of Beaverton was a wasteland of fast food and big box stores.

"Healthy? What am I going to do with you?" Selena said. "I know a place that serves fried poutine and a drink that's all whiskey-soaked cherries."

chapter 16

They were quiet as they Ubered across town,
but the silence felt warm to Cade, and the bar Selena
picked felt like the perfect place for quiet conversation.
Dim lamps hung from a low ceiling. A fire crackled in a
fireplace. Cade recognized the bartender, one of Selena's
friends from the funeral.

"Cade, you remember Beautiful Adrien," she said.

"Welcome." Beautiful Adrien began taking bottles off
the shelves, pouring little samples for Cade and Selena.

The first one tasted like peaches, campfires, and a hint
of cotton candy.

"Sadfire Dreaming Cowboy Reserve. It's supposed to
taste like unrequited desire," Beautiful Adrien said.

"I always wondered what unrequited desire tastes like."
Cade glanced at Selena as she said it. Because it was
normal to look at people in a conversation. It didn't
mean—

"You wouldn't be the first." Beautiful Adrien chuckled.

"Adrien!" Selena hissed.

"You know I've been unrequited for you for years," Beautiful Adrien said.

"You have not."

"I'm the only one then."

Selena scoffed. "Don't listen to him."

Cade finished her whiskey samples while Selena and Beautiful Adrien chatted about the Aviary co-op's annual auction. Luckily, the dim lights hid her blush. Then Cade ordered unrequited desire over ice. Selena ordered a drink called Sweetened Condensed Fall of Adam, which was, as she had promised, a glass filled with liquor-soaked cherries. They took a seat at a small table tucked in a corner.

"Beautiful Adrien was the last person I slept with before I took my vow of celibacy," Selena said, as though that was a normal way to start a conversation with your coworker.

Cade tried not to cough on her drink.

"I thought about it for a while. I wanted it to be someone I knew was a good lover. Beautiful Adrien is probably the best man I've been with. His edging technique is perfect. I wanted it to be someone I trusted, but someone who wasn't going to fall in love with me. TMI?" Selena asked.

"No, no, of course not."

Yes. What was edging? Cade did not have an edging technique. Had anyone edged her? Probably not. Maybe that was her problem.

Cade wondered how to continue that line of conversation, but she didn't have to.

"I've been thinking," Selena said. "The Full Spectrum bar has happy hour trivia every Thursday, but they lost their trivia master. I was thinking we could ask if we could have that spot. We could do sex trivia and have an anal bead raffle."

Words Cade never thought she'd hear someone say, at least not to her. Oh, well, if she was reading the questions, she wouldn't have to answer them. She nodded hesitantly.

"Is there a Trivial Pursuit deck?" Cade asked.

"We have to write our own questions," Selena said enthusiastically. "It'll be more fun."

The answer would be edging. What would the question be? It'd be like sex-anxiety Jeopardy.

"You'd be so good at that." Cade took a big sip of her whiskey. "Maybe you could do that, and I could work on getting Ruth's files into QuickBooks."

"Okay," Selena said cheerfully. "And I'll do Pour and Paint Your Vulva, and we'll both go to the Sexpo. Do we need to go to some more lectures?" Selena bit a cherry in half, its dark juice coloring her full lips.

Not that Cade was watching how Selena's lips curved around her words or how she looked like she was kissing the cherry before she bit into it. Nope. Not looking.

"I will go to another lecture." Selena popped the other half of the cherry in her mouth. "Because I believe in you, but can we get high first? I get really talkative, and I ask a lot of questions."

Cade pictured Selena high at a Chamber of Commerce lecture with all the insurance agents and small-time lawyers.

"I should say no." Cade chuckled. "But that would actually be fabulous."

"We'll do it." Selena leaned forward. "You sure you don't want to get high too?"

"Yes."

Selena rolled her eyes. "That's probably a good choice, but growing up where I did, you had to get high. What else were you going to do?"

"What was Tristess like?"

"It's two potholes and a Walmart, but it's gorgeous. High desert. At night you can see all the stars, and there're mountains in the distance. I love it, but I couldn't stay there, so I moved to Portland, started out waitressing, then shaping Christmas trees. I worked at a bank for a couple days. That was a mistake. But I always thought…" Selena traced a crack in the wood table. "When I left Tristess, I thought I was going to be an artist. I was going to go to college and be a famous painter."

"And you did go?" Cade wasn't sure if she should have asked.

Selena glanced at one of the bar's few windows, a faraway look in her eyes.

"That's where Alex came in." Selena wrapped her arms around herself. "I met her and we had a fucked-up relationship and I dropped out."

"I'm so sorry." Cade reached her hand out to take Selena's, then stopped. What was she thinking? But to her surprise Selena clasped her hand for a second.

"Thanks." Selena seemed to shake off a cloud. "I was too old to be painting with those eighteen-year-old kids. It was a silly dream. I also thought I'd run a dispensary and move to the Caribbean."

Cade wished she could go back in time and take Alex aside. *Leave her alone. You don't get to date your student and do...* whatever it was Alex had done to Selena. There was a bigger story there, but the way Selena raised her voice and rushed the words, "Tell me about you in college," told Cade not to ask.

"I was boring. Mostly. I rowed crew. That was the best part."

Cade didn't talk about it much. No one cared what sport she did in college, even if the hours on the river were the brightest she could remember.

"Were you good?" Selena asked.

"I was great." Cade could see mist rising off the river in early spring. "But I quit."

"Here's to quitters." Selena raised her glass with a rueful shrug.

Cade touched her whiskey glass to Selena's cup of cherries.

"We did okay in the end, though," Cade said.

Selena tipped a few cherries into her mouth.

"You did good," she said. "Did you quit because you got hurt?"

"I was back and forth between Boston University and the gallery. I just couldn't make enough races."

"I'm sorry." Selena pulled her hands into the cuffs of her surprisingly conservative sweater.

It occurred to Cade that Selena must have dressed up for the lecture...or dressed down, depending on what you thought about bustiers and fake fur. That was sweet, and boardroom gray looked good on her, although purple fur fit her better.

"It was okay. I was sad I didn't get to row, but whatever," Cade said.

"But you loved it."

"Sometimes the river would be so bright." Cade could still feel the sun reflecting off the water. "And sometimes it was like the arctic. But we were all in sync. I've never felt so together with people." She remembered every muscle of her body aching. "It's the most painful sport. In other sports, it hurts if you get injured, but in crew it hurts if you're doing it right, but then there's this moment when it all fades away and you're at peace."

"I know that feeling." Selena smiled gently. "It's special."

"I try to get that at the gym." Cade had never told anyone how she pushed herself, straining for that feeling she could never recapture, but she knew Selena's favorite dildo, she'd met Selena's ex, and now she knew the last person Selena had slept with. It seemed like Cade should share something. "Sometimes I exercise until I'm going to pass out, but I can't get that feeling."

Selena nodded thoughtfully, like a doctor considering her diagnosis. Then her face brightened.

"I could flog you, if you liked. It doesn't have to be sexual. I mean, it is, kind of, but I've flogged people I wasn't sleeping with. I'm not thinking BDSM, more just for the endorphins. It's a lot less effort than going to the gym; not that I go to the gym, but I've seen them."

What? Should she say, *Um, no!* or *That's nice of you. Maybe later*? If she said yes, would Selena actually whip her? Like go back to the house and bend her over the sofa? And how did you whip someone in a non-sexual, not-BDSM way? And...would she like it?

"Um," Cade said.

Selena let out a sweet, musical laugh that was definitely *at* Cade, not with her, but somehow wasn't mean at all.

"Maybe later," Selena said. "You know life is more than boiled chicken." She picked a cherry out of her drink. "Close your eyes and open your mouth."

Cade froze for a moment.

"Go on," Selena said. "I don't bite. You're the one who could bite."

Was Selena's flirtation a joke? *Look at me playing seductress because you're so uptight and you need someone to shake you up a bit?* Was it wishful thinking that told Cade that—somehow, improbably, and in contradiction to everything else Cade had ever experienced with women—the answer was no. Selena was teasing, but she wasn't joking.

Cade's mind reeled. Cade closed her eyes and parted her lips. A second later, Selena slipped a cherry into her mouth. The sweet, intoxicating flavor exploded on Cade's tongue, but that wasn't what Cade noticed. She noticed that Selena's fingertips rested on her lips for a half a second longer than they needed. Every cell of her body focused on that point of contact. Golden ripples spread from her lips through her body.

Cade's eyes flew open. Selena held Cade's gaze, her dark eyes full of implication. Cade's heart froze between beats.

Then Selena leaned back as though nothing had happened. Had Cade imagined it?

"So tell me more about rowing crew," Selena said.

And, unlike all the women who asked because they really wanted to know *how do I get into the Elgin Gallery?*, Selena actually listened to the answer.

chapter 17

Morning was not Selena's time of day unless she was getting tater tots at a diner after staying up all night, but Cade was working so hard to save the shop. After they'd gone out for drinks the night before, Selena had suggested they watch TV, but Cade said she had to write a grant application for something called the Gentrification Abatement Coalition. Apparently, they gave money to failing businesses that made Portland feel like Portland. Cade was still up, her profile silhouetted in the window, when Selena went to bed. If Cade was working that hard, Selena could do one early morning.

She dressed quickly in the closest thing she had to work clothes and rode her motorcycle to the shop. The breathing cats looked eerie in the six a.m. darkness. Selena switched on the neon clitoris and then the overhead lights. The shelves really were too crowded. And Cade had been right about the store catering to one kind of person. It looked like the home of a sexy Red Hat Society lady. In other words, it looked like Ruth. But there were so many people who wouldn't feel comfortable here.

She closed her eyes and imagined Ruth's face.

"You wouldn't mind if I cleaned up around here? Would you?"

She pictured Ruth petting the breathing cats and greeting each merman by name. She saw Ruth waltzing around the store with a feather duster. *If you have time to lean, you have time to clean*, Ruth always said, but it was a joke because Ruth loved to lean. To talk. To sneak whiskey in the back room.

"This place is so you," Selena said. "That's why I didn't want to change it, but I think Cade might be right. It was you, but it's not…us."

She trailed her fingers along a shelf. It was dusty…and sticky in places. Cleaning sex toys (and sterilizing them if you were sharing with multiple partners) was very important. The shelves did not set a good example.

"Cade put all your papers in folders and labeled them with what's actually in them, and she's applying for a grant." Selena picked up one of the mermen. She gazed at his smiling face, but she was talking to Ruth. "I'm glad you sent her. I couldn't have done this without her."

She put the merman back and walked around the store, then stopped. Images of Cade kept breaking through her thoughts. Cade in her tight, rain-soaked exercise wear. Cade trying as hard as Selena to look interested at the lecture on inventory. Cade's grin when they fled. Cade's gray cashmere sweaters and how sweet it was to be wrapped in Cade's arms.

"Don't be sad. Please. I still love you." Selena felt a lump in her throat. "I'll always love you, and I'll keep the mermen and hang them on the Christmas tree just like we said we would. You'll be there, right? But I just…I just don't think we can sell all this stuff and make the store work."

The clitoris light flickered. Did that mean, *I'm mad,* or *It's okay. You go girl*?

"I promise you'll like it," Selena said. "It's going to be a place for everyone."

With that, she went into the storeroom and scavenged some boxes and packing material. She started with the mermen.

Cade came in about an hour before opening. Her eyes widened at the state of the shop. In Selena's mind, it would all be perfect by the time Cade arrived. There would just be clean sex toys on wide-open shelves. No kittens. No YOLO pillows. No aprons. It'd be like an art gallery of sex toys.

"I didn't realize it'd take so long," Selena said, looking up from where she was sitting cross-legged on the floor surrounded by boxes.

Cade looked around.

"Wow," she said.

For a second, Selena thought Cade was angry. Her heart sank. *You were supposed to love it.*

But Cade said, "You're cleaning it up."

"No more breathing cats."

Cade sat down next to her.

"It's just going to be sex stuff. Super clean. Super modern," Selena said. "Vibrators over there. Dildos on that shelf. Anal play near the window. BDSM with—"

Cade touched Selena's knee.

"Are you okay?" Cade asked.

"Of course."

Selena had pushed down the lump in her throat. Cleaning was actually comforting. But now she felt her sadness come back.

"I'm sad," Selena said. "But it's okay. I'm glad I get to be sad about Ruth. That means I got to love her…get to love her. If she hadn't been in my life, I wouldn't get to be sad about her now."

Cade kept her hand on Selena's knee. Selena felt the warmth spread through her body.

"I told her I was going to clean up, and the clitoris light flickered." Selena felt herself tear up. "I thought maybe that was her sending a sign. Isn't that dumb?"

Cade had to be the last person to believe the dead talked to you through neon clitorises, but Cade just said, "That's not dumb."

"I hope she's not mad or hurt," Selena said.

"It could be a sign that she's okay with it," Cade said. "And she's an Elgin. If you tell a real Elgin—not me—that you're going to do something totally different and change everything just to see what happens, they'll be like, *Hell, yeah. Let's have a bonfire too.*"

Selena laughed.

"Come here." Cade opened her arms.

It was an awkward hug, Selena sitting cross-legged, Cade kneeling in front of her. But that didn't matter. Cade's body was warm and strong and comforting. Selena slipped her hands under Cade's overcoat and nestled her cheek against Cade's impossibly soft sweater.

"When we're done here," Cade murmured, "we'll find someplace to donate the things we're not selling. A nursing home or a shelter...but we'll not tell them it came from a sex toy store, or if we tell them, you have to be the one to go in and talk to them."

chapter 18

It was near closing. After several more hours of work, the store was looking great, great enough that Cade had retreated to the back room to review the specs for the Gentrification Abatement Grant one more time before hitting send. At least she was pretending to. The curtain was open between the back room and the store, so she'd know to come out if Selena needed help. Of course, Selena wouldn't need help. There weren't enough customers to need help with, and, plus, Selena was a wonderful sales-person. Easy. Friendly, not too friendly. Knowledgeable.

The door chimed. An older couple came in laughing and shaking the rain off their coats.

"Come in. Get out of the rain," Selena said warmly.

Cade watched the sale. The couple had come in for a cock ring. Selena had a long conversation about anatomy, and somewhere along the line they got into stories about lost sex toys. Selena picked up the Titan.

"Carry-on only," she said. "It's too good for cargo."

The woman held up a cock ring.

"He could wear it on," she said.

"I should get one with metal. Really give everyone a thrill," her partner joked.

Selena rang them up with a cheerful "Come again soon."

The couple laughed.

Cade turned back to her laptop before Selena could catch her watching, but she looked up when the next customers came in.

It was a pair of teenage girls. One had green hair, the other a jean jacket with QUEER AS FUCK stenciled on the back. They walked around the store without touching anything, exchanging glances. Finally, they stopped at the dildos.

"Just pick one," Queer As Fuck whispered.

"Which one?"

"I don't know."

"They're big. What about those?" the girl with the green hair said, looking at the butt plugs.

"I don't think they're for..." Queer As Fuck winced.

"Oh."

Selena stood in front of the bookshelf, adjusting the already perfectly straightened books.

"If you have any questions..." she said.

"No," the girls said in unison.

"No problem." Selena turned back to the books.

It occurred to Cade that the girls were probably underage. There were laws against minors in sex toy stores, but the chances that the Portland police would send two undercover officers to bust a failing sex toy store for selling—or probably not selling—dildos to teenagers was low.

The girls looked at the door.

Green Hair said, "But we took the bus all this way."

"It's kind of overwhelming, isn't it?" Selena said, putting the last book in its place. "A lot of choices."

The girls nodded.

"The first time I bought one, I ordered it online." Selena approached them slowly, like approaching a skittish cat. "It came to my dad. I forgot I was using his Amazon account."

"What happened?" Queer As Fuck asked.

Selena shook her head.

"I love my dad, but we weren't the kind of family that talked about things, you know, out loud. He tried to tape it up, so it looked like he hadn't seen it." Selena affected a gruff voice. "Then he said, *I think this got mailed to you.* Then he tried to talk to me about the birds and the bees, and he got as far as, *When a man and a woman.* Then he went on a really long motorcycle ride."

The girls laughed.

"We don't know which one to get," Green Hair blurted.

"Let me show you what we got," Selena said.

When they'd picked one, the Milo, Selena rang them up and grabbed a handful of lube samples. She held them up.

"Really important," she said as she added them to the bag. "Lube makes it better. Always." After they left, she called to Cade. "Closing time?"

"Yeah."

Selena turned off the open sign and the overhead lights and wandered into the back room.

"You staying late?" she asked.

Cade nodded. There was so much to do.

"You eat anything?" Selena asked.

Cade picked up the protein shake on the table beside her. Selena took it from her hand, examined the label, then handed it back.

"People drink these things because they hate themselves," she said. "Don't hate yourself."

"They're good."

"No," Selena said, as though it were scientific fact.

"Have you tried one?"

Selena took the bottle back, uncapped it, and took a sip. Cade watched her lips as she sipped, her mouth touching the bottle where Cade's lips had been, leaving a sheen of burgundy lipstick.

"Why did you make me do that?" Selena said.

She rested her hand on Cade's back. It was just a casual touch. Becket came in the store sometimes, and Selena hugged her like they were long-lost lovers. It wasn't a big deal, but it felt wonderful.

"I'm going to get you some real food," Selena said.

She came back an hour later with a huge carton.

"Make some room." She indicated the desk.

Cade moved her papers.

"Chopsticks." Selena opened the box.

There were enough noodles to feed a committee. Selena pulled up a chair and dug in.

"What they say about carbs being bad for you, it's a lie," Selena said through a mouthful of noodles. "Conspiracy. Probably from the beef industry. Carbs make people happy."

The back room was messy. The light was soft. Selena was beautiful slurping noodles gracelessly off her chopsticks. And Cade *was* happy. She tried a bite. The noodles were delicious. They ate in silence for a while.

"You're really good at selling toys," Cade said, breaking the companionable silence.

A noodle disappeared into Selena's mouth, and she wiped her lips.

"Thanks."

"I make people nervous," Cade said.

"You don't." Selena twirled her chopsticks in the noodles without taking any. "You're dignified…like British royalty. You're really good with the customers who want to take this seriously and get out quickly."

Cade put her chopsticks in the container, and Selena tapped them with her own, as if to say, *I'm just playing.*

"You do talk a lot about charging speeds." She put her chopsticks down. "It's hard selling sex toys. It's personal, and people come in with baggage."

"So if you had to write a book on sex toy sales, what would be your sales technique?" Cade asked.

"I guess I just try to meet people where they are, talk to *that* person." Selena cocked her head and pursed her lips. "Not what they look like or *do I think they'll be into bondage* or *they're trans so I think they might like this.* I just see *them,* and then I'm there to help. It's like painting someone's portrait. You have to see the whole person. You have to see their soul." She stopped and added, "That's what people say. Artists who paint. I don't know."

"I don't think I can see people's souls."

But could she glimpse Selena's? That sweet, incongruous

blend of burlesque hipster and country girl? The way she shared way too much, too soon, and all in one breath, and then the shadow that had crossed her face when she talked about art school. She had stories she didn't tell. Everyone did. Selena was a little over the top sometimes, but she was human too. Cade wanted to cup Selena's face between her hands and...well, that wasn't going to happen.

"The other trick," Selena said, breaking Cade out of her reverie, "is just to describe whatever they're holding." She snagged an enormous nest of noodles between her chopstick and shoved them in her mouth. "Want to practice after dinner?"

When they'd finished their noodles—well, one or two pounds of their noodles; there were plenty for leftovers—they went back into the store.

"Imagine I just walked in," Selena said. "See if I look comfortable. Really comfortable, picking things up, eye contact. Then you say, *Hi, can I help you. Looking for something special?* But if I'm like those girls, you wait. Four, five, ten minutes. Then you just let them know they can ask questions." Selena picked up a vibrator. "Pretend I'm in between. Kind of nervous. Kind of okay with everything. Go ahead."

"Can I help you?" Cade sounded stilted.

"I don't know. I'm just looking for something new." Selena looked at her expectantly.

"I can't ask what they have already?" Cade said.

"Describe what I'm holding." Selena held out the vibrator so Cade could see.

"That's the Vibrant, it's...one of our smallest insertables," Cade said.

"Good."

"It has a variety of vibration patterns."

"Exactly."

"But they all do," Cade said.

"And they're all fabulous."

"And if you'd like something bigger, we have the Vibrant II," Cade offered.

"You got it." Selena turned the vibrator on and held it against her palm. "But what about the charging speed?" she asked in a sultry voice.

Another woman teasing her like this would have made Cade feel bad. *You're so uptight. Millennials aren't having sex. Not much of a life. Six times. No orgasm.* But she didn't feel bad now. She felt seen and appreciated, like Selena thought she was charming just the way she was, with her charging speeds and her British royalty sex toy selling techniques.

Selena looked at Cade, her face suddenly serious.

"Are you okay with this stuff?" Selena asked. "If something happened to you, if this brings up past stuff, you don't have to work the floor. I can do it if you don't want to."

"No," Cade said. "I'm lucky. Nothing bad has happened to me like that." She paused. "I just never had much luck with sex toys."

She was surprised. It was easy to say. Not a big deal. The elliptical didn't give her a good workout. Cilantro tasted like soap. And sex toys weren't her thing.

"That's okay," Selena said.

"But I always felt like I was a bit of a fail. Everybody likes them. I want to like them," Cade admitted.

She felt comfortable telling Selena. Not comfortable enough to tell her the whole story, but comfortable.

"You're never a fail because you don't want to do something you don't like," Selena said. "You don't have to be anything you're not."

Cade didn't realize how much she wanted to hear those words until Selena spoke them.

"You're perfect," Selena said.

Their eyes met. Cade was suddenly aware of how dim the store was without the overhead lights. It was just them and their eyes locked and the giant, neon clitoris.

And Cade had to admit it; she had a crush so big she felt like her heart filled the whole room. *Selena.* Cade turned away, closing her eyes, trying—and failing—to hold back the wave of longing that washed over her. She hadn't had a crush like this since she was a teenager. And even if Selena had touched her lips and given her a cherry, it was all impossible. Selena was celibate. Cade had a return trip ticket to New York on her Delta app. It would be fun to flirt with Selena for the few weeks they'd be together, to dream, to pretend, but Cade liked Selena more than that, and the happiness she felt was mixed with something bittersweet. *Don't hope.*

"And if you want to like them, you can practice," Selena said. "And we sell books with exercises. Or you could find someone to help you."

"You're a good teacher," Cade said, realizing a second too late that it didn't sound like she was talking about sales techniques. "I...I didn't mean..."

Selena walked past Cade to the counter. As she went by, she trailed her fingertips across Cade's lower back, just a whisper of a touch.

"I know what you meant."

chapter 19

A few days later, Selena sat beside Cade on the Trimet, watching the streets whiz by as they headed to the Sexpo. Cade held the box of flyers Selena had made. She opened it for the third time.

"These look great," Cade said. "You're just so good at this."

Her words made Selena's heart sing. Design had never been Selena's specialty, but she'd taken classes. She had an eye.

"The colors here." Cade pointed to the stylized clitoris Selena had created as a logo for the store. "The curve here. Brilliant."

Selena's heart floated above the train like a kite. Cade thought she had talent.

"You're the opposite of Alex," Selena said.

Cade *was* the opposite of Alex. Kind when Alex had been mean. Encouraging when Alex had been critical. And Selena loved Cade's dry sense of humor. Every time Selena had joked with Alex, Alex had taken her seriously, which made whatever Selena had said sound stupid.

Selena probably shouldn't have said it though. Alex was her ex, and Cade was her friend...coworker...co-inheritor. Something.

"Sorry, that's weird," Selena said.

"I want to be opposite to her." Cade looked at Selena with kind eyes. "She's an asshole."

Selena looked down at the flyers. "I'm glad you like these."

Cade ran her finger down the flyer. Selena tried not to notice the perfect architecture of her hand. Like Rodin marble. Those hands could...Selena stopped herself. Her mind had been turning toward Cade's hands, Cade's lips, Cade's everything. And it wasn't because she was celibate and the idea of anyone's hands on her body was enticing. It was Cade.

"But the calendar." Cade's finger came to rest on the calendar of events. "It goes through June."

"We can move the dates around if we need to."

"Yes," Cade said tentatively. She put the lid back on the box. "But we're not doing as well as we need to. I called Swing Set. I think they'll work with us. But the others...We shouldn't get our hopes up."

Selena had been trying not to. Cade had a return trip ticket. She had a life in New York. The thought was starting to make Selena sad, a kind of sad that kept her up at night staring at the lights strung across her ceiling.

Selena pulled herself out of her thoughts.

"We'll make it work," she said. "We're handing out

a thousand flyers, so everyone knows that Satisfaction Guaranteed is Portland's best sex toy store."

"I am going to give a thousand people a picture of a clitoris," Cade said with mock distress. Then she added, "A very well-designed clitoris."

"Only five hundred. We'll share."

"We're not going to split up in there?"

"We'll get out faster if we do."

"How could you leave me?" Cade clasped a hand to her chest.

How could you leave me? Leave the shop? Leave Portland? How silly to even think about wanting Cade to stay. They hadn't known each other a month. But still...

The train's automatic message announced their stop and they got off with the rest of the crowd. People streamed toward the expo center, dressed in everything from fleece to full bondage gear.

"You'll love it," Selena said.

Selena liked the way Cade rolled her eyes.

"They have live demonstrations." Selena raised her eyebrows.

"Oh, god," Cade said.

"You could volunteer."

"You learn something new every day," Cade said.

"You'd be a wonderful subject."

Selena was flirting. She shouldn't. It was just so tempting. She loved the way Cade tried to hide a smile, the way she ducked her head and hid behind the perfect sweep of her blond hair. Cade was gorgeous, and she was Cadence Elgin of the Elgin Gallery, but somehow it seemed like she was always surprised when Selena complimented her, like Selena was the first woman to pay attention to her. It made her want to lavish Cade with her attention. The wrong choices were always so much more attractive than the responsible ones.

"What do you want to know?" Selena said. "I could teach you."

Cade blushed.

Do not flirt.

Selena looped her arm through Cade's. They were both wearing coats, but the touch still gave her a thrill.

"Come on. Let's get in there," Selena said. "You're going to beg me to stay all day once you see what it's like."

"Optimist." Cade gave her a little shove with her shoulder, then pulled her back, their bodies almost touching as they strolled in arm in arm.

Inside, Selena led Cade to the check-in table. They took their place at the end of the registration line. It was more of a registration cluster. A man knocked into Selena. The crowd pressed them together. It was wonderful. But too soon they were through the line. Inside, the space was filled with stalls selling sex products. Some stalls played porn on big screens behind their stuff. Famous porn stars signed autographs for fans. Nearby a maker sold hand-made purses that looked like vulvas.

Cade's eyes were wide.

"Okay, it's a lot," Selena said. "But it really is cool. It's an experience."

"Everyone likes an experience." Cade looked at a stand of blow-up dolls. "Wow."

"Want to give me my flyers?"

Cade split the stack in two and handed half to Selena.

"You ready to tell everyone how fabulous we are...the store is?" Selena asked.

"Yes." Cade looked like she was trying on a power pose: shoulders back, chin up. "We *are* fabulous."

"You got this."

There was a map of the conference on an easel nearby. Selena walked over and studied it. "We could meet up at the Bouncy House of Breasts in, say, two hours?"

"Of course. Everyone meets at the Bouncy House of Breasts." Cade shook her head with a look of amused disbelief.

She looked adorably formal in her starched shirt and overcoat, all gray. Formal and hot. People would notice her. They'd hit on her. For sure. And that was none of Selena's business, and she shouldn't mind. At all.

"Thank you for doing this," Selena said.

Selena rose up on her toes and planted a kiss on Cade's cheek with a loud smack. She'd kissed Becket like that a thousand times. But this was different. Their eyes locked for a second. Cade opened her mouth but said nothing.

God, you're lovely.

"Now go," Selena said. "Talk about the clitoris."

"I'm doing this for you," Cade said over her shoulder as she walked away. "Appreciate it."

Selena did, and she watched Cade's back until Cade disappeared into the crowd.

Selena arrived at the Bouncy House of Breasts twenty minutes early, which was good because it was a twenty-minute wait to get in. Cade arrived as Selena was nearing the front of the line, handing her last flyer to a random person as she joined Selena.

"How was it?" Selena asked.

Cade raised her arm over her face. "I know how to talk about art."

"Sex is the sacred human art."

"Not the kind of art you can wrap in bubble wrap and ship to the Hamptons."

"Whatever works for you. There's nothing wrong with a little bubble wrap," Selena drawled, delighting in Cade's blush. "I'm sure you did great."

"Is this what I think it is?" Cade nodded toward the large, pink bouncy house ahead of them.

"It's here every year."

"Full of breasts?"

"Giant inflatable breasts."

Cade groaned.

"You're secretly having fun," Selena said.

"Now that I'm back with you."

You're celibate. Don't flirt. The smile Cade gave her weakened Selena's resolves.

"Next!" the man at the entrance called.

"That's us."

The bouncy house manager glared at them for not taking their shoes off while they were still in line.

"No sharp objects in your pockets. You get two minutes. If you panic, call for help."

They crawled through a plastic flap into the bouncy house. Inside, it was like being in a cloud of giant bubbles, only they were breasts. Different colors. Different nipples. Inflated like a backyard party bouncy house except so very different. The light in the house came from the soft, pink glow of the ceiling.

"I can't believe someone made this," Cade said, stumbling against a dark brown breast.

Cade looked around.

"Bounce." Selena jumped on the springy floor, feeling like a kid.

Cade jumped too, her perfect hair flying around her. The young CEO letting loose. It was the cutest thing, and hearing Cade laugh, Selena felt like she'd done something wonderful, something she wanted to do again and again: make Cade happy.

"One minute," the bouncy house master called in.

It went so quickly.

Cade launched herself off one of the breasts. Selena bounced off another. The inflatable breasts sent them toppling in different directions. Then before she realized where she was going, Selena collided with Cade, losing her footing and falling backward. Cade grabbed her to steady her, but the floor shifted, and Cade fell forward. She caught herself at the last minute, bracing her whole body in a push-up, hovering above Selena, her body swaying as she held her pose on the shifting floor.

She was so strong. She would be a wonderful lover, strong enough to hold Selena down, gentle enough to lift her up. Kind. Attentive. Thoughtful. All the things people forgot to look for when they looked for lovers. All the things Selena had never had with Alex. And Selena's whole body cried out for Cade's weight on top of her.

And for once the universe agreed to give her exactly what she wanted. The bouncy house quivered. The floor sunk beneath them. Cade lost her hold, and she collapsed on top of Selena, the whole length of their legs touching, their hips pressed together.

"Oh, my god, I'm sorry," Cade said. "I'm sorry. I…"

Selena put her arms around Cade's waist before she realized what she was doing. She heard Cade gasp, but Selena had been with enough people to know the difference between distress and delight.

"I'm sorry," Selena breathed, but she didn't let Cade go and Cade didn't struggle.

Selena felt like time froze. Surely outside the bouncy house everyone had turned into a statue. Her breath sounded loud in her ears. She could feel Cade's heartbeat.

Kiss me.

"You're done," the bouncy house manager called out. "Next."

Cade seemed to remember where she was. She tried to scramble away, blushing furiously, but the floor pushed them together, like sinking into the middle of a mattress. It felt right.

"You get two minutes with the breasts. If you don't share the breasts, there will not be enough breasts for everyone," the manager called out.

Cade burst into laughter. It was contagious. And suddenly, Selena was laughing so hard she could barely catch her breath. Cade got hold of a nipple and pulled herself up. Cade pulled Selena to her feet.

"Out!" the manager yelled.

"Are we going to get a ticket for spending too much time with the breasts?" Cade was still laughing. "Can I contest it in court?"

They crawled out of the bouncy house through a pink tube with an inflatable vulva on the outside.

Cade looked back, grinning. "Think we could get one of those for the backyard?"

"We could." Selena was so focused on Cade she nearly walked into a man in a condom costume. Cade caught her around the waist and guided her out of his way.

"You're actually thinking about it," Cade said.

"We could throw a party."

"Okay. We'll throw a bouncy house party, maybe for Arbor Day."

Selena laughed. "Don't you think Valentine's Day would be more traditional?"

"Too obvious." Cade raised her eyebrows. "No one expects the Bouncy House of Breasts on Arbor Day. It would be an experience."

Of course they wouldn't have an inflatable-breast-house party for Arbor Day, but it was fun to pretend. *And dangerous*, a voice in the back of Selena's mind whispered. She really would like to throw a party with Cade. She could picture it, just like the parties Ruth threw. Food and drinks and lights and music, her and Cade standing on the sidelines admiring the festivities. She couldn't remember when Arbor Day was exactly, but it was not in the next few weeks before Cade left. What day was Cade leaving? Had Selena forgotten or had she pushed it out of her mind? Whatever. She pushed the thought away again.

They walked toward the train in perfect step with each other.

"Do you think anyone really panics in the bouncy house?" Cade asked.

"Maybe." Selena laughed. "If they're claustrophobic or they're afraid of women. Female power and all that. Everyone's got their phobias. I'm afraid of amusement park rides."

"Riding a motorcycle is more dangerous."

"But I'm in control. Back in Tristess, there were these traveling fairs that'd show up in an empty lot. Overnight. There they were. You could see there were lights burnt out on the rides. The paint was coming off. I don't know that the guy who runs the Zipper wasn't drunk last night."

Cade laughed. "I would have thought you'd love rides."

"What are you afraid of?" Selena asked.

"Plane crashes. Climate change. The usual stuff." Cade put her hands in her pockets. "Dying alone and being eaten by my cat."

"Sociopath?"

"He'd eat me before I was dead if I didn't move fast enough."

Cade's voice was light, but when Selena glanced over, Cade's brow was furrowed.

"Are you really afraid you'll die alone? Sorry. That's heavy."

Cade shrugged.

"My friend Amy says I don't have enough fun, don't go out enough. My parents say I'm old before my time, and I need to meet someone." She smiled ruefully. "Thanks, Mom."

"Why don't you go out?"

"I do go out, and I do meet women."

Selena felt a sting of jealousy.

"But it's always for work," Cade added. "And they're not interested in me, just the gallery and my parents."

Selena doubted that.

"Do you like working for your parents?" she asked. "If it takes up so much of your life?"

Cade looked over with mild surprise.

"I don't work for them. I own a third of the gallery."

She owned it, part of it. The thought made Selena's heart sink a little. Cade was even more tied to the gallery than she'd realized and even more über professional.

"I do more than a third of the work, though," Cade said, "and I like it. I'd love it if I could run it without fighting with my parents over alpacas or whatever. If I could just work with someone responsible, who did what they were supposed to do, and didn't make crazy decisions because the Spirit of the Universe told them to."

That was to say, Cade didn't want to work with a person like Selena. Selena let out a tiny sigh.

They'd reached the train stop. Cade scanned the tracks.

"And I love the art," Cade said. "I love the opening where everything is perfect. The work is amazing. I get to see the artist go from some guy who paints on plywood in an attic to…a star. It doesn't always make them happy to be famous, but at least they'll never wonder *what if.* And people get to see great work. You know what's dumb, though," Cade said, still staring into the distance. "They transferred a third of the ownership to me when I turned twenty-one. I get a third of the gallery's profits. It was a huge gift. But I didn't want it. Spoiled kid, right?" She turned back to Selena. "I just didn't want it yet. I felt like…" She trailed off.

"What?"

A dusty wind blew up from the train tracks. Selena shivered and stepped closer to Cade.

"I feel like I missed out," Cade said.

"On what?"

Cade pursed her lips, thinking. Then the shadow that had fallen over her seemed to lift.

"The Bouncy House of Breasts." She grinned. "On this."

chapter 20

Selena beamed with pride as she looked around Satisfaction Guaranteed. She'd had to rent tables from the party store. The attendees were packed tightly together with pots of paint and glasses of wine in front of them. Everyone was talking. A few women had shared their vulva selfies with one another. It already felt like a party. Plus, Selena had borrowed a camera from Becket. It sat on a tripod behind the group ready to capture everything for the forty-two people who had signed up to watch the session on Zoom.

Cade stood behind the counter looking a little bit like she was about to preside over a board meeting. And adorable. She also looked adorable.

Selena slipped behind the counter and leaned close to her.

"Don't be nervous," Selena whispered.

Cade straightened the collar of her sweater.

"I'm not nervous as long as I don't have to take a Polaroid of my vulva," Cade whispered back.

"A selfie?"

"No."

"Mirror?"

"No."

Selena had brought a glass of wine for Cade.

"Wine? It's more fun if you're relaxed."

"I love you." Cade took a big swig, then coughed. "I mean..." She trailed off.

"I am your goddess of the vine?"

"Exactly." Cade took another large sip of wine.

"If you change your mind about painting"—Selena let her fingertips trail across Cade's back as she walked away—"I'm sure she's beautiful."

"Who?" Cade blushed as she must have realized what Selena meant.

So much for not flirting with this funny, sweet, hot woman...who was going to go back to New York and wanted to date an accountant.

"Let's get started," Selena said to the crowd.

Her heart raced. That always happened when she taught. It wasn't as bad as giving a eulogy, but she always got nervous. Except the heady tingle of adrenaline she felt now wasn't for the students watching her. It was for Cade standing behind her.

No.

Selena wouldn't. They were just playing. She turned around. Cade smiled at her encouragingly.

You got this, Cade mouthed.

Did she?

Selena took a deep breath and started the class as she always did, with a photograph of Jamie McCartney's *Great Wall of Vagina* installation: plaster casts of four hundred women's vulvas. *"Great Wall of Vagina* is just a catchy name," Selena said. "They're vulvas, not vaginas. That's important." She went on to describe the anatomy of the vulva and the clitoris, gesturing to the neon clitoris to demonstrate. Then she covered safe space rules.

"Remember, everything you create is beautiful because it's part of who you are," Selena finished. "Let's pour some wine and paint something beautiful."

As the students worked, Selena walked around the room, refilling wineglasses and complimenting paintings.

"I love how you used a big glob of paint for the clitoris," she said to one student. "That three-D touch is great."

Another student complained that her labia looked like crinkle fries.

"Everyone likes crinkle fries." Selena took a closer look. "There's a lovely textural quality to the crinkle, and look here. How sweet is that blend of pink and gold? Lovely."

When everyone was happily painting and drinking, Selena leaned against the front of the counter while Cade stood behind it.

"They love it." Cade leaned across the counter to speak the words near Selena's ear.

"You would too if you tried," Selena teased gently.

She turned to look at Cade. Cade's lips parted. Selena wanted to taste her. She wanted to feel Cade's hair running through her fingers as she drew her closer.

She could too. She could break her vow. This room full of students said, *I've got my shit together.* Yes, technically, Selena still wasn't paying rent. And her phone was crap. And having your shit together probably meant exercising and drinking hateful protein shakes. But she owned half a business that she and Cade were rescuing from the brink. The store looked fresh and bright. She'd charmed everyone she met at the Sexpo. The class was packed and fabulous, which meant there'd be even more students next month.

Becket had told her not to expect one dazzling moment when she suddenly knew she'd gotten it together, but Becket was wrong. This was it. And that meant…

"I have to get something." Selena rushed into the back room.

Inside, she leaned her head against the wall. If it was just sex, she'd have pulled Cade into the back room with her. But sex was only one part of what she wanted. The realization made her chest tighten. She wanted to fall asleep next to Cade. To wake up in Cade's arms. She wanted to kiss Cade at the Aviary New Year's Eve party. She wanted to take Cade home to Tristess.

And Selena knew just how she would paint Cade if she were still a painter. She'd catch Cade as Cade tried not to smile. That self-deprecating tilt of her head. The laughter in her blue eyes. Selena would layer grays until they were as soft as Cade's sweaters. She'd capture how Cade could be so warm, even though she was reserved. And she'd paint Cade's lips in pink cream so rich people would kiss the canvas.

Selena texted Becket.

Tell me not to kiss Cade. Only that was a hard sentence to write on her phone with all the letters it didn't type reliably. No one could interpret *T nt t* but Becket knew her well.

Do you need me to tell you not to break your vow? Becket texted back.

Ys

If she broke her vow with Cade, Cade would leave and break her heart. That was a fucked-up thing to walk into. Maybe she didn't have her shit together. If she had her shit together she could break her vow, but if she broke her vow with Cade, that meant she didn't have her shit together because Cade was a bad decision, so that meant she shouldn't have broken it in the first place. She tried to explain the paradox in text.

Becket texted back, *You know I have no idea what you're saying. Want to talk?*

But Cade had just poked her head through the curtain.

"Everything okay?" she asked. "The woman with the crinkle fries wanted to know if we have any more yellow paint."

It was a good night despite the existential crisis. Selena loved leaning over a student's shoulder and taking their brush. *May I?* Just a touch. Just a quick blend of red and orange. Not painting, just remembering. The students left laughing and talking, each with their vulva painting balanced on a piece of cardboard.

"You're a good teacher," Cade said as they started to clean up. She touched the paint with her finger, then drew a smiling face on her hand. She held it up. "Will I get into MoMA?"

"Definitely."

"Will you paint me something?" Cade asked.

I can't. Alex's criticisms flooded her mind. Selena was

talented but not disciplined. When she tried to be disciplined, she was stiff. She'd had such a gift when she started, but then her work got derivative.

Selena hurriedly gathered an armload of paints and dumped them into a box. She forced a laugh.

"You're Cade Elgin of the Elgin Gallery. I am not painting you anything. You see the best of the best."

"You could tell the landscape painter."

"I guessed."

"You guessed right."

"I was a horrible painter, and I only did a few."

"What happened to *everything you create is beautiful because it's part of who you are*? I'm not judging."

"It is literally your job to judge art."

No one from the Aviary would press her like this, but Cade didn't know what had happened after Alex broke up with her, how Ruth had burned Selena's paintings for her so that Selena would not have to watch her dreams go up in flames. Cade was just teasing.

"We're drinking boxed wine from Solo cups in a sex toy store." Cade took another sip of wine. "If you don't get in the Louvre with this, I'm not going to think you're a failure."

"I gave it up."

Cade looked at Selena more seriously.

"You don't have to. If you gave it up, you gave it up," Cade said.

Selena looked at the box of student-grade paint. Basically, pigment in glue. It called to her with a force that made her heart ache. And suddenly Selena was sick of being the painter who gave it up, the failed artist whom everyone tiptoed around because she was so broken. The woman who gave it up for an ex she didn't even want to see on caller ID.

"I will paint something if you paint your vulva," Selena said.

Cade made two swoops of paint on a piece of scratch paper.

"That is not a vulva," Selena said. "That's two half circles. Put a little effort into it, and I'll paint you something."

"Yes, teacher." Cade sat down.

Except for the Solo cup she sipped from occasionally, Cade looked like a dutiful student, head bent over her work. They sat at different tables, but as Selena slowly opened a jar of brown paint, she felt the space between them shrink. She applied the first layer, just a backdrop to hold Cade's image.

She blurred an edge of black paint with the side of her hand, then dipped her finger in white and smoothed it into the dark. It felt like touching a woman, wet and delicate. Across from her, Cade kept her eyes on her paper, and Selena studied her. The way she sat up straight, even when she was looking down. Elegant. Strong. The edge of her blond hair, sweeping her cheek and never falling in her eyes. Her slight smile that made it seem like she was dreaming of something beyond the paper in front of her.

After a few minutes, Cade sat up and downed the last of her wine.

"I'm done," she said, "but first show me yours."

"It doesn't look like anything," Selena said, but when she looked at her work it wasn't bad. It was pretty good, actually.

"We're at Pour and Paint Your Vulva." Cade walked over to Selena's table. "I really expect you to make a master-piece. I did. I…" She put a hand on Selena's shoulder. Then she saw it. "It's me!"

"You're prettier."

"I love it." Cade spoke quietly. "And it doesn't matter, but, Selena, it *is* good. That's *me*. No, that's who I want to be. It's like…" She shook her head. "You said you dropped out of art school. You said you just did a few paintings."

Selena bit her lip.

"I guess I did a few more than a few."

"Can I have it?" Cade asked.

Remember me forever.

"Okay," Selena said. "But only if I can have your vulva."

Cade held up her painting. It looked like a symmetrical daisy with a ring of clitorises around the edge.

"I love it," Selena said, "and I think we need to talk about anatomy."

chapter 21

Cade could tell Selena was trying to keep a straight face. She was too.

"Every vulva is different." Selena held Cade's painting across her palms. "But this is more different than most."

"It's a mandala."

"Different sizes, shapes, colors. That's normal. But I see here, you've put in"—Selena counted the ring of dots—"eighteen clitorises."

"Mandala!"

"That's a nice word for it."

"It's part of a very serious spiritual practice," Cade said.

Selena dipped her chin and looked up at Cade with sultry eyes.

"It's definitely part of my *spiritual practice*," she said. "Is the purple your vaginal opening or is it this whole flower structure? And you vajazzled your sixth labia. Very festive."

"You're terrible."

Cade pretended to grab for her painting. Selena brushed

her hand away, her fingers grazing the back of Cade's hand. It should have been nothing. Cade shouldn't even have noticed. Cade had ridden the subway when every single part of her body pressed against a stranger, and she hadn't noticed. But Selena's feather-light touch made her head swim.

"I don't want you to feel self-conscious about your eighteen clitorises." Selena's eyes twinkled with humor. "But just in case you, maybe, got the anatomy wrong, would you like to take a Polaroid, just to make sure?"

"If God meant you to look," Cade said, imitating the coy dip of Selena's chin, "he would have put it somewhere obvious."

Selena pressed her hands to her chest. "How can you work here and say that?"

"It's like looking under your tongue."

Selena opened her mouth and exhibited the underside of her tongue, managing to look sexy. A tingle ran through Cade's body. She wanted to kiss Selena. She wanted to feel Selena's tongue against hers. She wanted it so much.

"If God hadn't wanted us to look," Selena said, "he wouldn't have invented the cell phone camera."

"You didn't study theology, did you?"

"I've been to church."

"I want to hear you recite some Bible verses."

Selena rattled off a few.

"You know I think it's...cool that you can do that," Cade said seriously.

"We all got religion in Tristess. Everyone in Portland thinks it's weird."

"It's cool," Cade said, "that you want me to take a

Polaroid of my vulva. You can do a portrait in ten minutes that's better than stuff people have spent years on. You've memorized the Bible. You're..." *Complex. Mysterious. Lovely.* "You are who you are. You're real."

Selena looked down. She traced the white space on the paper around Cade's painting.

"Well, shucks," she said with a country twang.

Silence welled up between them, full of things they weren't saying.

But finally, Selena pulled out a phone and said, "If you're not going to take a Polaroid, do you want to see mine?"

Cade opened her mouth and closed it again.

"Artemisia in the flesh," Selena said.

She was holding a cell phone selfie of her own vulva. She was offering it to Cade. The six times Cade had had sex—what a sad number—she hadn't thought about what her lovers' vulvas looked like. They were just mysterious places where she would do something wrong.

"She's beautiful, and no one has seen her for a long time," Selena said.

Was there etiquette for looking at vulvas? Should Cade say, *Sure*, like an invitation to look at a nice picture someone had just posted on Instagram? Or, *No, you don't have to*, like when an acquaintance offered to pay for dinner? She'd pretend to look but not really look. That was polite but modest.

Cade nodded. Selena handed her the phone. Of course, Cade looked. Selena's body was a deep, dusty-rose pink. Asymmetrical. Her clitoris was hidden in the folds of her labia. All of it was a little squished and dry, like Selena had been wearing tight jeans.

Cade stared for far, far too long.

"She has that effect on people," Selena said. "Pretty, right?"

A kind of longing Cade had never felt before washed over her. Her whole soul wanted to unfurl Selena's labia with her tongue. She wanted to touch Selena. She wanted to be touched. She had never wanted anything the way she wanted Selena.

There was only one thing to say.

"How on earth do you still have a flip phone?"

Selena's laugh was so big it filled the store.

"Oh, my god, you are a hard woman to impress, Cade Elgin. Come on. Let's go home and drink some absinthe."

Selena snapped her phone closed and stood up. Cade stood too, her chair clattering. She felt like every muscle in her body had gone limp and taut at the same time. They looked at each other, frozen, as though they were both about to speak. Then a person Cade had never been but was apparently becoming reached out and wrapped her arm around Selena's waist. She pulled her close. Their hips touched. Electricity ran through Cade's body.

"Oh, Cade," Selena breathed.

And Cade kissed her, slowly at first. Selena's lips were soft, her breath sweet, her body like sunshine itself. But as they kissed Cade felt Selena stiffen, heard her give a little moan. When Cade finally parted her lips, Selena plunged her tongue into Cade's mouth, rolling her tongue against Cade's.

Cade's heart raced. The kiss filled her whole body.

Selena walked Cade backward, both of them stumbling,

then she pressed Cade's back against the counter, still kissing her. Caressing her face. Fisting Cade's hair in her hands. Her leg pressing between Cade's. The pleasure made Cade's knees tremble. It was so good and so not enough. Did Selena know what she was doing to Cade? Of course she knew. Selena was rubbing against Cade too, moaning softly. The sound made Cade's body contract with need. She buried her hands in Selena's hair, torn between the desire to devour her and the desire to hold her as lightly as a butterfly.

I want you. I need you. Selena. Darling. Sweetheart. Friend.

Cade felt herself melting into Selena. They were one body. One need. One purpose. And even though Selena gripped her hard, Cade felt Selena's affection in every movement.

Then without warning, Selena pulled away, her eyes stormy with desire. She cupped Cade's cheek in her hand.

"I'm not ready, Cade. I'm so sorry."

Back at Ruth's house, Cade draped herself across Ruth's bed, her mind swimming. It was too late to call Amy, but she wouldn't have called her if she could. She wanted to rest in the moment, to savor the ghost of Selena's kiss, to memorize every second before reality set in.

And with that thought, there it was: reality.

Sales at Satisfaction Guaranteed were getting better and better, but it wasn't nearly enough. There was no way they'd make the money they needed. The grant was the longest of long shots. And so little time left. Even if Cade threw in her savings, they wouldn't be close. She'd have to go back to New York. She couldn't stay in Portland hoping that one day Selena would be ready. Even if Cade found an excuse to stay and Selena was ready, there was still the matter of six times, no orgasm, and got-kicked-out-of-bed-for-poor-performance. There was still the matter of even-my-mother-thinks-I'm-boring. Cade wouldn't hold Selena's interest for long. She sighed. Amy would say encouraging things about long-distance relationships, dating while they were celibate, growing as a couple.

Don't hope too much.

Cade's body was still glowing from the pressure of Selena's leg between hers. She crawled under the blankets, unbuttoned her pants, and slipped her hand between her legs. She tried a variety of touch and pressure. It was all right, nothing like Selena's body against hers. She got up again and got a vibrator out of the bag of merchandise she'd taken from Satisfaction Guaranteed. They all came fully charged. (Cade had emphasized that feature to customers in hopes that they wouldn't ask about anything else.) She turned it on and pressed it to about where her clit was.

Fine.

She increased the vibrations.

Okay.

She switched to one of the twelve patterns of vibration. It felt like Morse code, but she wasn't getting the message, until…there.

There it was. Right there. Twenty-nine years and she hadn't, but now…yes…that was it…a little harder.

But what if she couldn't? The pleasure of the vibration faded a little. She increased the vibrations again. A car passed by the house. They were driving too fast. Could someone see her from the road? Selena probably

masturbated in broad daylight. Was it wrong to mastur-
bate in her aunt's bed? Thoughts popped into her mind
like the notifications on her phone. The pleasure she'd felt
faded into the dull ache of need. She turned the vibrator
off and tossed it in the bedside table drawer. Apparently,
she wasn't ready yet either.

chapter 22

Cade wandered into the kitchen the next morning around six. Cade's head was still spinning. She hadn't slept. She felt elated and rejected at the same time.

She texted Amy.

We kissed but she doesn't want anything.

Amy called instantly.

"You kissed? When? Where? Did you sleep with her?"

Cade could hear Amy tucking her phone under her ear as she tended to something in the food cart.

"It wasn't that big a deal." The lilt in Cade's voice made her a liar. There was no feigning cool. "She was teaching a class, and afterwards we were just playing around, painting vulva, except she painted me, and I painted a mandala, and then she showed me her vulva on her phone, and I kissed her." She sounded like a teenager. "She's amazing."

"Hold on. You were painting your vulva?" Amy asked. "Naked?"

"On paper. With clothes. But she's celibate, and she said

she wasn't ready." Cade sat down at the table. "And I'm leaving. We were drinking boxed wine. It really wasn't anything."

She knew Amy wouldn't let her get away with that.

"You like her." Cade heard Amy slap the food cart counter with satisfaction. "You. Cade Elgin. A crush. Finally."

"There's no finally about it."

"When was the last time you crushed on someone?"

"High school."

Amy let out her big, loving I-told-you-so laugh.

"And maybe she can help you with your…problem."

Cade picked up a cat-shaped saltshaker and poured out a pile of salt. If Selena decided to break her vow and Cade was the first person she was with…what a sad reentry into sex.

"Anyway, it's nothing, but I wanted to tell you," Cade said, "so you wouldn't think I was totally frigid."

Cade heard Selena cough behind her. Cade spun around. Selena was never up this early.

"I'm sorry," Selena said.

Selena's moonlight robe swung around her hips, and her dark hair was loose. She looked like a pin-up girl and an angel all at once.

"Let me talk to her," Amy said.

"Why?!"

"I want to get to know her, the woman who got you out of your tax books."

"You cannot talk…" Cade didn't finish the sentence.

Selena looked at her, a slight smile pulling at the corner of her lips.

"I need to go," Cade said.

"Just tell her I'm your ride-or-die and I want to say hello," Amy said.

"I love you and no way." Cade hung up and put her phone on silent.

"Hey," Selena said. "Sorry. Do you want some cereal?"

Cade needed a protein shake and two hours at the gym to clear her head.

"You're up early," Cade said.

Selena sat down across from her, looking more serious.

"I wanted to talk to you. Are you okay? Last night..." Selena trailed off.

"Of course?" It came out as a question. Who wouldn't be okay with kissing Selena Mathis? But then who would be okay with Selena Mathis not wanting to kiss them again?

"I told you I was celibate," Selena began.

And Cade had kissed her anyway. And after that, she'd been so excited and flustered and happy. She hadn't even thought about what she'd done to Selena. They sold T-shirts that read CONSENT IS MANDATORY. She was a creeper, one of those people who didn't listen to women when they said no.

"I am so sorry." Cade covered her mouth. "Shit. I wasn't thinking. I can go. Do you want me to go?" She started to stand up. "I know you're celibate, and then I just...you didn't want that. You didn't give me any sign—"

Selena caught Cade's hand before Cade could stand all the way up. The touch rushed through Cade's body.

"If I weren't celibate," Selena said, "I would eat you like a peach."

Cade froze, half standing. Selena's grip on her hand softened, but she didn't let go.

"I gave you every sign," Selena said. "The only sign I could have given you that was more obvious was a text saying *please kiss me now.*"

Cade sat back down. Did that mean...?

"I thought I was ready." Selena released her hand.

No. It didn't mean.

"Last night," Selena said. "For a second. I had this moment, with all those students, I thought, *I've got my shit together.* But I don't. Not like you. There's things I need to figure out." She gave a little laugh. "I lied to my ex about being engaged to Cadence Elgin. That's not shit-together territory. I didn't mean to lead you on."

Cade felt hurt and giddy at the same time. She stirred a heart in the salt on the table, realized what she'd done, and erased it. Selena sat on her hands, waiting for a response.

"I know what it's like to like someone and have them play games," Selena said when Cade failed to speak. "Not that I think you like me." She rushed the words out in half a breath. "Just, I like you, not like that, I mean...not that I wouldn't like you like that...but we're coworkers, roommates...sort of roommates...and I'm celibate, and I knew that, and I hope you don't feel like I took advantage of you."

Selena hung her head, her messy black hair falling over her face. Cade stared at her.

"Forgive me?" Selena said. "I have a way of fucking things up. Did I?"

Cade replayed the kiss in her mind. Not hard to do since she'd been playing it on repeat all night.

"You didn't take advantage of me," Cade said. "I kissed you first."

It was hard to believe but true.

Selena looked up, a smile lighting her face.

"You did." Then in a breath so quiet that Cade barely heard her, Selena whispered, "I was so into it I couldn't remember."

And Cade melted into a pool of lust and longing and confusion and delight.

"We're cool?" Selena asked.

"Of course."

"Good. You can wear mine."

Cade hadn't even noticed the two motorcycle helmets on the table. Selena put her hand on one.

"I borrowed Becket's spare," she said. "Now you can ride with me."

Half an hour later they were dressed and standing in the driveway. Selena had changed into pleather leggings and her purple fake fur, but she held an armload of leather.

"These things are terrifying." Cade eyed the bike.

"Don't worry." Selena winked. "I started riding dirt bikes when I was four."

"For real?"

"Yeah," Selena said a little defensively. She hugged the leathers to her chest. "It was normal back home."

"I didn't mean it like that." Cade allowed herself to look at Selena and really take her in. Her glittery boots. Her hair pulled back in a knot that looked utterly untangleable. The mischievous asymmetry of her smile. "That's cool. I wish I'd seen you as a kid."

Selena's face softened instantly.

"I was an awesome kid. Come on. Let's get you dressed." She laid the leathers out over the bike. "Chaps. Jacket. Gloves."

Cade gave her a look. "I'm wearing that?"

"Yes. And please don't say I have to wear all this too because we are just going around the block. If you knew what I've ridden in. But I've reformed. No high heels. No short shorts."

"Have you ever crashed?"

"Of course." Selena handed Cade the chaps. "Plenty. Don't worry. You don't want to ride with someone who hasn't. You don't want to be their first crash."

Cade blew out a breath. She was going to do this. No point in dragging her feet. She struggled into the chaps. The concept was obvious. Getting her legs through the right holes while standing up was harder. But soon she was dressed. The leather was heavy but supple, like Selena had worn it for years. The thought made Cade tingle.

Selena put her hands on her hips, accentuating every curve.

"You look like a prep schoolboy gone bad," she said.

Cade spread her arms. "A look I've always wanted."

Selena laughed.

"Let me give you a tour." Selena identified the parts on her bike.

Cade knew a quarter of the words Selena used.

"Now when we ride," Selena went on, "I'll get on first. Then you'll swing your leg over like this." She demonstrated with a graceful swoop of her leg. "Now when we're riding, it's a lot easier for me to keep my weight upright, so you can lean into me. I can hold us both. You don't ride with someone if they can't hold you. Make sure you always have at least one arm around me. And if our helmets bump, that's my fault for being too jerky." Selena mounted the bike. "And I'm used to riding fast, so one tap on my shoulder means slow down. Two means stop soon. Three means stop now."

Cade didn't ask if there was a tap to speed up.

"I've been a lot of people's first ride. I got you."

For a second, they were silent, as though they were both about to speak or both saying something without words.

"Ready?" Selena said quietly.

She picked up one of the helmets that had been dangling off the handlebars and stepped toward Cade. For a second, Cade thought Selena would kiss her, but Selena placed the helmet on Cade's head and pulled it forward. The black sphere covered her face. The foam inside hugged Cade's cheeks. It smelled of Selena's perfume and her shampoo. Selena took the helmet in both hands and adjusted it.

She was so close. Black glitter sparkled on her long eyelashes. Her lipstick was a perfect burgundy. She shifted the helmet on Cade's head, then ran two fingers along the inner edge of the foam where it pressed against Cade's neck. She was checking the fit, but Selena's touch made Cade's knees tremble and her head expand. As long as Selena was touching her, Cade didn't care if her parents bought an alpaca farm or ran the Elgin Gallery into the ground. She didn't care if she lost her QuickBooks password or never saw her walk-up apartment again.

Selena rubbed her fingertips gently against the back of Cade's neck.

"Don't be tense."

Cade thought she might faint.

"Remember, you can always tell me to slow down or stop."

With that, Selena mounted her bike and patted the seat behind her. Cade got on. The seat angled down. She slid forward. Her chest pressed against Selena's back. Her thighs touched Selena's ass. Yearning lit like a match. She didn't know this feeling. This pressure. Her legs open. She pulled back, resisting the slope of the seat.

"Scoot forward." Selena reached behind her and tugged Cade's waist. Put your arms around me." Selena's helmet muffled her voice. "You're your own seat belt. Don't be shy."

And with that, Selena engaged some clutch, and the bike rumbled to life. Cade locked her hands in front of Selena. Selena clasped her hand over Cade's.

Cade half expected Selena to tear off in a smear of rubber, but she puttered down the street so slowly Cade wasn't sure how the bike was still upright.

"This okay?" Selena asked.

Cade gave her a thumbs-up.

"Faster?"

Thumbs-up.

The turns were frightening, but when they'd circled the block and Selena asked if Cade wanted to go again, Cade did. Selena made a wider sweep of the neighborhood. Then they tried busy MLK Boulevard.

Finally, Selena pulled into a gas station parking lot. She pulled off her helmet, shaking out her dark hair.

"You're a natural. You should get a bike."

Cade struggled out of her own helmet.

"It's not as terrifying as I thought it'd be."

"I told you I'd take care of you."

If only Selena would take care of her the way Amy kept suggesting. Cade shut the thought down quickly. Selena was celibate. Cade accepted that. Really, she did.

"Do you want to try the freeway? Just one exit up?"

Cade would have tried a drag race just for the chance to lean her helmeted head against Selena's shoulder. She nodded.

"One for slow down. Two for stop soon. Three for stop now," Selena reminded her. "And squeeze my shoulder for keep going."

Riding on the freeway was so much faster than riding on the roads, it wasn't even the same thing. The streets were a moving sidewalk. This was a roller coaster. But Cade didn't tap Selena's shoulder. Selena gestured thumbs-up, middle, and down. Cade returned thumbs-up and squeezed Selena's shoulder.

Selena accelerated. The engine roared. And they were off, Selena weaving through traffic like it was standing still, taking the curves at an angle that felt like it defied the law of centrifugal force that held them upright. Cade should have been screaming, *Stop!* but she felt utterly at peace. It was like rowing. Maybe it was like being flogged in a non-sexual way.

Selena slowed down as they crossed a soaring bridge. She pointed left. Cade could see all of Portland, shimmering blue and green like an underwater city.

When they finally returned home, Selena said, "You were amazing."

"You are amazing," Cade said.

She felt a pang of something much bigger than any crush she'd ever felt before.

You'll be my first crash.

chapter 23

The next day was all work. Probably for the best. Cade got an email from the Gentrification Abatement Coalition saying they liked her application but had concerns because of the "unique" nature of the store. They wanted to see an in-person presentation. She skipped her workout to start putting together the financials.

When she arrived at the store around noon, Selena was juggling three customers at the same time, and there were four more perusing the shelves. Some had heard about the Pour and Paint class. A trio had received bridal shower gifts from Satisfaction Guaranteed. Several people had met Selena at the Sexpo. The rest of the day was almost as busy. The last customer left after closing time.

"I never thought I'd say this," Cade said, "but lock the door before anyone else comes in."

"That was great." Selena grinned.

It was the first moment they'd been alone together since they returned from their motorcycle ride.

Selena glanced at her phone.

"Becket's having a movie night," Selena said.

Was that an invitation or a statement?

"Her movies are terrible," Selena added. "But in a good way. She collects film reels. Russian cartoons from the eighties. Sexploitation films. Black-and-white Swedish porn."

"Who doesn't like black-and-white Swedish porn?"

"So, you'll go with me?"

If there were a thousand alternate universes there wouldn't have been one in which Cade said no.

They rode together on Selena's motorcycle. Cade loved the way Selena patted Cade's hands as Cade clasped them to Selena's belly.

"Lean into me," Selena said as they took off. "I can hold you."

Please hold me.

Becket's house did not look like the home of a burlesque performer. A low wire fence circled the small house. A few rangy plants sagged in the yard. But music poured out of the open door, and Cade could see people moving around inside. Selena flung open the door without knocking. Inside, the house looked like a cross between a costume shop and a gamers' lair. Enormous monitors filled one side of the living room. Two sewing machines and piles of fabric occupied another.

"Mathis!" Selena's friends called out.

Cade thought she heard someone say, *and the roommate,* in a way that didn't sound like they thought Cade was Selena's roommate.

People milled around drinking from Solo cups and balancing plates of food.

Selena took Cade's hand and pulled her in.

"This is Donald." Selena waved at a man with a beard down to his waist. "And Vita, Wine Barrel, Thomas. You know Beautiful Adrien. You met Zenobious at the funeral. Where's Becket?"

Becket popped out of the kitchen, looking like a blue-haired sprite.

"The movie starts at eight," she said. "If you are late, the doors will be locked."

"Your door's never locked," someone called out.

"Fine cinema awaits you cultureless heathens." Becket spread her arms.

"Are we watching *Vampiros Lesbos* again?" the man named—probably not by his parents—Wine Barrel asked.

"*Godzilla versus Mothra?*" someone else suggested.

"You won't know if you're all out here eating potato chips," Becket said.

Becket's theater had once been the master bedroom, but she had furnished it with two rows of sofas and piles of pillows on the floor. The walls were papered in red velveteen wallpaper. Stage curtains revealed a screen at the front of the room, and a cabinet in the back held a reel-to-reel projector.

Selena motioned for Cade to take a seat on the sofa. Selena sat on the floor and tucked herself between Cade's legs, her shoulders resting against Cade's knees. If Cade had leaned over, she could have curled her whole body around Selena's.

She gingerly leaned back in the sofa, trying to hold her legs so she wasn't touching Selena and wasn't not touching her.

The rest of the party piled into the theater.

"She's been hiding you away," Zenobious said to Cade.

"I have not." Selena swatted at him.

"She has. Her *business* partner."

"Be quiet." Beautiful Adrien sat down in Zenobious's lap. "We could be business partners."

"You have only to ask." The way Zenobious said it sounded like he and Beautiful Adrien had joked like this a thousand times. Whether they had or hadn't been "business partners" wasn't any of Cade's business. But she liked their obvious affection. Was that what she and Selena had? That easy, flirtatious friendship. If only she could figure out how many millimeters to put between her knees and Selena's shoulders.

Selena answered the question by draping her arms over Cade's knees and pulling them around her.

Across the room, Cade heard a woman say, "She's from New York."

"I can't believe she hasn't brought her to the Aviary," someone else said.

Then—was Cade imagining it?—she thought she heard someone say, "Selena's right. She is cute."

"Have you talked about me to your friends?" Cade leaned over enough to speak in Selena's ear but not so much that she touched her any more than they were already touching.

"I wouldn't," Selena said.

She obviously had. It made Cade's heart swell.

Becket stood in front of the screen.

"This is a classic nineteen sixties pre-feminist exploration of gender and power." Becket hit a light switch, and the room went dim.

All Cade could think about was Selena leaning against the low sofa, her body between Cade's knees.

The film started. A woman in a gold bikini had sex with a mobster and then killed him. Maybe it had a plot. Cade wasn't paying attention. Selena turned around, draping her arm around Cade's knee.

"I've seen this one before," Selena whispered. "The girl fight is coming up soon."

"Why are they fighting?"

Selena tipped her head back so she was looking up at Cade. Cade could have leaned over and kissed her.

"Because the one in red stole the other one's mafia boyfriend," Selena said. "You weren't paying attention."

One of the women took off her shirt and squirted tanning oil over her body.

"I was distracted."

Was that too much? Cade was about to say, *but I'll pay more attention.*

Selena said, "I always fight naked covered in oil in my living room in a gold bikini."

A collective groan of disbelief and appreciation went up from the group of friends as the women ripped each other's clothes off.

Midway through the film, Becket called intermission.

"But do not get drunk and miss the psycho-sexual Cold War anxieties in the second half," she said with mock seriousness. "This film had a strong influence on the modern action film."

The crowd was already tumbling into the kitchen in search of drinks. Selena and Cade were the last to get up.

Cade could have stayed there forever enjoying Selena's closeness, but Selena hopped up.

"Get Cade a drink," Becket said cheerfully. "Cade, let me show you around."

The house was so small you could pretty much see the whole place from the front door, but Becket led Cade to the one door that wasn't open.

"I want to know what you think about this," Becket said as she opened the door.

Cade didn't need to ask what.

A painting dominated the room. It was a portrait of a man sitting naked on the edge of a bed. Behind him a window opened on a blue landscape bathed in either dawn light or dusk. If it was dawn, his posture was hopeful but worried. If he was going to bed, his downturned face radiated peace. It was two paintings in one or one truth that was bigger than the frame that housed it. A masterpiece.

"Oh, my god." Cade stared.

The technique was flawless, but technique could be learned. It was the insight and the empathy that radiated from the painting that took Cade's breath away.

"To see so clearly," Cade murmured.

"It's *Geoffrey in Cobalt Teal*," Becket said reverently.

"Is it someone you know?"

"Geoffrey? Acquaintance-friend. He moved to Missouri or Dallas. I'm not sure."

Portraits were hard to sell. People didn't usually buy paintings of strangers. Painting portraits on commission could be lucrative, but it didn't bring out artists' best work.

"Who did it?" Cade took a step closer. The signature

had been scraped off. "It's by the same person who did the portrait of Ruth."

Of course it was.

"Yeah," Becket said.

"It's amazing."

"Yeah."

"Who did it?" Cade asked again.

"Selena didn't tell you?"

"She said she didn't know. But she said the painter only did that one of Ruth."

"There's only these two," Becket said.

"But you don't know who did them?"

Becket closed the door behind them.

"Selena knows," she said.

"Was it her ex?"

Becket gave a short, harsh laugh.

"Alex is a hack." Becket might be the size of a pixie, but there was a fierce protectiveness in her eyes. "She put Selena through a lot of shit."

"How could anyone do that? To have her and..." *Not love her?*

Becket's face softened, but her voice was still serious.

"Selena took her vow because she wanted to get her life together, and a big part of why it wasn't was Alex." Becket held Cade's gaze. "Don't do that to her again."

"She's not interested." Selena had said *ready.* "I wouldn't."

Cade didn't know what Alex had done, but if it hurt Selena, Cade wouldn't do it.

"Alex is an asshole," Becket said.

Cade loved Becket for the anger that flared across her face. Selena deserved a friend like that.

"She had power over Selena because she was her professor and she was rich and privileged and Selena—and me—we're just trailer park girls who took a swig off the Everclear and made a run for it," Becket went on. "And Alex knew she was breaking Selena's heart, but Alex still wanted her. Selena was her trophy."

"Because she's beautiful."

Becket scowled. "Because she was so fucking talented she made us all want to cry. Alex fucked her because Alex wanted to be her, and then Alex left and it broke Selena."

Cade wanted to race out of the room and throw her arms around Selena and hold her close. *You deserve better. I would never do that to you.*

"You'll do that to her if you're not careful," Becket said.

"She doesn't want me like that."

Becket's face said, *Don't be stupid.*

"You won't mean to, but you will if you get with her and then go back to New York like she was just—"

Outside the door, Cade heard Selena call out, "Becket? Cade?"

"They're in the bedroom," someone said.

"Jealous?" another voice teased.

Selena opened the door.

"There you guys are." Her face fell. "Beck, what are you doing?"

"Cade wanted to know who painted *Geoffrey in Cobalt Teal,*" Becket said.

"And?" Selena asked.

"I said you might know."

"Cade." Selena held out her hand. "Beck, you are not my

father. You do not get to get your rifle and tell Cade not to get me pregnant."

Despite the tension in the air, Cade's heart soared. Selena might not be ready yet, but if Becket wanted to get the rifle, it meant Selena wanted to be with Cade.

"Okay, okay. Get back to my movie," Becket said cheerfully, but when she passed Cade in the hall, she clasped her arm and whispered. "Don't break her heart, Elgin."

They returned to Becket's theater. Selena resumed her seat between Cade's knees. Cade pretended to watch as she replayed her conversation with Becket. *Geoffrey in Cobalt Teal. She was so fucking talented. Don't break her heart, Elgin.*

Selena reached up and undid the rubber band holding her hair. Then she leaned her head on Cade's thigh. Cade stopped breathing, but it was okay because she no longer needed oxygen. She could live on the light of the film caught in Selena's black curls. Very tentatively, Cade stroked Selena's hair. Just once. Selena lowered her chin, inviting Cade's touch. Cade ran her fingers through the silky curls. Selena sighed.

"That feels good," she whispered.

Becket was watching them. Cade couldn't read her expression. Disapproval? Threat? Or something kinder? Like Becket was thinking, *Good luck, you two. You're probably screwed, but if you're going to try, try hard.*

When they returned to the house that night, they lingered in the driveway talking about the movie. When Selena finally returned to her apartment, Cade wandered around the house for an hour, looking out the windows and picking up knickknacks and putting them back down again. Everything felt more…real. Like she was really *seeing* after a life of just pretending to look at things. This vase. This raindrop on the window. All of it glittering and mysterious and wonderful.

chapter 24

The next evening, Selena and Becket sat at a booth at their favorite dive bar. It was old Portland, iceberg not arugula, Bud Light not Wolf Eel Ale. It made a girl from Tristess miss home.

"We're moving forward with renting that theater." Becket sipped her beer. "The question is whether or not our sponsors are going to pay for the capital investment. We need ADA bathrooms. That's a one hundred percent must. The stage needs to be refinished, and I want to get it checked for mold. There are three kinds of mold we need to worry about."

Becket was the unpaid therapist to everyone in her burlesque troupe, so Selena always made an extra effort to listen to her, even if Becket wanted to talk about mold.

"What are the three kinds?" Selena asked, her mind tracing the contours of Cade's shoulders, savoring the feel of Cade's fingers in her hair.

"There are actually five kinds," Becket said. "Alternia, aspergillus, cladosporium, penicillium, and stachybotrys.

I'm only worried about the first three. Do you want to hear more?"

"Of course."

"No, you don't." Becket laughed. "You are dying to talk about Cade Elgin."

"I want to hear about your mold. Is penicillium like penicillin? Is it bad, or do you not get infections if it's in the building?"

The waiter arrived with their tots.

Becket popped one in her mouth. "Cade is cute. I like her."

"I thought you took her aside to show her your shotgun."

"I took her aside to show her *Geoffrey in Cobalt Teal.*"

"Thanks for not telling her."

Selena pulled a napkin out of the holder and crushed it into a ball.

"What's wrong with telling her you were the best painter McLaughlin ever saw?" Becket asked.

"I don't want her to know."

Her paintings had gone up in flames, at her request. It was kind of Ruth to burn them, so Selena didn't have to watch it happen, but it made her sad too. All that work. All those faces. A shit-together person would never have done that. A shit-together person would still be painting.

"Why not?"

"I burned all my work because my ex dumped me. That is so massively dumb." Selena ripped a piece off her napkin ball. "I don't want Cade to think I'm some sort of loser who's going to crash my bike or overdose because I didn't get what I wanted."

"Your relationship with Alex was borderline abusive.

Maybe not border. And I'm sure Cade has done some crazy things. We all have."

"She hasn't ever fucked up."

Becket raised a skeptical eyebrow.

"We tell people we like about the things that've hurt us," she said.

"I don't want her to think I'm a fuck-up."

"You're not a fuck-up."

"I have strong fuck-up potential."

"What would you tell me if I said I was a fuck-up?" Becket asked.

"That you're a great person, and it's okay to make mistakes."

"Exactly."

Becket pushed the tots in Selena's direction. "Eat something."

"I can't."

"There's always room for tots."

"Tell me not to fall for her." Selena leaned her head against the side of their booth.

"Why waste my breath?" Becket took a sip of her PBR. "I saw you sitting in her lap, all blissed out, at movie night. What happened when you got home?"

"Nothing."

"Did you sleep with her?"

"When was that nothing?"

Becket's shrug said, *I'm not going to tell you you've had a lot of nothing sex.*

"The other day at Paint your Vulva, when I texted you…" She hadn't told Becket about their kiss. It felt too big, too important. She couldn't put it in words. Becket would say something practical and tell her not to break her vow. "She kissed me."

"And?" Becket's eyes widened.

"I kissed her back, and then I told her nothing could happen, and we should go back to the way we were."

"Oh, Mathis." Becket shook her head.

Selena remembered the look on Cade's face. It wasn't just disappointment. Lots of people had been disappointed that Selena turned them down. But behind Cade's disappointment had been a look of such concern. Selena had almost changed her mind and kissed Cade again. That concern said, *I will never hurt you.*

Except Cade would. She wouldn't mean to, but she'd break Selena's heart in the end.

"You could date her and not have sex," Becket said.

Selena picked at the label on her beer, then poured a lake of ketchup onto her plate and sunk a tater tot into it.

"You could at least take her out for tater tots and a beer," Becket said.

"She doesn't like tater tots."

"That's just weird."

"We talk about…anything. Everything," Selena said.

"Except your paintings."

"Except my paintings."

"So, help me out here, or I *will* start talking about mold. You like her. She kissed you. You talk about everything. What's the problem?"

"Aren't you going to tell me not to break my vow?"

"You told me to tell you that every time you thought about it. Don't break your vow," Becket said perfunctorily.

"But maybe Beautiful Adrien is right. Maybe she would be good for you."

Selena pushed her tater tot around in the ketchup.

"Eat it already," Becket said gently.

"She's leaving," Selena said. "I want her to stay and she's not going to."

"You can be long distance."

"Maybe for a few months." Selena's heart ached at the thought. "But Cade Elgin is not going to stay with *me*. She's a rock star. She owns a third of the gallery. She *is* the Elgin Gallery. She's a rower. God, she wears white suede and it doesn't get dirty. I know I'm not really a fuck-up, but she's not going to want me long-term. She wants an accountant."

"Well." Becket took a definitive swig of her beer. "Nothing I saw last night said, *I'd rather be with an accountant.* But if you're set on being tragically in love with her—"

"I'm not in love."

Was she? The question echoed through her mind.

"If you think she's so wonderful, and you're not good enough—which you are—there's a Portland Community College ad on literally every bus in Portland. Take a class on accounting. That's the least romantic way anyone's seduced a woman." Becket grinned, coaxing a smile from Selena. "You do you."

The lights were on when Selena got home. Cade was working at the dining room table.

"I should be helping you," Selena said.

Cade rubbed her shoulder, stretching her neck to one side.

"I'm looking at the accounts," Cade said. "QuickBooks stuff."

"How are we doing?"

Cade's frown told Selena everything she needed to know. "No good?" she asked.

"We've paid off four months of the mortgage, but we've got to make six more payments to hold the bank off, and I've been paying the bank out of the store's profits, which means we still owe the vendors a lot of money."

Selena had been so focused on Cade leaving, she hadn't been thinking about Ruth's store closing and the house and the banks. "How are we going to…?"

"I don't know." Cade stretched her shoulders with a sigh. "For the grant we need to show all our finances—and not in a box labeled *Clitorises, etc.*—so that's what I'm working on here." She gestured to stacks of papers on the table. "I need to get this all input by tomorrow."

There were a lot of papers. The forms on Cade's computer screen looked complex. *See?* Selena thought to Becket. An accountant could help. But maybe she could help too.

Gently, so as not to startle Cade, she put her hands on Cade's shoulders and rubbed light circles at the base of her neck. Cade's muscles were as tight as a bronze statue. Selena could feel the weight of responsibility in her shoulders. Cade was trying so hard.

"I…" Cade dropped her head.

Selena massaged her softly. It was a mistake to try to wrangle muscles this tight. Cade's whole body must have ached from the tension, and she'd tense up even more if Selena dug into her. Instead, Selena pressed gently and stroked the place where her neck met her shoulder.

"That okay?" Selena asked.

"God, yeah." The sigh that escaped Cade's lips sent a shiver of desire through Selena's body.

Cade bent her head as Selena rubbed her neck with knowing fingers. Selena could have stood there all night. Touching Cade made her own body melt. She closed her eyes, just feeling Cade's skin. She wanted to kiss Cade's neck, her back, her flat abs, her thighs...but after a few minutes, Selena opened her eyes.

She wasn't going to seduce Cade Elgin. She was going to help.

"Do you want to show me how to put stuff into Quick-Books?" she asked.

They worked almost to dawn. Luckily Cade had two laptops. They got through all the papers. A miracle.

"Thank you," Cade said, as she closed her laptop. "Get some sleep. I'll open the store."

"I'll come with you," Selena said.

Her eyes were blurred with fatigue, but she didn't want to leave Cade. They only had a few precious days left. Selena wanted to savor every minute, even if they were just friends, even if all they did was input numbers into QuickBooks.

"You're a rock star." Cade turned to go, then paused. She glanced at Ruth's painting. "Are you sure you don't know who painted this?"

Selena gave an infinitesimal nod. The smaller the nod, the smaller the lie.

When Selena was back in her apartment, she turned on the strings of lights and sat by the window. She closed her eyes.

"You screwed me," she said to Ruth's ghost, but her heart was brimming with love for Ruth and love for Cade. "You knew I would fall for her. I'm learning QuickBooks. That has to be love."

Love.

"You think she's worth the risk."

If someone else told Cade she was cool, but she wasn't worth risking their heart over, Selena would kick that person's ass. Cade deserved to be loved completely, worshiped, body and soul.

"Of course she is."

Selena thought the lights twinkled a little bit brighter.

"Remember those movies you made me watch? The ones where the shy woman moves to Italy or whatever, and she kisses a sexy lifeguard, and then goes back to America and starts her own company and dates a ton of gorgeous men and has everything she wants? No one ever thinks about the sexy lifeguard she leaves in Italy. He's just there to help her get self-actualized, but what if he really liked her?" She paused for a moment, taking in the space. If they lost the shop, they'd lose the house too. She'd lose this room. But it wouldn't matter if Cade stayed. "I don't want to be Cade's sexy lifeguard."

She pictured Cade sitting at her laptop and lifted her finger like a brush and traced Cade's silhouette in the air. She longed to touch every curve and plane of Cade's body, both on canvas and in life.

If having her shit together meant knowing what she wanted, she had that part figured out. She unplugged the lights.

"Good night, Ruth," she said to the darkness. "Good night, Cade."

Then she felt around in her dresser drawer for a vibrator and a dildo. She covered the dildo in lube, lay down, and slipped it inside. She worked the vibrator over her clit. It was a reliable position. The fullness, vibrations, and clitoral stimulation covered all the bases, and she came in five luxurious waves of pleasure. Then for no reason and for every reason, she burst into tears.

chapter 25

Cade called Amy the next morning, still lying in bed.

"So how are things?" Amy said. "I'm heading over to Marco's for coffee. Wish I could get you one, but you're probably having fun over there. Are you having fun?"

"Yeah." The thrill of happiness that vibrated Cade's body came through in her voice.

"You and Selena! You did it?" Amy lowered her voice as though anyone on the street was listening. "Did you hit the big O?"

"We didn't sleep together."

"But? Turn on your video."

Amy switched the call to video. Cade turned on her video as well.

"You're in bed," Amy said with surprise. "You're not up doing one of those awful exercise routines?"

"Time difference."

"It's noon over here."

Nine o'clock. Cade couldn't remember the last time she'd slept in until nine.

Amy's face bounced around the screen as she walked.

"I have to hear the whole thing."

Cade recounted everything from the portrait Selena painted at Pour and Paint Your Vulva to the languid feeling that suffused her body as she ran her hands through Selena's hair. That was probably too much detail, but Amy didn't seem to mind.

"So what's next?"

Cade caught glimpses of the city behind Amy.

"Is she still celibate? Are you going out? When do I meet her?"

"It's not going to be anything," Cade said, "but it's wonderful just to have—"

"No. You're not going to say it was wonderful to have one memory, like some tragic, slow movie about British people."

Cade laughed. "I was kind of going to say that."

"Your face says you don't want to be a tragic British movie."

"She helped me with QuickBooks too."

"She kissed you and showed you her vulva on a flip phone and you want to talk about QuickBooks?"

"It was sweet," Cade said. "You know my parents. If I told them, *I will drop dead at dawn if you don't help me input this data into QuickBooks*, they'd say, *You've got this, honey*, and go out with their friends."

"Your parents love you."

"Fine, but they don't…" What was it that had touched

Cade so deeply about Selena sitting down in front of the laptop? "They don't take care of me. She did."

Selena brought her coffee and real food. She laughed at Cade's jokes and listened to her stories. She'd gone to the horrible lecture on inventory and cleaned the store.

"We're going to my aunt's cabin tomorrow," Cade said. "I've got an appraiser coming out to see what it's worth. Selena's going to drive me because she says there's a storm on the pass and the roads are a mess."

"On her motorcycle?"

"She's borrowing a friend's SUV."

"*There's a storm on the pass*," Amy repeated. "Look at you all rugged and outdoorsy."

"Not."

"Have you thought about staying?" The wind blew Amy's hair around her face as she walked. Her cheeks were rosy from the cold. "I would miss you like crazy, but you'd have to visit, like, every month to make sure your parents are feeding the alpacas."

Cade had thought about it as she lay in bed dreaming of Selena's dark hair cascading through her fingers. She'd thought about it as she sat on the counter next to Selena drinking coffee and feeling cozy on a rainy afternoon. *What if this was my life?* It wasn't that easy.

"My life is in New York." Cade sighed. "What would say *stalker* more than selling my apartment, leaving the gallery, and totally moving my life because I kissed her once?"

"Saving her fingernails. Making a life-size doll with her face on it." Amy flipped off a taxi that cut too close to her as she crossed a street. "You don't have to sell your apartment. You can say you want to help with Satisfaction Guaranteed. You stay. She falls in love with you. You figure out what you do next."

"If we don't get the grant and get an offer on the cabin and get the vendors to float us for a few more months, we're not going to keep any of Ruth's property."

"Well, tell her you want to look for West Coast artists. You fell in love with Portland. You need a vacation." Amy rounded a corner, heading toward their favorite coffee shop. "Or you could just tell her how you feel and see what she says."

Cade couldn't do that. What would she say? *I've never dated. I've barely had sex. We haven't even known each other for a month. I'll give up everything for you.*

"I suppose that'd be more efficient than hanging around Portland pretending I want to go hiking," Cade said, but she knew she wouldn't do it. She was the boring Elgin, switched at birth with an accountant's daughter. The one who never missed a payment, who only stayed up late to work. The one who never made a bold, life-changing move for passion.

Selena was right. A snowstorm had hit the pass hard. Enormous snowflakes landed on the windshield in a dizzying flurry. The winding highway was packed snow and patches of ice.

"See those?" Selena pointed out the window to orange-tipped poles sticking out of the snowbanks that lined the road. "It's to tell you where the edge is. There's usually a drop-off."

Selena cruised around a curve, her hands resting lightly on the wheel.

"I can't believe you passed a snowplow," Cade said, shaking her head.

"That last one was just slow."

"They're all slow."

"If I do it again, I'll tell you to close your eyes." Selena made it sound sexual. "Trust me, I'm not good at much, but I drive like a goddess."

"You're good at everything," Cade said.

"Flattery will get you…" Selena didn't finish the sentence.

Instead, she turned up the radio and sang a bit of "Wish I Knew You." Cade closed her eyes, although there was no plow in sight. She could see the shadows of passing trees behind her eyelids. This moment: she wanted to hang on to it forever. Just the two of them, in the woods, going on an adventure. She loved New York, but she couldn't imagine going back to her clean, sparse apartment alone.

After about two hours, the highway split. Selena took the narrower leg. A mile or two later, she turned onto a forested road. In another mile, she turned onto a gravel road deep in snow. Cade was sure they would get stuck, but they didn't.

"There it is," Selena said after a little while.

At the end of the road sat a small wooden house. Behind it, a pine forest glowed with new snow.

When they got inside, Cade could see it was definitely Ruth's cabin. Tasseled lamps. Velvet paintings. Dolls. There was an all-in-one kitchen and a living room, a fireplace, and doors that must have led to the bathroom and a bedroom. The living room was dominated by a ridiculously puffy red sofa and a futon mattress that took up most of the floor and was covered in a harem of pillows and velvet blankets.

Selena walked over to the kitchen running her fingers along the counter and touching the cupboards. "It was like she was just here." She stopped. "She left a letter."

She held the piece of paper out to Cade, tears forming in her eyes.

"Do you want me to read it to you?" Cade asked.

Selena nodded.

"*Dear Selena,*" Cade began. "*I hope it's you, and I hope you brought Cade. The cabin always filled me with joy, and I want you to be filled with joy too. Some people want a legacy. I just want to leave the world a happier place. Have fun. Relax. The bedroom is locked. I've put some old treasures there. Sort through them and keep what you want, but don't do it the minute you get here. It's hard to look at old things. Wait 'til tomorrow.*" Tomorrow the appraiser was coming. Cade put the thought out of her mind. She read on. "*I've ordered you some treats from the Market. Call and tell them to deliver Ruth's basket to the cabin. This is your place now, yours and Cade's.*"

"We have to sell it," Selena said, "if we want to pay off the bills."

"Yeah."

Selena wiped her eyes and nodded.

Cade should have loved Ruth more. Cade had barely known her the last few years. Cade had been so busy, and Ruth was just another crazy Elgin. But everything she saw of Ruth's life was full of... *life*. Love. Pleasure. Flowers. Friends. YOLO pillows. Messages from the beyond.

"It's okay to be sad." Cade handed Selena the letter.

Selena nodded again, her lips quivering. Cade put her arms around her, but she held her lightly. She wanted to lead her to the pile of pillows and cradle her while she cried or talked or lay quietly in Cade's arms. But was that right? Was that too much like kissing Selena in the store? *I'm not ready, Cade. I'm so sorry.*

"I'm glad Ruth had you in her life," Cade said.

"Me too." Selena looked down at the letter. "I got to have her in my life, and I got to meet you. Ruth told me we'd be friends."

"Before she died?"

"No. Afterward. I felt her. She said she wanted us to..."

Cade wished Selena would finish the sentence, but she didn't.

"Do you think that's dumb? Talking to her. I know she can't hear," Selena said.

"Are you sure?"

Cade didn't think Ruth could hear, but it'd be nice to think Ruth was following along behind Selena, loving her and protecting her.

Selena folded the letter carefully and set it on a decorative plate on the counter.

"Ruth wanted everyone to be happy." Selena turned to Cade, her eyes bright. "Let's have a perfect night. For Ruth. We will only be happy, and we will only have fun."

"One perfect night." Cade nodded solemnly. "For Ruth."

chapter 26

"You want to see something, City Girl?" Selena asked. "We need to light a fire. Don't take your coat off."

She took Cade's hand and led Cade outside. Cade thought as long as Selena held her hand, she'd never get cold. Selena led them to a dilapidated shed behind the cabin.

"Is this where the Revenant lives?" Cade said.

Selena opened the door and switched on a single, exposed bulb. Inside were neatly stacked rounds of wood. Selena dropped Cade's hand, picked one off the top of the stack, and carried it outside, setting it on a stump. Then she retrieved an axe.

"Stand behind me." Selena leaned the axe against her leg and twisted her hair into a knot, showing off the beautiful curve of her neck. "If the axe head comes off, it'll fly forward."

"I love that you know that and I am afraid of you."

Selena laughed, looked over her shoulder at Cade standing a safe distance away, then raised the axe over her head and swung it in an effortless arc, landing perfectly on the round and splitting it in two. Cade wished she were a photographer so she could capture the surreal beauty of Selena wielding an axe in purple fur. Selena picked up the halves of wood, set them on the stump, and split them again. It only took her a few minutes to produce a pile of wood.

"I've never seen anyone split wood," Cade said.

"Impressed?"

"Yes."

"You want to try one?"

When Cade swung the axe it stuck an inch in the wood, the wood unsplit. She tried again. Same thing.

"How do you do it?" she asked.

"You have to split *this* log. Really look at it. Where does it look like it should split?"

Cade tried again to no avail. Selena took the axe from her. She motioned for Cade to step back again and split the log in perfect halves. As she walked past Cade to retrieve the wood, she planted a kiss on Cade's cheek, so quick Cade thought she might have imagined it.

"You have other gifts," Selena said. "I'll split your firewood for you."

Back in the cabin, Cade went looking for her phone to call the Market so Selena wouldn't see the longing in her eyes.

As promised, a basket of food and wine arrived an hour later. Cade and Selena sat on the futon, their backs propped against the sofa.

"I have never seen so many throw pillows in one place," Cade said.

Selena nibbled a cracker.

"Ruth used to have parties up here. Sometimes a bunch of us would camp around the cabin. Sometimes, we'd stay up so late talking everyone would just fall asleep on the futon. Ruth said that's how puppies slept."

Cade could not imagine falling asleep on a futon with a bunch of other people, but she could imagine falling asleep beside Selena. But she would take the couch. Selena would take the futon on the floor. Or the other way around. Cade knew she wouldn't sleep. She wouldn't waste a moment of this night. They were quiet for a while, watching the fire through the glass window on the woodstove.

Eventually Selena moved her plate aside and slid down onto the futon so she was looking up at Cade.

"What are you thinking?" Selena asked.

How beautiful you are. Nothing in my life is like you. And how can this be so perfect and not enough?

"Nothing," Cade said. "This is nice."

"It is."

Selena gazed up at her.

"Do you think you'll meet an accountant when you go back to New York?" Selena asked.

"An accountant?"

"You said your perfect girl was an accountant."

"I did?"

"When we first met. I asked you if you were dating, and you said you weren't, but if you were, you'd date an accountant."

I want you.

"I think I was being practical." Cade's heart quickened.

Was Selena asking…? Cade kept her eyes on the fire. If she looked at Selena, Selena would see everything written on her face. If that wasn't the question Selena was asking, it would break her heart.

"You're a good person," Selena said. "You're responsible. You listen. You don't push things."

"I'm boring."

"You're not."

The passion in Selena's voice turned Cade's head. She gazed into Selena's dark eyes, then gently reached out and stroked a lock of hair off Selena's forehead. Selena sighed.

"I could take an accounting class," Selena said.

Never in the history of accounting had those words ever filled someone's heart with the wild, reeling joy Cade felt. Selena wanted her. Cade didn't move.

"You'd be good at it," she whispered.

"I'm just saying," Selena said, "if you wanted to push a girl to break her vow, you could."

All the longing of the past weeks, all Cade's impossible hope rolled into this moment.

"I would never push you," Cade whispered. "I would never do anything you didn't want me to."

Selena smiled.

"Well, then, Cade Elgin, would you kiss me? I'm ready."

Selena sat up. They looked at each other. Selena cupped Cade's cheek.

"You're so beautiful," Selena said.

Cade didn't know if she moved first or if Selena did. All she knew was that Selena's lips were warm and soft on hers and that Selena's kiss was full of need and tenderness. They kissed for a long time. Eventually they slid down onto the futon, lying side by side, arms wrapped around each other. Cade loved the feel of Selena's body against hers, but Cade didn't rush anything. Selena hadn't said what *ready* meant. If all they did was kiss, Cade was already in heaven. But Selena's kisses grew more urgent. She moved from Cade's lips to her neck. Her legs wrapped around Cade's. Selena moaned in the back of her throat. Cade felt the same aching longing consume her.

Selena broke her kiss long enough to ask, "Do you want to? We don't have to do anything you don't want to do."

Yes, Cade wanted to. She was trembling with how much she wanted to. But before she did, she really should mention the bit about six times, kicked-out-of-bed, and pre-orgasmic.

"Yes," Cade breathed. "But I'm afraid I won't be good enough for your new first time."

"You will," Selena said.

Selena didn't know what an optimist she was, and Cade didn't tell her. Instead, Cade lifted the hem of Selena's shirt and drew it over her head. Selena was even more beautiful than Cade had imagined, her breasts full in a bra of translucent black lace. Her belly was soft, her skin smooth. Cade marveled at her until Selena said, "Now you," and pulled Cade's sweater over her head. She unbuttoned Cade's shirt and undid Cade's bra with one hand. Cade loved the urgency in Selena's touch.

"Can I take off your pants?" Selena asked.

This was happening. Cade wanted it so much.

"Yes."

"You're gorgeous," Selena said when Cade was naked.

Selena took a breath as if steadying herself. She motioned for Cade to lie in front of her. She touched Cade's

ankle and slowly caressed her, all the way up to her ear-
lobes, rubbing them between her fingers, making Cade's
toes curl with desire.

"It's been a long time," Selena said. "Tell me if I go
too fast."

Cade wanted to tell Selena she could go as fast or
slow as she wanted, but she could barely form the words,
"Don't worry."

Then Selena slipped out of the rest of her clothing,
straddled Cade, then leaned over and kissed her, deep and
desperate. Tasting her. Claiming her. There was nothing
but Selena's lips and the fire of their hips touching.

And although Cade didn't have experience, she found
she had confidence. The confidence of running the gallery.
The confidence of looking at a piece of art and knowing if
she was looking at a star. Maybe it even helped that she
was good with QuickBooks. She was strong and smart and
thoughtful and attentive and so desperately in love.

Love. How had it happened so quickly? Maybe because
her soul had been searching for Selena her whole life
without even knowing it. Her body knew where to go
from there.

She lay on top of Selena, bracing herself on one elbow.
Selena's kisses sent sparks shivering along the back of her
legs, lighting up her center...or as Selena would insist
she call it: her vulva. But more than her own pleasure, she
wanted Selena to be happy.

"May I?" Cade rested her hand on the dark hair between
Selena's legs.

"Oh, god, please," Selena moaned, guiding Cade's hand
between her legs.

Cade had never paid attention to the shape and size of a woman's vulva. Now she traced every swollen fold of Selena's labia. She wanted to know everything about her. She dipped her finger into Selena's body. She circled her clit. Selena groaned, and the sound made Cade's body throb with a kind of hunger she'd never felt before.

"It's been so long since someone touched me," Selena whispered. "It feels so good."

Selena was so responsive, it wasn't hard to figure out what blend of touches worked for her, and when she was close, Selena clasped Cade's hand to her body, moving Cade's fingers in a fast, hard rhythm, whispering, "Yes, yes, yes, yes," until she went mute. She clutched Cade's shoulders. Her eyes squeezed shut. The whole beautiful length of her body arched. Then she fell back to the futon and pulled Cade to her. Cade lay half on her, half beside her, holding Selena tightly.

"That was so good." Selena pressed her face against Cade's shoulder. "And I needed it to be you."

Cade would have been happy to have Selena fall asleep in her arms, but after they had relaxed together, Selena rose up on one elbow and kissed Cade's stomach.

Selena's eyes twinkled. "I've wanted you since the first time I saw you."

"At my aunt's funeral?"

"I know it's wrong."

"If only I'd known."

"Is that a yes?"

Selena brushed her hand over the hair between Cade's legs.

Cade closed her eyes.

"Yes."

Selena kissed down Cade's belly and down her thighs. Then she parted Cade's legs a little bit more. Cade felt the whisper of Selena's breath on her.

"Yes?" Selena whispered.

Cade's "yes" came out in a cry that held in it all her lonely nights, all her failed attempts with one toy or another, all the swelling love she felt for Selena.

"Please," Cade murmured.

With that, Selena swept her tongue from Cade's opening to her clit.

"Oh," Cade gasped.

Selena lingered there, her tongue pressed lightly against Cade's clit. It felt like the universe expanding and the sun coming up and the best massage ever, and every breath Cade exhaled was a yes. Selena ran her fingers through Cade's pubic hair. Selena caressed her with her lips and tongue and chin and nose. She massaged Cade's thighs, and the pressure amplified the pleasure of her kiss.

"You can tell me how you like it."

Cade trembled. She felt like a coiled spring. She couldn't speak.

"That's okay," Selena said. "How about this?"

Cade managed, "Yes."

"And this?"

Everything felt good.

Cade was climbing higher and higher. She clutched the futon. Her thoughts were a jumble of *Don't stop!* and *I can't take it.* People did this all the time. They got here, and then they went over the edge, and it was nothing surprising, but Cade didn't know what to do with the feelings in her heart or the feelings in her body. She couldn't bear it if Selena took her higher and there was no release. She'd explode. She'd cry.

"I've never had an orgasm," Cade blurted out.

The part of her brain that could still form thoughts half expected Selena to sit up, wipe her lips, and say, *How is that possible?*

Instead, Selena whispered, "You don't have to."

Then she placed her hands on Cade's thighs and held her down. She slowed her kisses, circling Cade's clit without stopping or changing her stroke. Around and around. The room disappeared. All Cade knew was the exquisite pleasure of Selena's mouth. Then from nowhere and everywhere at the same time a wave of pleasure broke over her, and Cade Elgin learned what she had been missing.

Cade woke slowly after the best night's sleep she'd ever had. She opened her eyes. Sunlight filtered through the cabin window. She was swimming in a sea of blankets. Selena watched her, propped up on her elbow.

"Hello, gorgeous," Selena said.

Cade couldn't believe this was her life.

"I had a wonderful time with you last night," Selena added.

"I had a wonderful time with you."

Wonderful did not begin to cover it.

Selena lay down. Cade put her arm around her. Selena rested her head on Cade's chest, trailing her fingers over Cade's hipbone and down her thigh.

"Are you happy?" Selena asked.

"Yes."

A thousand times yes.

"Are you happy you broke your vow?" Cade asked.

"I didn't break it," Selena said thoughtfully. "I decided it was finished. And you were worth waiting for." Selena snuggled closer. "God, you were worth it."

Cade chuckled. "I thought I'd be a huge disappointment."

Selena lifted her head for a moment. "How is that possible?"

Cade hadn't meant to cry out *I've never had an orgasm.* That was not how you shared that bit of information with a lover. But she was glad Selena's kisses had undone her. Now words came easily.

"I haven't had a lot of sex," Cade said.

"I didn't notice." Selena took Cade's hand and drew it to her lips and kissed her fingertips.

"I've only had sex six times." It didn't sound so bad now. Maybe she'd been waiting for Selena all these years.

"Did you just not want to? There's nothing wrong with that," Selena said.

"No. I wanted a girlfriend. I had one in high school. Then in college I was back and forth so much between school and the gallery. I didn't have time to date. Then I took over managing the gallery full-time, and then…it started to feel like it was too late."

Selena kissed Cade's palm. "Who got to be your six times? And you don't need to tell me if you don't want to."

Cade wanted to tell Selena everything.

"There were three people. My girlfriend in high school," Cade said. "We slept together four times, and it was probably awful, but I was in love with her, so I didn't notice.

Then a girl from the UMass crew team on a pile of boat covers. And an art purchaser who literally kicked me out of bed because she said I sucked...not like that. Or like that in the wrong way. She said I fucked like a virgin."

"That's terrible. If she said you didn't know what you were doing, she didn't know how to ask for what she wanted."

"I thought I should tell you all that before, but I didn't know how."

It felt so easy now. How had she ever thought that Selena would judge her? Maybe she was just judging herself.

"So last night was number seven," Selena said.

"And my first orgasm."

"With another person."

"Ever."

Cade could feel Selena's smile as Selena kissed her breast.

"I am not supposed to be proud," Selena said, her voice glowing with pride. "You're not my accomplishment. But I'm glad I was there." She relaxed against Cade, their bodies melting together. After a moment, she added. "I'd have been so jealous if it was anyone else."

And Cade's heart filled with so much happiness, she felt like she might grow wings and fly.

chapter 27

Selena could have lain in bed with Cade all day. All week. All year. Their bodies fit together perfectly, and cuddling and talking was as sweet as making love, although Selena's body ached for the next time and the next time and the next time. There were so many things she wanted to do with Cade, things she wanted to show her and ask her for. She wanted to learn everything about Cade's body, and she wanted to watch Cade discover her own pleasure. Six times. Seven now. What an honor to be with someone on that journey, and not just someone: Cade. But that did not change the fact that the building appraiser was coming at three. It was noon, and they were still naked.

Reluctantly, Selena said, "Do we have to get up?"

"We should stay here forever," Cade said.

They both knew they couldn't. That truth hung in the air for a moment.

"Should we look at that room?" Cade asked.

Selena didn't want to open a room full of Ruth's

mementos. She didn't want to think about death or fore-
closures or all the reasons that soon Cade would be back
in New York. But they had to.

"Okay," she said. "I'll probably cry."

"I've got you," Cade said, drawing Selena to her.

They lay in each other's arms for a moment longer,
then rose and dressed. They found the key in a bowl of
keys in the kitchen cupboard. Cade opened the door, and a
draft rushed out. Selena peeked in. She expected boxes of
photos and souvenirs from Ruth's travels. Cade switched
on the light. Selena covered her mouth and stepped back,
knocking into Cade.

"Oh," Selena whispered.

The room was full of her paintings. Beautiful Adrien
hung on one wall, smiling seductively. Becket glared at
her from a stack by the window. There were portraits
of strangers too—*Man Dancing on Burnside*, *Trans Girl
with Cherry Blossoms*. She'd forgotten how many she had
painted. And Ruth had saved them. Selena had carried
those paintings out to Ruth's patio. She'd lit the firepit.
And at the last minute, Ruth said, *Let me do it. You
shouldn't have to see it*. Of course Ruth hadn't burned
them. Ruth would never destroy something Selena had
worked so hard to create. Tears welled up in Selena's
eyes.

Thank you.

Memories of the paintings flooded back. She could feel
the wind on Burnside Bridge. She remembered the day she
painted Becket and how they'd talked about God. She saw
an ancient drag queen whose aggressive eyelashes and
wide, Carol Burnett lips said *fuck you* to all the death and

oppression she'd seen. She could remember every stroke, every challenging line, every time she got it right.

Selena could tell Cade was waiting for her to speak, but she couldn't find the words. She took a step into the room.

"I know they're yours," Cade said quietly.

Selena was still staring at her work.

"Did Becket tell you?"

"No."

"Then how?"

"This is the best portraiture I've ever seen," Cade said. "And when work is that good, you can see the artist's soul."

Selena opened her mouth to deflect the compliment. *They're not. You're just saying that because you like me.* But she turned to speak to Cade, and the look in Cade's eyes stopped her.

"I don't paint anymore," Selena said quietly, "but when I did, I was good."

"What happened?"

She was a fuck-up. That's what she'd always told herself. But suddenly she saw herself from the outside, as though she were sitting for her portrait. She wasn't a fuck-up.

"I got scared."

Cade came up behind her and put her arms around her.

"I bounced around when I got to Portland," Selena said, "but I knew I wanted to go to art school. My dad loved to paint. He got me into it. When my mom split when I was five, she just dropped me off with my dad and told him she was moving to Santa Fe. They're not the kind of people who get attorneys, so he just said, *Okay, what does she eat?*

Most of my dad's art was drawing eagles and skulls for his tattoo shop, but in the evening, he'd take his watercolors onto the porch and paint the desert."

Cade held her tighter. Selena felt the comfort of Cade's touch throughout her whole body.

"I must have been upset about her leaving," Selena said, "but I don't remember it. I just remember my dad taking out his watercolors and us sitting on the porch. He never gave me kids' paints, always his own artist grade."

Selena stepped out of Cade's embrace and moved aside a small painting to reveal a larger one.

"This is my dad."

She examined the painting. There he was, laughing his gruff laugh. Next to him, his best friend, Chet, sat with hands on his beer belly and the rangeland in his eyes. She turned around.

"Finally, I got up the courage to go to school…and figured out how to go to school. No one in my family's ever gone to college. Then I met Alex. Professor Alex Sarta." The name didn't make her tremble. "She was a dragon to her other students. People took semesters off so they could get out of her classes, but when I started, she loved my stuff. She told everyone I was a genius, and then she wanted to be my advisor. And then one night I was at her house, having dinner with her and her husband. She invited me upstairs to look at something, and we had sex, standing up against the bathroom wall."

"You deserve more," Cade said, her eyes full of sympathy.

"I liked it. I was proud." Selena shrugged. "Professor Sarta liked *me*. But it didn't last. Becket says Alex couldn't be me, so she wanted to own me. I don't know. She started to say my work was derivative."

"Of what?" Cade frowned. "The grand masters of the sixteenth century and everything we've learned from modernism?"

Selena picked up another piece. It felt strange to hold her work again. Strange and wonderful.

"It is good, isn't it?" How had she not seen it? Forget modesty. If this was someone else's work, she'd say it was pure brilliance. "I thought I was in love with Alex. And I thought if I was good enough, if I painted a true master-piece, she'd leave her husband."

"And she did," Cade said with a shrug. "You are that good."

Selena laughed, walked across the room, and tucked herself back into Cade's arms.

"When she dumped me, she did it in her office. We were coming out of class and she actually said, *Ms. Mathis, can I see you in my office for a sec?* She told me I had no discipline as a painter. She said some people paint a few good things right at first, but they don't have anything after that. I shouldn't keep trying at something I'd never do." Selena felt herself getting teary, but it felt good to find the words to sum it all up, get out all the hurt and bitterness and let it go. "And she couldn't be with someone like that. She definitely wouldn't leave her husband for me."

"Oh, my god, she is such an asshole," Cade said.

Selena laughed.

"Yeah."

"And you didn't know these were here?" Cade asked.

Selena took a deep breath. All her friends knew that

she'd tried to burn her paintings. It was a crazy, stupid, impulsive thing to do, but they didn't judge her. Cade's strong arms around her told Selena Cade wouldn't judge her either.

"I tried to burn my paintings."

Cade held her tighter.

"I was standing at the firepit in Ruth's backyard. I lit it. I was going to put the first one in, and Ruth stopped me. She said I shouldn't have to see them burn. She'd do it for me. I should have known she wouldn't." There was something missing from the collection though. "I think she burned the ones of Alex."

"Alex didn't deserve you or your portraits." Cade kissed Selena on the forehead. "Sometimes my family does the right thing."

"Ruth was so kind," Selena said.

"And if she hadn't been kind," Cade said, "she would have kept these for the money."

"To sell?"

"If Josiah finds out about these, he'll never leave you alone."

Cade turned Selena around and put her hands on Selena's shoulders, looking deep into her eyes. "You know it doesn't matter to me how well you paint. If you shot paint balls at a canvas, I'd—"

Love you.

"I'd like you just as much."

The appraiser came and went. Afterward, they returned to the room with Selena's paintings. Cade asked her about each one. Who was it? Which had been the most challenging to paint? Which ones did Selena like best? Looking at her work was like reuniting with old friends, and as she told Cade about her process, she thought *I could do that again.*

The whole time they found reasons to touch. Selena took Cade's hand to lead her to a painting. Cade rested her hand on Selena's shoulder when Selena knelt down. Their hips touched when they stood side by side. In between studying the paintings, they kissed.

When they had looked at each painting, Cade said, "We'll have to get a van to get these into climate-controlled storage. The temperature and humidity are going to be all over the place in the cabin."

This was real work. Real art. And Cadence Elgin—of the Elgin Gallery—cared about how it was stored. It was a thrilling thought. But more wonderful was the fact that funny, sweet, sexy, hardworking Cade cared about something Selena had made, not because it had to be good, but because Selena had made it.

Cade surveyed the mess they'd made of the cabin floor. The futon was a tangle of blankets and pillows. Their clothes were strewn everywhere.

"I can't believe we didn't clean up for the appraiser," Cade said. "You're supposed to stage your house with beige furniture and fake baking-cookie smell."

"I'd buy this house," Selena said.

"Me too." Cade picked up a red velvet pillow and squeezed it. "Do you think your friends would cover the store if we stayed another night?"

Selena beamed.

"I already asked Beck and Adrien if they'd cover for a few days."

"You were planning on seducing me."

"Yes, and I wanted to make sure I had enough time."

"I don't know how you thought I'd be hard to get." Cade dropped the pillow and gave Selena a playful kiss. "Good," Cade said. "I don't want to go back to reality yet."

They walked through the snow to the Market, ordered coffee and hot sandwiches, and ate them at little bistro tables in the back of the store. The walk back took longer, as they stopped to kiss and toss snow at each other. When they got back to the cabin, the winter light was fading. Selena added more wood to the fire. They lay down again. Desire pulsed between them. Selena needed Cade again, and she knew one orgasm would only stoke Cade's hunger. But there was no need to rush. They had all night. Selena reached over for a bottle of wine and poured a glass for them to share, and they talked.

But eventually, talk became kissing, and kissing became touching. Their clothes came off piece by piece until they were naked. Selena ran her hands over Cade's small breasts and tight belly. Her own breasts tingled as she felt Cade's nipples stiffen between her fingers.

"You look like a Greek statue." Selena lay down and stretched her arms over her head. "Kiss me more."

Cade stretched out next to her and kissed her deeply, sucking on Selena's upper lip, then her lower, then biting her lightly, then sweeping her tongue around Selena's. And Selena savored Cade's lips. For a while nothing else existed. Then languid pleasure gave way to need.

Cade rested the heel of her hand on Selena's mons, rubbing a slow circle. Selena was so wet, swollen, ready to explode and melt at the same time.

"Can I kiss you more?" Cade asked.

Selena wanted it so much.

Cade lowered herself between Selena's thighs, parted her legs. She kissed Selena's hair.

"You smell good," she said.

"I smell like sex."

"I like it," Cade said.

"Is Artemisia beautiful?" Selena asked.

Her whole body shuddered as Cade parted her labia with her fingers.

Please. God. Now. Yes.

"She's lovely," Cade said.

Cade kissed all around the outside of Selena's labia. She breathed on Selena's clit. Sparks of desire shot through Selena's body. Cade settled into a teasing rhythm that made Selena sing with pleasure, lapping up and down Selena's vulva, catching her clitoris every few strokes. Selena pushed her hips greedily toward Cade's lips.

There. There. There! And there too!

Selena tried to delay her orgasm. She even tried thinking about Tristess high school football to slow down and make it last. But then she pictured herself lying in a sea of pillows, desperate to come and thinking about football, and that image turned her on even more, and she startled them both with a sudden orgasm that left her shaking.

She put her hand on the back of Cade's head. "Just a little more," she gasped. The first orgasm had turned her inside out with pleasure, but she still felt like she was seconds away from climax. She needed that second orgasm like she needed air. "Really soft like you're starting over from the beginning."

Cade obliged. Selena was so sensitive. After a few light strokes, Selena's second orgasm washed over her in a warm wave, and she was certain her life had never been more perfect.

chapter 28

Cade sat at the dining room table after work, her laptop open to the draft of their presentation to the Gentrification Abatement Coalition. She wanted to be in bed with Selena and, if not in bed, sitting on the floor of her bedroom, leaning against the bed, talking about their childhood dreams and what they thought about the *Great British Baking Show* and everything in between. But more than that, she wanted to save Satisfaction Guaranteed, not because she needed a fifty-percent share in a sex toy store. She wanted it for Selena. Desperately. She couldn't fail. She couldn't watch Selena pack her things and leave Ruth's place forever. Even if they never saw each other after this, even if Selena said, *You're fun but not long-distance fun*, she wanted Selena to be happy.

Cade closed her eyes. Amy had once dragged her to a meditation retreat. The teacher had told them to imagine a spark of light in their chests. With each breath the light expanded until it filled the whole body. Cade hadn't felt that sitting on her mat. She felt it now.

"Whatcha doing?"

Cade's eyes flew open. Selena leaned in the doorway, Cade's second laptop tucked under her arm. Cade's heart leaped. Selena was so beautiful standing there in a long T-shirt and leggings, her hair messy, her feet bare and flecked with mud from the soggy lawn. So perfect.

"I...um...Working on the presentation for the grant," Cade said.

Selena sat down next to her.

"Me too." Selena kissed Cade on the cheek, and opened the laptop. "Here are the slides I've done so far. We can put your info in them."

Selena's PowerPoint presentation made all other Power-Points look like clip art from the nineties. The layouts were beautiful, and the colors in the slides picked up the colors in the photographs she'd included. The photos made Satisfaction Guaranteed look fabulous.

"I love these," Cade said.

Selena smiled. "I have untapped corporate potential."

"Is there anything you can't do?"

"The list is so long," Selena said, "but I can kick this presentation's ass."

They worked all evening. Selena put the financials into her PowerPoint in elegant graphs and charts. Then they practiced the presentation, standing in front of Ruth's portrait and talking to her like they'd talk to the Coalition. Selena talked about the history of Satisfaction Guaranteed, Ruth's vision, and why the store mattered to the community. Cade presented the financials in the best possible light...which was still terrible.

*   *   *

Around eleven, they both yawned.

"Call it a night?" Cade picked up a pile of papers and tapped them into a neat stack.

Selena stood up, but she was still looking at the laptop, stopping on each of the spreadsheets.

"I just want to make sure I understand the money," she said without looking up. "You're talking about it, but I don't want them to ask me a question and be like, *I have no idea. That's her job.*"

"I love that you're reading my spreadsheets."

Should she have said *love*? Everyone said love. They loved French fries. They loved the opera. But now, standing in the intimate glow of the chandelier that hung over the table, the word held a special charge.

"What's *internal theft*?" Selena asked. "There's five hundred and thirty-four dollars there." She looked up with a smile. "You don't think I'm embezzling?"

"It's me," Cade said. "I stole from the store."

"You can't steal from a store you own."

"You still need to log the loss."

"So responsible." Selena looked from Cade to the laptop and back again, her eyes sparkling with amusement and desire. "What did you steal?"

A few weeks ago, Cade would have been embarrassed. She wasn't now.

"YOLO pillows." She shrugged innocently.

"Really? Where are they?"

"I hid them."

"You're hording throw pillows." Selena nodded knowingly. "That's the sign of a problem."

Cade gave Selena a kiss.

"I stole sex toys. What else?"

"Five hundred and thirty-four dollars," Selena said. "Go big or go home. What did you get?" She pulled Cade closer to her. "And will you show me?"

Anticipation pulsed in Cade's body. So strange to have been dead (at least very, very quiet) down there and now to feel this delicious urgency.

Back in Selena's room, Selena lit a candle and turned down the lights. They sat on her bed, the Satisfaction Guaranteed bag between them.

"You didn't even take them out of their boxes," Selena said.

"I tried some."

"Hmm." Selena picked out the Lucy, still in its package. "A classic vibrator. Does it charge quickly?"

Cade reached around the big pink bag and gave Selena a playful shove.

"So, these aren't a no-go for you, just a haven't-worked-yet?" Selena asked.

"I think I need someone to teach me." Cade glowed. She wanted to rush out of her clothes.

"I know you'll be a good student." Selena gave her a look so seductive it made Cade's body pulse with anticipation.

Selena shimmied out of her pleather pants. Cade tossed her sweater on top of a pile of Selena's dresses. Soon they were lying naked on top of Selena's Crown Royal quilt. Desire pulsed between Cade's legs. She whimpered and sighed, sounds she'd never made before. But Selena didn't rush. Selena kissed her for a long time. The desire building up inside Cade felt unbearable and unbearably wonderful.

"Yes?" Selena asked.

"Please."

Selena adjusted the pillow under Cade's head, then gently parted Cade's legs.

"You don't have to like it." Selena propped herself up on one arm. "Tell me if you don't."

Selena found the vibrator and touched the toy to Cade's body, moving it slowly, never quite touching her clit. The vibration felt better than it had when Cade was alone.

"Do you like it?"

"Yes," Cade breathed.

Selena moved the toy across her clit for a second, then moved it away. Cade's hips bucked.

"Now this one has eight intensity levels and nine vibration patterns," Selena said, putting on her salesperson voice. "That'll be seventy-two variations. We'll try each one, and you can tell me what you like."

"I think I'll die," Cade gasped, as Selena teased her clit again.

"I can't let you come. We have seventy-one left to go." Selena moved the vibrator up and down Cade's thighs and then back to her sex.

Cade sunk back into the bed.

"Relax every muscle in your body," Selena said.

Cade tried. She felt like her body was seeing stars. Selena did not make her go through all seventy-two variations. A moment later, Cade moaned as an orgasm built inside her. Selena took Cade's hand and brought it to the vibrator.

"You try," she said gently.

Cade closed her eyes. She held the vibrator. The vibrations found their way through her skin, into the wings and bulbs of her clitoris that were hidden inside her body. Her whole world distilled to the spirals behind her eyelids and the pleasure mounting inside her. She loved this. How had she not enjoyed this before? And how wonderful to have waited for Selena. She clutched the vibrator, not holding it right, just grinding it against her body with both hands. She wanted to increase the intensity of the vibrations, but that would mean pausing to find the controls and she couldn't bear that. She pressed harder.

"Yes, yes, yes."

Selena clutched Cade's thigh as if urging her on.

"You are so hot," Selena whispered.

Then Cade came, gasping and laughing, and much better prepared to discuss the merits of Satisfaction Guaranteed's most profitable merchandise category.

"I get it now," Cade said when she caught her breath.

Selena leaned over her.

"Good."

Cade turned the vibrator over in her hand.

"Who knew," she said.

Selena kissed her.

"Women," she said.

Selena rolled onto her side. Her eyes were dark with unspent need. She cupped her hand around Cade's breast, stroking her thumb over her nipple.

"So...you're so athletic," Selena said slowly. "How do you feel about wearing a strap-on?"

Cade quickly scanned her memory for product descriptions. *Easy to wear.* That came up a lot.

"You'll have to tell me what to do."

"I'm sure it's just like rowing crew."

Selena pinched Cade's nipple. Cade lifted her chest toward Selena, savoring the delicious nip of pain.

"I'm sure it's not," Cade said. "It'll be more fun."

Selena rolled over, half sliding off the bed, and pulled a box out from beneath it. She rolled back into bed, sat up and opened the box, setting out a dildo, harness shorts, three vibrators—one bullet, two wearables—and lube. Everything with Selena was comfortable, but it was still an intimidating amount of equipment.

"Am I going to mess this up?" Cade asked.

"You won't." Selena popped a bullet vibrator into the base of the dildo and unceremoniously put one of the other vibrators inside herself. She handed Cade the other one. "If you like."

Cade slipped the U-shaped vibrator inside. Selena wrestled the dildo into the rubber ring in the shorts. Cade tried to pull on the shorts. It was like getting into a wet sports bra one size too small.

"You're so sexy," Selena said, as Cade struggled to hitch the shorts over her thighs.

"You lie."

The dildo bobbed above her knees.

"No." Selena looked at her like she was contemplating dessert.

"The website said these were easy to wear." Cade tugged.

"They never are," Selena said, her smile full of affection. She got up on her knees and inched the shorts up Cade's body.

A month ago, Cade would have picked a bad trip to the dentist over getting stuck in a pair of harness shorts in front of a beautiful woman. Now she laughed as Selena grabbed the base of the dildo and yanked.

"It's not like rowing crew," Cade said.

Then the shorts snapped into place, tight and surprisingly comfortable.

"There!" Selena said.

Cade looked down. She looked silly...but also powerful.

"And after all that"—Selena rubbed lube on the dildo and lay back—"I won't last. It's a lot of getting dressed for a short show. Come."

Selena pulled Cade on top of her. Selena still had the small vibrator inside. Cade had read the specs. You wore it during penetration. It still seemed like a lot.

"I don't want to hurt you," Cade said.

Selena tilted her head back, closing her eyes.

"Bae, you won't."

Bae. Cade didn't have time to take in the endearment. Selena guided the head of the dildo inside her, moaning luxuriously as she shifted it into place.

"Thrust hard," she said. "God, it's been so long." Her eyes flew open. "I need this, Cade."

As thrilling as it was to be on top of Selena, wielding a dildo in a harness felt as precise as a pick-up-a-toy game in a grocery store lobby. No one could pick up a plush Minion with that rickety claw. Cade hesitated.

Selena grasped Cade's ass. "Please."

With that Cade thrust into Selena with the strength of a crew team rower and the confidence of a blindfolded driver.

"Yes," Selena sung out. "Right there."

Cade thrust again.

Selena clutched Cade's hips, holding Cade to her, undulating her own hips. Her whole face contorted. "Oh, my God, that's fucking perfect."

Then she came with a beautiful, hawklike cry.

It was the sexiest thing Cade had ever seen.

When Selena opened her eyes, she said, "Sorry. I told you I wouldn't last."

"I love it." Cade laughed.

Why not use the word *love*? This was better than fries or the opera.

When they were curled up together under the Crown Royal blanket, Cade said, "I always thought toys would make sex feel...I don't know...impersonal."

"Did it?"

Sex toys were strewn across the bed. The bottle of lube was leaking on the bedside table. The scene looked triumphant.

"I feel like a winner," Cade said.

chapter 29

Becket pulled the last pin from the suit she'd tailored for Selena's presentation to the Gender Abatement Coalition. She stuck the pin into a pin cushion on the sewing table that occupied a large corner of her living room.

"Put this on," Becket said.

Selena rose from Becket's couch and let Becket put the jacket on her. Becket had transformed the thirty-dollar Goodwill suit. Selena admired herself in the three-way mirror Becket used for fitting her burlesque troupe.

"I look like a CEO," Selena said.

"Sexy but professional," Becket agreed. "Professional for the committee. Sexy for Cade."

Selena sat back down on Becket's sagging sofa. Becket didn't waste money on living room furniture.

"What if I mess it up?" Selena pulled at a bit of stuffing that was escaping the sofa cushion. "You heard my eulogy." Her stomach clenched at the idea of speaking in front of a bunch of people, knowing that what she said would decide the fate of Satisfaction Guaranteed. It made her want to pass out.

"And I've seen you teach. You're a great teacher, and you're teaching them why Satisfaction Guaranteed is so important. You've got this."

"But what if we don't get the grant?"

Becket sat down next to Selena and put an arm around her.

"We have gone over this. You and Cade being long distance is not the end of the world. If she goes back to New York, you'll make it work."

"We'll be three thousand miles apart."

"You don't have to take the Oregon Trail to visit her."

But how long before Selena saved up enough money for an apartment, let alone plane tickets? Selena imagined Cade in New York, wearing her subtle gray sweaters at parties with other people who wore subtle gray cashmere and owned their own apartments, which they probably called flats. Selena was sexy and fun. She knew that. It wasn't a life plan. And she had once been a great painter. And now she understood QuickBooks (at least the basics). But would that hold Cade's interest when they saw each other a few times a year? When Cade had to pay for everything because Selena worked at a grocery store? When everywhere Cade went there were people like Cade? Cade wanted a partner, in business and in life. Someone she could count on. Someone responsible. As much as Selena wanted to throw herself at Cade's feet and cry, *Stay...or take me with you*, that was not a life strategy, and not a way to keep a woman like Cade. People with their shit together didn't go around clinging to their lovers' ankles begging, *Don't leave me. I'll do anything.* People with their shit together said, *I like you. I'd like to see where this goes. Let's see what happens and be sure to communicate.*

"Can I practice my presentation to you again?" Selena asked Becket.

Becket's face said, *Oh, god, not again.*

"Of course," Becket said.

"You look amazing," Cade said, when Selena walked into the kitchen, her copy of the presentation in a folder tucked under her arm.

Cade was dressed in her everyday clothes which, of course, meant she was dressed to give a make-or-break business presentation.

"Are you ready?" Cade asked.

Twenty-three run-throughs had made Selena feel as ready as she was going to be.

It was dark by the time they got to the Gentrification Abatement Coalition. The Coalition was housed in a small brick building beside a park.

"This used to be a schoolhouse," the head of the selection committee told them as he led them into the conference room. "The Coalition actually started because we wanted to save the park and this building from development. Now we work with all sorts of landmark buildings and businesses."

Three people waited for them in the conference room, two other men and a woman in a colorful knitted scarf. They looked like classic Portlanders, all wearing fleece, with frowzy hair and travel mugs sitting in front of them, each one printed with the good cause that had given it to them or sold it at a fundraiser. Selena saw the Pride House, something about whales, and two for a past mayoral candidate. She knew this crowd.

They sat down, and everyone introduced themselves.

After a little bit of conversation about the rain, the head of the committee said, "You can understand why we asked for an additional presentation beyond our usual grant application."

The committee shifted in their seats. The room suddenly felt tense. The woman frowned. The men sipped their coffee in unison, which would have been funny except that Selena's heart was racing. This was it. Their one chance to save Satisfaction Guaranteed. If they didn't get the grant or they didn't get enough, the creditors got the house. Cade had said they'd have to sell everything in the store, even the shelves, and give whatever they made to the vendors.

"Satisfaction Guaranteed is a very different kind of store," the head of the committee added.

They'd anticipated this comment. Cade gave Selena an encouraging nod.

"It's actually not," Selena said. "I can understand why a lot of people would say that. My co-owner"—Cade was so much more than a co-owner—"definitely had that feeling when she learned what she'd inherited."

"True that," Cade said. "I was hoping to get some teacups."

"Ruth has those teacups with the naked Greek goddesses on them," Selena said.

Cade chuckled ruefully. Selena shrugged. They were perfectly in sync.

"But the fact is Satisfaction Guaranteed sells a product that makes one aspect of people's lives more interesting, hopefully happier," Selena went on. "It's like selling succulents. Someone lives in a small apartment. They miss being outside. They want to bring a little bit of nature into their space. They buy an arrangement of succulents, and it brightens their life."

She and Cade exchanged a smile.

"Satisfaction Guaranteed does that for a different aspect of people's lives, and we need stores like this because our society makes it hard to talk about sex in an open, comfortable way."

She went on to talk about Ruth's vision, the charity work Ruth had done, the value of pleasure education. The committee relaxed. They laughed at her jokes. The woman nodded as Selena described the pleasure gap and how important it was to educate women about their bodies. Cade presented the store's financial situation. She made it a story about hope and dreams.

"My aunt was a visionary," Cade said in conclusion, "but like many visionaries, her vision didn't extend to smart inventory management…or paying bills. But Selena and I have both vision and accounting skills. This store is a gift to the community. It's been a gift to me. And if it goes under, it's quite likely that Portland will never have another store like this."

* * *

"We were good," Cade said, when they were on the street.

"Do you think so?" Selena clasped Cade's hand.

"If we didn't win them over, no one could," Cade said, but her eyes were dark. "I don't know if it's going to be enough though."

chapter 30

The following evening, Selena found herself climbing out of an Uber into the bustle of the Portland Art Walk. "I haven't been to the Art Walk in years," she said.

It looked just like she remembered. The area had once been warehouses. Now the old brick buildings glowed with gallery lights. Lofts graced the upper stories of old factories. Sleek, LEED-certified highrises boasted windmills on their rooftops. And now she was here with Cade. On a real date. Like normal people. Not like two people whose lives were soon to be determined by a grant committee.

The rain had stopped. A few bistros had set up tables outside. Everything glittered.

"I love this," Selena said. "Everyone at McLaughlin used to go. They'd all complain about it. It was all boxed wine and string quartets. *If I hear one more Pachelbel's Canon…*" She affected a snooty accent. "Back in Tristess, you didn't complain about free booze, and if someone picked up a fiddle or their old guitar and played you something, that was a gift." Selena turned and gave Cade a quick kiss. "But if we see Alex will you still pretend to be my fiancée?"

Cade smiled.

"Yes, but I get to choose the monogrammed napkins."

If only. Selena caught herself. She'd been with a lot of people. Some she cared about deeply, some she had had fun with for a night, some not so much fun. But she'd never thought, *Sure, you can choose the napkins.*

"You can have anything you want," she said.

"I can think of a lot of things I want," Cade said.

Selena linked her arm around Cade's, leaning into her as they set off down the sidewalk.

"When I first got to Portland, I'd ridden my motorcycle in," Selena said. "I went to the Art Walk. The day before I'd been on the road. I'd had lunch in Brothers. If you think Tristess is the end of the world, Brothers has fallen off the map. But they had sandwiches and gas. That was cool. Then I got to Portland, and I was...It was like nothing I'd ever seen."

"You'd never been to Portland?"

"Biggest city I'd been to was Burns. That's about three thousand people," Selena said. "You probably go to things like this all the time, openings and shows and stuff."

"It's just free Chardonnay and cheese cubes without you."

Cade stopped them on a street corner, swept Selena up in her arms, and kissed her on the lips. Selena kept her eyes open while they kissed so she could experience everything: the taste of Cade's mouth, the glimpse of Cade's hair as it swept her cheek, the bistro diners watching them. It felt like everyone on the street was happy for them, although realistically some of them were probably annoyed that she and Cade were taking up the sidewalk. Selena didn't care.

"This is wonderful," Selena said when they stopped kissing. "A perfect date."

Cade took Selena's arm again, and they continued down the street.

"So you haven't been to New York," Cade said.

"No."

"I'd like to take you."

Was she offering in a casual way? Did she mean it? *Would you ask me to stay there?*

"I'd love that," Selena said.

"I'll take you to all the tourist stuff," Cade said. "We'll take pictures in front of wax sculptures of Bill Clinton. We'll go to the Stonewall Inn."

"I'll wear an I Heart New York thong," Selena said.

"You will be the most beautiful person to ever wear New York tourist gear."

They turned into a gallery at random. A caterer came by with flutes of white wine. They stood in front of a painting of daisies, sipping their box wine. Selena didn't see the art. She was just enjoying Cade's presence. They were about to move on to the next painting when Selena heard an unmistakable voice.

"I wouldn't say that Derrick had an influence over my creative process. I wouldn't give him that much power, but our marriage created a space of normativity."

Alex. Why? Selena was having a perfect date with a woman she adored, and Alex had to be here.

Cade must have felt her stiffen. Cade glanced over her shoulder.

"Alex," Cade confirmed.

"Let's go," Selena said. "I don't want to deal with her."

"She's such a douche. *Space of normativity*. We can go. Anyway, I have a present I want to give you while we're downtown."

But a voice behind them said, "Is that the brilliant Ms. Mathis?"

It was one of the older professors.

"Want to run?" Cade asked.

"No," Selena said with a sigh and turned around. "Hello, Professor Rutherford."

Alex stood with old Professor Rutherford and a younger woman Selena didn't recognize.

"Ms. Mathis, where have you been hiding?" Rutherford said. "Off to bigger and better things, I'm guessing." To the younger woman, he added, "Ms. Mathis was one of our best students." And to Selena he said, "This is our new dean, a wonderful leader for our ship of fools."

"When did you graduate? I just took the job at McLaughlin. I probably missed you," the dean asked conversationally.

"She dropped out," Alex said under her breath.

"Such a shame!" Rutherford said. "We old dogs do stifle your young minds, though. Better to get out while you can. What genius work have you been up to?"

"I believe she's an entrepreneur now." Alex's thin smile said, *Aren't I good for saving you the embarrassment of telling them what you're really doing?*

Alex wasn't good.

"I run a sex toy store," Selena said. "Satisfaction Guaranteed in NoPo."

Alex's eyes traveled down her body.

"I trust you are still painting," Rutherford said.

Cade rested her hand on Selena's waist. The touch steadied her.

"I am," she lied.

"Really?" Alex said.

"I've been trying to talk her into doing a show," Cade said. "My parents and I own a little gallery. Selena's way above our pay grade, but hope springs eternal."

Cade sounded so calm. This was her world.

Professor Rutherford shook Cade's hand.

"I am the ignoble Professor Rutherford. And besides escorting the talented Ms. Mathis to the Art Walk, you are?"

"Cade."

Rutherford pursed his lips in a dramatic O. "Is it possible that you are…? Would it be presumptuous to guess that we were in the presence of the daughter of the famous Roger and Pepper?"

Cade shrugged as if to say, *Yes, if you insist.*

"*My father owns a little gallery.*" Rutherford laughed approvingly. "So, you're thinking of showing Ms. Mathis's paintings? I am not surprised."

"If she agrees," Cade said. "She hasn't said."

Alex stepped forward, edging out Professor Rutherford. "A little conflict of interest?" She looked from Cade to Selena.

"Alex?" The dean frowned.

"Anyone would be lucky to show Ms. Mathis's work," Rutherford said. "Ms. Mathis, when you have your next show, email the department and call the alumni office.

We've been waiting with bated breath for your entrée into the light."

"You should come back to McLaughlin," the dean said. "We have some exciting programs starting in the fall. Why not finish your degree?"

"Yes. Why did you leave us?" Rutherford clasped his hand to his heart. "Except that the academy had nothing to offer a woman of your talent."

"Selena had a problem with financial aid," Alex said, a warning in every word. "It can be hard for first-generation students to navigate that system."

That was true. Many maxed-out credit cards attested to that.

"We can help you sort out financial aid," the dean said. "I was first gen too. I get it."

"I wasn't great with money," Selena said, "but I dropped out because Alex and I were lovers, and she dumped me." She had said it. Out loud. She waited for the realization that this was yet one more time when she should have thought before she spoke, but that realization didn't come. "I was young and dumb." She held her hand to her forehead like a swooning debutante. "I was devastated."

Rutherford's mouth dropped open.

The dean said, "Alex?"

Alex's eyes burned with rage.

"So now I own a sex toy store," Selena said, and with that, she took Cade's hand and whisked her away as though it was very important that they look at the display of topographical woodblock prints. She was not going to give Alex the satisfaction of running out of the gallery.

But she nestled close to Cade as they stood in front of the largest woodblock print, letting Cade's strong, solid presence ground her. Cade put her arm around Selena.

"That was fantastic," Cade said without moving her lips. "They are going to have the most awkward walk home."

"I can't believe I said that," Selena whispered.

"I love it." Cade squeezed Selena's hand. "If she didn't think it was wrong to sleep with you, she shouldn't mind you saying it in front of her colleagues."

"Do you think they'll really disapprove?"

"It's wrong. I'm sure it's against college policy. And she might have broken the law. Even if they didn't care that she slept with you, which they should, you dropped out because of her. They missed out on having the great Selena Mathis on their alumni list. If you had finished your degree, you'd have been on every promotional flyer. The website would be like, *Hello. Selena Mathis went here.*"

"Nobody cares about my paintings."

"If you show at the Elgin Gallery, the whole world will care." Cade looked around. "She's gone."

Selena sunk into Cade's arms, laughing in relief.

That was me!

When they were back on the street, Cade said, "I want to give you your present. It's this way."

They strolled down the street. When Cade stopped, it took Selena a moment to realize where they were. Blick Art Supply. Open late for the Art Walk. Cade held the door open, and the familiar smell of paint and canvas washed over Selena.

"There's a thousand dollars of credit for you," Cade

said. "They have it in their system. I'll wait for you at the bar across the street."

Selena stopped in the doorway.

"We should put that money into the store." She gazed into Cade's eyes.

"This is even more important." Cade's eyes echoed the sentiment in her words.

"Oh, Cade."

"Go." Cade held the door a little wider.

Inside, the store was so familiar. So wonderful. She knew exactly what a tube of Maimeri Classico would feel like in her hand. A filbert brush. The feather of a fan brush.

"And, sweetheart," Cade called after her, "you don't have to be good. Whatever you do is beautiful."

Back in her apartment, Selena cleared off her desk for the first time in years. Slowly, one by one, she set out the paints. Cade knocked on the door a few minutes later, two drinks in hand.

"Do you want me to leave you alone?" she asked.

"No," Selena said quickly.

It was late. They'd stayed at the Art Walk until after nine. They had to work the next day. And she wouldn't be able to fall asleep next to Cade without sampling Cade's beautiful body. But a canvas rested on her new easel. She'd peeled off the plastic seals on the paint and the thinner.

"I'm going to let you paint," Cade said.

"Can I paint you?" It was the only thing Selena wanted as much as she wanted to kiss Cade from the crown of her head to the soles of her feet. "You could just have a drink and talk to me. But it's late. You don't have to. Modeling is boring."

"Nothing with you is boring," Cade said. "How do you want me?" Cade made it sound dirty.

Selena loved that.

Selena posed Cade naked in bed so that Cade could fall asleep if she got bored and so that Selena could enjoy Cade's body naked. She invited Cade to turn toward her, and she draped the Crown Royal quilt around her. Cade looked powerful, sexy, proper, and vulnerable all at once. The room was warm. The string lights illuminated Cade's face without shadows. Selena considered the rainbow of colors before her. She'd want a blend of manganese and cerulean blue for Cade's eyes. She picked up a brush.

It was just a stick with sable fronds. The paint was just pigment in linseed oil. Products with a price tag attached made by a company that did or did not pay their employees enough. Just stuff. She looked back and forth between Cade and the brush in her hand. And she remembered Cade holding her on the patio. The taste of Cade's body. The way Cade listened to her stories like Selena was the only person in the world. And she touched her brush to a tube of paint. Everything would be okay. The store. The house. This beautiful thing that was starting between her and Cade. She had nothing to worry about. The world went quiet, and there was only her and Cade's soul and the sheen of oil on stretched canvas.

chapter 31

Cade got the email a few minutes before the store opened. She was sitting on the counter, waiting for Selena to come back with coffees. She opened her email on her phone. Somehow, she'd thought the Coalition would call. Somehow, she'd forgotten that the news was almost certainly going to be bad.

Dear Ms. Mathis and Ms. Elgin, We regret to inform you... very competitive process... felt that other applicants were more... the coalition's mission...

What happened to *everything will work out the way it's supposed to?*

Cade stared at her phone. There must have been dozens of applicants. And a sex toy store run by a Portland hipster and a New York art dealer wasn't exactly an iconic deli or a shoe repair shop that had been in business since the eighteen hundreds. But she'd lain in Selena's arms, listening to Selena's deep, regular breath, and imagined how she would hug Selena if they got the grant. *We did it!* They'd invite Selena's friends to the store after closing and drink champagne. Becket would pull Cade aside and say, *Thanks for taking care of Selena.* Then Cade would have an excuse to stay. She couldn't leave Selena to run the store until they could afford help. The house needed repairs. Just another month or two. Then, in a month or two or six, when they'd had more time, Cade would say, *What if I stayed in Portland? Or you came to live in New York?*

Now she only had a few days before she was supposed to leave.

The door chimed. Selena walked in, holding cups of coffee. She beamed.

"Hello, lover," Selena said. Then her face fell. "What is it?"

Cade took a deep breath.

"We didn't get the grant."

"But they loved us." Selena hurried over and put the coffees down.

"Love wasn't enough."

The grief on Selena's face broke Cade's heart. A month ago, Cade would have preferred Ruth will everything to bulldog rescue so Cade wouldn't have to deal with it. Now she desperately wanted a feminist sex toy store with a giant, neon clit over the counter. She wanted to see Selena happy.

"Is there anything we can do?"

"We'll talk to Delmar," Cade said.

Selena stepped into Cade's arms, leaning her head on Cade's shoulder. She wasn't crying, but her breath sounded ragged.

* * *

Delmar's office felt darker than Cade remembered it. The
wood paneling was almost black. He hadn't lit a fire in
the fireplace. Selena sat silently beside Cade, her head
up, her face set in a blank look. It was as sad as seeing
her cry.

"I've been in communication with the creditors," he
said. "Palace Perfect and Adult Playground are ready to
repossess the inventory and the house. I tried to get
another month, but no."

"If we sell the cabin?" Cade saw the sea of pillows,
the firelight, and Selena's body, naked before her for the
first time.

"Ruth didn't own the land," Delmar said. "Ruth was a
wonderful woman." Delmar capped and uncapped his pen,
then set it down. "She wanted this to work for you. You
two did an amazing job. You did the best anyone could
have done."

"What happens next?" Cade asked.

"We have to do a short sale. Legally have to. We liquidate
everything as quickly as possible. Including the store."

"That'll take a lot of work," Cade said.

Give me an excuse to stay.

"There are companies that can run those going-out-of-
business sales," Delmar said. "I've talked to a couple. Cade,
I know you're headed back to New York. You don't have
to do it yourself."

Cade wanted Selena to stand up and say, *No! There has to
be a way. You have to stay. You owe Ruth.* But she didn't.

"You have three days to move out of the house," Delmar
said. "If there are things of value—antiques, furniture,
jewelry—those have to stay. But anything you'd sell at a

garage sale and sentimentals, photos, keepsakes, you can keep those."

Finally, Selena spoke. "Can I take Ruth's portrait?"

"Do you think it has a monetary value?" Delmar asked. "Could you sell it for more than...a hundred dollars or so?"

"Of course not," Selena said.

"Then it's yours."

The next two days passed in a blur of moving boxes. There wasn't time to sort Ruth's things. Every room was full of treasures, but Cade couldn't figure out which ones to keep, and there wasn't time to ask Selena about each teacup. They worked in different rooms. Selena was quiet and efficient, packing boxes and stacking the borrowed van. At night they lay in Selena's bed. Selena kissed Cade and told her she was beautiful. Selena went down on her with the same attention as always, but Cade didn't come, and Selena's moans were quiet and restrained.

The last night, the house was more a disaster than the night of the funeral. Selena stood in the kitchen around midnight, surveying the mess. Cade took her in her arms.

"How are you doing?" Cade asked.

Selena leaned against her. "They take the keys tomorrow, right?"

"We drop them off at Delmar's," Cade said.

"And you're flying home."

"I have a ticket."

Ask me to stay.

Cade buried her face in Selena's hair, breathing in the

smell of jasmine and musk. This was the moment. Cade wouldn't let it slip away. She was an Elgin. She had not been switched at birth with an accountant. Elgins made big, wild moves. They bought alpacas and joined communes and drank kegs of whiskey at funerals.

So, I was thinking...I don't have to go.

Cade's mother would tell her there was never a wrong time to share your love. Her father would tell her something about the bacchanalia or Athena, but what he'd mean was YOLO.

"Selena," Cade said quietly.

"Yes?"

"I was thinking about what comes next," Cade said.

I can't imagine coming home every night and not seeing you. I don't want you to go to bed alone. We've never been to the movies. I haven't met your father. I want to see springtime with you.

"With the sale?" Selena asked.

Cade hesitated. "With us."

I want to watch the sunrise reflected in your eyes.

"I've been thinking about that too," Selena said.

Selena pulled away just enough to look at Cade. Cade loved how Selena's emotions showed on her face. Tenderness. Hope. Optimism. Selena looked like she was going to make a declaration, like she was gathering up a torrent of words to release in one long breath.

Yes! I'll stay with you. I'll dream with you. We'll make it work.

Selena leaned back into Cade's chest, tightening her arms around Cade until she was clutching her, pressing her face against Cade's shoulder, then Selena stepped away.

"I know you're really busy," she said.

It took a moment for the words to register. Selena had already gone on.

"You have a career. You've worked hard for it, and you own part of the gallery. I guess I've got a lot going on too. Time to update my résumé…make one. Becket won't let me sleep on her couch forever."

It sounded rehearsed.

"But long distance isn't out of the question for me," Selena went on. "I know it makes people feel…split. Like they're not really in one place, and I know you meet a lot of people. Women. But if you'd like to see what happens, I'll give it a try. This has been really fun. The most fun you could have going bankrupt."

This has been fun? Cade felt like she'd been punched. Everything she wanted to say died on her lips.

"I…" she began.

Amy would say, *Just tell her.* Her father would suggest an extemporaneous poem. Her mother would suggest an interpretive dance. But *let's see what happens* meant *I'm not that interested. Let's see what happens* meant *chill out.*

Don't scare her off.

"Definitely, let's see what happens. Of course, long distance is difficult, but…"

Cade swallowed the lump in her throat. This wasn't the end. Selena didn't say, *You're fun but not if I have to fly to New York.* Selena was saying they could keep going. Cade would get her a month or two or six. They'd miss each other. Maybe Cade would leave, and Selena would wake up the next morning and think, *How could I have let her go?* Cade's heart turned toward the possibility. *Maybe.* But what she'd wanted to hear was *Yes! Yes! Yes! Be mine forever.*

"I'd like to see what happens." Cade put her gallery manager face on. "This has been a special time for me."

Selena nodded.

"Me too."

It felt like they were finishing a business deal.

Who was she kidding? What made her think she could win over a woman like Selena? Selena would probably wake up and think exactly what she had said: *That was fun.* Then she'd be off to the Aviary to paint and eat tater tots with Becket. Maybe she'd present Adrien with a to-do list of sex acts. Afterward she'd sprawl out beside him, casual friends who didn't think sex was a big deal. *I needed that,* she'd say.

The thought tore Cade's heart apart.

"Of course, it doesn't have to be exclusive," Cade said. "Unless you want to?"

Say yes. Make me stay.

"Of course," Selena said.

"Yes."

Cade wasn't sure what she'd said yes to, only that it was a shadow of a shadow of what she wanted. She drew Selena back into her arms, and they held each other. But that night when Selena stroked the hair between Cade's legs, Cade stayed her hand.

"Of course," Selena said. "I understand."

Then Selena curled up behind her, tucking her knees behind Cade's and wrapping her arm around Cade's waist. They fit perfectly, and Selena's body was as warm and soft as always, but it didn't feel like being cradled. It felt like goodbye.

chapter 32

It was midafternoon when Cade arrived at her apartment. The air was cold, and a few flakes of dry snow flurried in the street outside her building. She dug her keys out of her laptop bag and climbed four flights. Her apartment was cold. The bed was made with gray sheets. She missed Selena's Crown Royal bags and Selena's warm curves pressed up against her.

Sociopath sat at the window.

"Still on my fire escape? The other ones aren't good enough?"

Cade approached the window.

"You can't curse me," she said. "I feed you."

Sociopath hissed, *I already did.*

Cade had grabbed a black coffee at the Starbucks down the street. She'd picked up some pods of creamer as well. She took out a bowl and poured half the cream in the bowl, half in her coffee. She put the bowl on the fire escape and watched Sociopath lap it up.

She texted Selena. *Made it safe.* She considered adding

a heart, typed it, deleted it, and added it again. What was she doing? Amy used six hearts every time she texted about quinoa.

She hit send with the heart.

Selena texted back instantly.

:)

Cade wanted to get *I miss you. Come back. My life is empty without you.* Of course, with Selena's phone that would be a difficult message to decipher. But :)? She didn't know someone could be crushed by two punctuation marks.

Cade took the subway to Amy's food truck. It was strange being back in New York. The city was still the city, but it didn't feel like home without Selena.

"Cade!" Amy exclaimed when she spotted her. She said something to the other workers, then left the truck, arms wide.

Cade let Amy squeeze her.

"Baby doll, what happened?" Amy asked. "A green smoothie, protein power pack extra," she called to her coworkers.

Cade's regular.

She held Cade at arm's length.

"Why are you back? Is everything all right?"

"I was always supposed to come back today," Cade said.

"Yeah, but you were supposed to stay with Selena and sell sex toys and have amazing sex." Amy's round, red face paled with worry.

"We lost the store," Cade said. "They'll take Ruth's house too."

Amy hugged her again. This time, Cade sank into Amy's hug, engulfed in the smell of warm saffron rice.

"I'm so sorry."

"It's not the store." Cade didn't cry on friends' shoulders. She made wry comments like, *That happened.* Now she sniffled, just a bit. Amy went into maternal overdrive.

"Tell me everything."

Amy's coworker ran the smoothie out to Cade. It would have been better with whipped cream. Amy led Cade to a sheltered stoop a little way down the street. They sat on the steps, protected from the wind. Cade sipped her smoothie through its biodegradable straw.

"Talk to me," Amy said.

"I miss Selena."

A delivery truck rattled by. At the end of the street, a busker tried to squeak out a tune on a cold violin. A few blocks away, Times Square glittered with lights. Selena would love it, and Cade would have loved to show Selena the city.

Cade wasn't going to cry.

"You didn't break up, did you?" Amy asked.

Cade took a deep breath.

"I don't think we were ever together." She recounted their parting conversation. "She's not that interested, not from three thousand miles away."

The man who believed the world was ending at midnight walked by, waving his placard, his beard wild.

"If I wake up one night and it is the end of the world, I'll be like, *Damn. He told me*," Cade said, but she felt like her world had already ended.

"But every night it doesn't happen," Amy said. "Surprise. We survived."

Cade wished she could fall asleep in her apartment and wake up in Selena's arms.

"Selena's just waiting for enough time to call it off without making me feel bad."

"It looks like you feel bad." Amy cupped Cade's cheeks in her hands.

"She probably didn't want to just blow me off right away. Didn't want me to think she was only with me for the store." God, how many women had wanted her for what they thought she could do for them. That wasn't Selena. It couldn't be Selena. But that didn't mean Selena wanted the hassle of a long-distance relationship, and obviously staying in Portland or inviting Selena to live with her in New York was too much too soon. "She could have anyone."

"And she wanted you."

"While I was there." Cade sucked on her green protein smoothie. "I think I fell for her the minute I saw her. That eulogy. She cared so much, and it was so wrong. It was like her whole heart was right there, like she was just going to say what she felt. Go big or go home."

Cade wrapped her coat tighter around herself. She could feel Amy watching her. It was hard not to cry with the cold wind stinging her eyes.

"I kind of thought..." Cade swallowed. "I thought she'd be like that with me. Make this big...declaration."

"She's an idiot if she's not into you."

Not really.

Cade didn't want to sound maudlin.

"I'd be good at doing her taxes."

"You'd be good at everything. You're kind. You're funny. You take care of people. You're smart. Every queer girl I know thinks you're hot." Amy pulled her into another hug, almost spilling Cade's smoothie. "Something will work out. I know it will."

"You sound like my parents."

Cade's heart was breaking, but it was impossible not to be a little bit cheered by Amy's hugs and her love and her totally unfounded belief that things worked out for the best.

chapter 33

Selena opened her eyes, cursing the morning light coming in through the windows. She was lying on Becket's sofa (now her bed until she saved enough for an apartment). It was hard and saggy at the same time. She didn't care. It fit her mood. Cade had been gone for three days. It felt like an eternity.

"How could I have let her go?" Selena moaned.

She and Becket had been over this before.

"Do you know that you went from dead sleep to angst?" Becket was sitting at her sewing table.

"I was angsting in my sleep."

"Coffee."

Selena wanted to weep, *Cade drinks coffee, and I bought it for her, and she drank it, and now I'm never going to see her again, and my life is over,* but that was dramatic, even for her.

"I'm too sad for coffee."

"Get up. Help me finish this." Becket flapped a piece of lace at her. "I wish we could do tots, but the auction is in a week. We're performing, and everybody has torn their outfits. How could they all tear everything a week before the show?"

That was Becket, taking care of everyone, as always.

Selena dragged herself over to the chair opposite Becket's sewing table.

"Hand me that seam ripper," Becket said.

Who could care about seam rippers or corsets? She'd sent Cade away like a bad hookup, and Cade had accepted the brush-off. Selena looked around for something that could rip seams.

"Little blue thing with the metal." Becket nodded toward a pile of sewing tools. She'd recently dyed her hair yellow. She looked like a sunflower, but that didn't cheer Selena up.

"I talked to her last night," Selena said.

"How is she?"

"She's fine," Selena said glumly.

Becket found the seam ripper for herself.

"She's getting ready for a gallery opening. The guy who did the nudes. She's worried that it's going to look crowded. His canvases are larger than he said they'd be. I told her you'd got me a space to paint at the Aviary, but that I'd have to bring in my own light because the window spots are all taken."

Becket put the seam ripper down.

"I don't want to be that friend who doesn't get you when you're sad, but what's wrong with that? You guys like each other and you talked about your day."

"It was the *way* we talked. Every time I call her, it's just *Good evening. How were things at the gallery?*" Selena affected an indifferent tone. "It's like we're strangers, or we started dating online and now we don't know how to break up with each other. That wasn't how it was here. We were together, a team. I could tell her anything. And the sex was amazing, but not just because she was a good lover but because it was *her*. And then she was leaving, and I thought I'd play it cool, not just be like, *Oh, my god, can I throw myself at your feet*. I know I can be a little extra. She thinks about things."

"A plus in a partner."

"I wanted her to know I'd thought about it. I wasn't just rushing in like a stalker. I have…had…my shit together. I was being"—Selena put the word in air quotes—"level-headed. Like her."

"I'm sorry." Becket was a patient friend.

"Then she was leaving, and I told her I *liked* her, and I wanted to see *where our relationship went*." Selena pulled her knees up and wrapped her arms around them.

"Not a horrible rejection."

"But as soon as I said it, I was like, *Fuck that. That's not me*. And I was going to tell her I'd move to New York with her in a second. Forget being cool. But she was totally on board with *let's see what happens*. She said we didn't have to be exclusive. She's not interested in making something work. I'm ready to get monogrammed napkins and she's not."

It happened all the time. Selena had turned down people who liked her. She'd strung a few people along, and she felt bad about it. Just because they'd shared a few magical nights together did not mean that Cadence Elgin of the Elgin Gallery wanted to throw everything away for a homeless, jobless painter.

"Call her and tell her." Becket reached around the sewing machine and patted Selena's hand. "Maybe she's waiting for you to declare your undying love."

"She's not."

Cade would be polite and embarrassed and kind. She'd try to let Selena down gently. That tenderness would hurt more than a simple *fuck off*, because Selena would remember when Cade had lavished that tenderness on her body and her soul. Or at least that's how it had felt in Cade's arms.

"It wouldn't have worked anyway," Selena said. "I'm not the kind of person she'd be with long-term." Tears welled up in her eyes.

"You're an amazing person," Becket said.

"Don't be nice. You know she wouldn't have stayed with me. I'm fine," Selena said, wiping her eyes. "I'll survive."

"Forget this corset," Becket said. "You want to get tots and Bloody Marys?"

Selena closed her eyes. Behind her eyelids she saw the painting she was working on: Cade in bed, half wrapped in Crown Royal bags, her hair still perfect. Selena wasn't done, but she'd captured the way Cade's body at rest remembered the tension of the day. She'd captured Cade's uprightness and her longing for release. And she'd captured *them*, although Selena wasn't in the frame. She'd caught the way Cade looked at her...the way she'd thought Cade had looked at her.

Selena wanted to lie on the floor and wail, but Becket really shouldn't have to put up with that. And Selena would probably get pins and bits of velvet stuck to her. It was time to get her own place: first, last, deposit, and utilities. Rent in Portland was ridiculous. If she saved up, she'd be on Becket's couch for months. There was only one way to get that money fast. Apparently, this was adulting: doing the right thing and still not getting what you wanted.

"Beck, I'm going to sell my paintings."

chapter 34

The cabin was cold when Selena and Becket arrived in two borrowed vans stuffed with packing supplies. Selena let them in.

"Let's get pictures of all these to Zenobious now," Becket said. "He's got to get them up on the promo stuff."

They looked around. Some of the paintings were propped in the living room where she and Cade had looked at them. The back room was full of the rest.

"You're amazing," Becket said, shaking her head. "How many are you going to sell?"

"All of them." Selena could remember every face she'd painted.

"Are you sure?"

"I'll keep the pictures of my dad and Ruth and you can keep *Geoffrey in Cobalt Teal.*"

"Of course, I keep Geoffrey. I stole him. He's mine. But *everything*? You're going to keep the picture of Cade, right?"

"Maybe." Selena ran her fingers along the top of *Sandy in the Blue Moon.*

"You'll want it later," Becket said.

"You said I was getting too angsty. I don't need a painting of Cade to remind me."

"I didn't say you were getting too angsty. I said you woke up angsty." Becket changed tactics. "I just think you should keep some of them. You won't be able to do a show or get commissions if you don't have work." Becket picked up a picture of herself. "This one's very handsome."

Selena smiled at Becket, flipping through a stack of paintings leaning against the wall. "I'll paint more."

"I like that." Becket still looked worried. "But you know you don't have to do this to get off my couch. I'll buy you an air mattress. You can save up for an apartment."

Selena wouldn't make a lot at the auction. She hadn't advertised. Her social media presence was an Instagram account with ten pictures of her father's dog. And she was an unknown with no provenance. Artists like that were lucky to make up the cost of supplies.

Selena picked up a portrait of a woman at a gas station, set it on the floor, knelt down, and wrapped it in a towel.

"Cade would kill me if she knew what we were wrapping these in," she said. "She said it had to be archival."

Cade had cared about her work. She'd recognized Selena's soul in her work. And she'd told Selena it didn't have to be perfect. It didn't even have to be good. *I thought I was enough.*

"Selena?"

Selena looked up. She didn't realize Becket had been talking to her.

"You're not doing this for Cade, are you?" The way

Becket asked told Selena that Becket was repeating the question.

"Of course not."

Becket sat down next to Selena. She seemed to be picking her words carefully. Finally, Becket said, "You don't think that if you make enough money or someone notices your work that she'll come back, right?"

"No."

Becket didn't look convinced.

"You did with Alex. You thought if your work was good enough, she'd love you."

Becket folded her legs cross-legged, making space for herself in the middle of the mess of paintings and last-minute packing supplies.

"*Are* you trying to make Cade love you?" Becket asked.

Selena had fantasized about it. She was standing on the stage in the Aviary, people crowding around her. She was a star. MoMA wanted her work. She'd pictured Cade calling her. *I didn't know how good you were. Come to New York.* But that wasn't the Cade she wanted. She wanted the Cade who told her everything she painted was beautiful because it was part of her.

"I wouldn't want her if she wanted me because I'm a good painter," Selena said. "Seriously. It's rent money. I remember painting every one of these. I don't need to keep them." She looked around the room. Too many memories. "I'm ready to let them go."

Selena tucked the corners of the towel around the woman at the gas station.

"Pass me the tape?" she asked.

Becket picked it up but didn't hand it to her.

"You know if Cade posts one thing about your work, you'll triple your profits. One post from the Elgin Gallery and you'll be a star."

Becket was right. Sometimes art sold because it was good. Sometimes it sold because it was famous. Sometimes it sold because someone thought it might get famous. She heard Cade's voice. *They only want to get close to my parents.*

"That's true," Selena said, taking the tape out of Becket's hands.

"Cade would do it for you."

Selena taped the painting she was wrapping.

"You're not going to ask her," Becket said.

"No." Selena didn't look at her.

"Shouldn't you get something out of having your heart broken by Cadence Elgin? And, in case I didn't say this before, you're having a lot of angst for a woman whose girlfriend has not *actually* broken up with her."

"You did say it before."

"Because I'm right."

"Everybody wants her because she's with the Elgin Gallery. I love her for who she is."

So simple. She didn't love Cade because of what Cade could do for her. And she didn't stop loving Cade because Cade was drifting away in a wake of polite voice mails and sporadic texts. Selena still wanted Cade to be happy. She wanted Cade to know that what they had together—even if it was short—wasn't about the gallery.

She waited for Becket to tell her to suck it up and ask. Cade wouldn't die because Selena asked her to tweet something, but Becket didn't speak.

When Selena was sure Becket wasn't going to, Selena said, "Before the auction, there's another thing I want to do."

"What's that?" Becket asked.

"I'm going to file a complaint against Alex at the academy." The thought of walking onto campus again and talking about Alex made her stomach knot, but she could handle it. "She should never have treated me like that. I don't want her to do that to anyone else."

Becket regarded Selena with a look Selena hadn't seen before.

"I'm proud of you," Becket said.

chapter 35

Selena parked her motorcycle in one of the
McLaughlin Academy parking lots, tucked her helmet
under her arm, and set off across campus. Students hurried
along the narrow sidewalks that wound around the thick
oak trees. Professors ambled in groups of two or three,
probably heading to lunch.

The dean's office was in a nineteenth-century house,
retrofitted to include spacious offices and a large waiting
room. Inside it was all polished wood and hushed footsteps. A secretary indicated Selena take a chair. A moment
later, the door to the dean's office opened.

The dean recognized Selena immediately.

"I'm so glad you came," she said. "Come in. Come in."
She shut the door behind her. "Still raining out there?"

They made a little small talk. It was raining. Not as
heavily as last year. Crocuses were coming up. There was
a nice patch of them by the gym. Selena should check
them out if she was parked in the north lot.

"I'll do that," Selena said.

Talking about crocuses calmed Selena's nerves a bit.

"Weather." The dean said when they seemed to have exhausted the subject. She pursed her lips. "Yes." She folded her arms on the table and leaned in, trading her reserved smile for a look of real concern. "You're here to talk about Alex Sarta."

Selena tucked her hands under her legs and nodded.

"That night at the gallery," the dean said.

"Not my best moment." Actually, it kind of had been. "TMI for the Art Walk."

"I thought you were amaz—"

The dean appeared to rethink what she was about to say, translating into something more dean-appropriate.

"There is no wrong time to come forward with a concern about sexual harassment. And I'm glad you're here now. Do you want to tell me about it?"

Selena had rehearsed her story more times than she'd rehearsed her presentation to the Gentrification Abatement Coalition. It never came out sounding quite right, but she took a deep breath and gave it her best shot. After she'd finished, she added, "I did consent. Alex didn't force me to sleep with her. She didn't say she'd get me thrown out if I didn't."

"But you did drop out because of her."

The dean's face said, *That shit is wrong*.

"That was my choice." She had to own it. She could have told Alex to leave her alone. She could have reported her back then. "But, yeah, she had a lot to do with it. And she had a lot to do with why I stopped painting. I get it that professors are supposed to criticize their students. That's how you learn. But it was different. I think she wanted me to fail, and that had everything to do with us being together."

"And Professor Sarta's colleagues didn't know that you were…involved." The dean tapped a pen against a notepad on her desk. "But after that night at the gallery several of them came to me and said they'd worried about her undermining you. There's a line between tough love and tearing someone down. They were never sure where you two were on that. Now they wish they'd done something."

"I wish I'd done something too. But I'm okay." Actually, she really was. A little shaky, but okay. She untucked her hands from beneath her legs and sat up straighter. "But I don't want her to do that to another student."

"I wish she hadn't done it to you," the dean said. "Would you file a formal complaint?"

"Yes," Selena said.

"Thank god. There've been others, but no one's been willing to come forward. They think Sarta will tank their careers. She needs to go down." The dean grimaced. "You did not hear me say that."

Selena smiled. They could be friends. The dean had the same fire in her eyes that Becket had when Selena told her she was dropping out.

"I didn't hear anything," Selena said.

"I know this may not be the time for you, but if you'd like to finish your degree, I can help you re-enroll. I could make sure you don't have any interactions with Sarta. And I'm not just being nice. Your professors say we need to get you back so we can say we're the school that graduated Selena Mathis."

chapter 36

Cade stood beside a couple at the Elgin Gallery. She stared into the near distance and nodded.

"This reminds me of Klimt," one of the men said.

Nothing about the large abstract reminded Cade of Klimt, but that was okay. If the man and his partner wanted to pay twelve thousand dollars for the piece, they could think it looked like whatever they liked.

"Yes," Cade said slowly.

"Or Maxfield Parrish," the other man said.

Maxfield Parrish? Were they even looking at the same painting?

"Yes," Cade said. "I see."

She stepped away so the men could discuss the purchase in private and went back to the counter where Amy and Cade's parents were drinking tea out of a Turkish coffee set and eating dolmas. Cade's father was wearing a top hat and monocle. Her mother wore some sort of beaded crown. Amy glowed in a yellow dress, striped leggings,

and matching fingerless gloves. They looked like something from *Alice in Wonderland*.

"Are you all on your break or something?" Cade
grumbled.

She wanted to sit down, but they'd taken up the three
metal stools, and, anyway, Cade didn't want to be associ-
ated with the smell of stuffed grape leaves.

"You can't eat your lunch at the counter." She glared at
her parents. "This isn't a dive bar."

"Oh, honey." Her mother popped one of the slimy green
packages into her mouth.

"Your parents love them," Amy said. "Try one. I used
za'atar this time."

It had been two weeks since Cade had left Portland. Two
weeks of sporadic texts with Selena. She was never sure
what Selena actually said. She got one message that read, *Ipn
fr Umy darregster.* It could have meant *I pine for you, darling.*
It could also mean *I finally got my motorcycle registered.*

Send a pic, Cade had texted.

In the photograph, Selena was standing in front of an
easel at the Aviary. Beautiful Adrien held a bottle of champagne. Becket was smiling next to them. Selena was back
in the artists' co-op. Cade wanted to hear all about it. And
every day, Cade thought of a million things she wanted
to say to Selena, but when they got on the phone Cade
remembered Selena's cool *If you'd like to see what happens,
I'll give it a try.* Their conversations felt stilted, with long
pauses followed by both of them speaking at the same
times, then saying, *You go. No, you.* They were like polite
drivers at a four-way stop. No one went anywhere.

"Have some tea. Your mom put weed in it," Amy said.

"You like to hang out with them." Cade nodded to her parents. "But this is *my* job."

Amy looked hurt.

"I'm sorry," Cade said. "No thank you. I don't want weed tea."

"Have a dolma?"

Cade ate one to be nice. It was tasty, but it caught in her throat. She just wanted the day to be over so she could lie in bed and stare at the ceiling.

"Your aura is all wrong," her mother said.

"Thanks."

Her mother poured her some tea.

"It's good for you."

"It's weed."

It was weed mixed with Earl Grey. It smelled a bit like Selena's perfume, floral and not floral at the same time, like flowers climbing a castle wall.

Cade was a lost cause. Why was love so hard? If only she'd known how much easier it was to be an almost-thirty-year-old almost-virgin...she'd have done everything exactly the same. One perfect night with Selena was worth it.

"If you guys want to hang out, I got the gallery," Cade said. "Go get a drink or something."

Across the room, the men were still considering the painting that did not look like Klimt or Parrish.

"Why don't you get drunk," her mother said kindly. "You look very sober."

Not a bad thing for a workday.

"Somber." Her father adjusted his monocle.

"It's Selena, from the funeral," Amy filled in for Cade's parents. "Cade misses her."

"That young woman who said all those nice things about your aunt's clitoris?" her mother said.

Words that should never be spoken out loud.

"I liked her eulogy," her mom added.

I did too.

"Did you have a romantic interlude?" her father asked.

Cade hoped he wasn't asking if they'd had sex. She shot Amy a look. *Don't talk to my parents about me.* Amy pushed the dolmas in Cade's direction.

"Your parents are worried about you," she said.

Cade's parents nodded.

"Your aura is dull," her mother said.

That probably was the problem. If she'd had a shiny aura, Selena might have wanted more than *let's see what happens.*

"Lusterless," her father added. "Lifeless."

"Depressed," Amy said.

"Thank you. That makes me feel better," Cade said.

"Talk to us," her mother said. "We're your parents."

That was a good reason *not* to talk to them. Cade took a sip of her tea. Probably a mistake, but it reminded her of Selena.

"Cade," Amy urged. "You've been walking around like someone died. At least tell them what happened, so they don't worry that you have cancer or something."

Cade sighed.

"Selena and I dated. Kind of. And we decided not to commit to anything when I went back to New York. We didn't break up; we just didn't make it a big thing."

Her parents looked at her expectantly. Cade looked back and forth between them. They'd been together forever.

Always eccentric. Always looking for the next alpaca farm to buy or the next ashram to join. Always perfect for each other.

Cade took another sip of her tea. "I had fun with her. She took me on her motorcycle. We drank whiskey. We talked." *We made love. I felt like I was free.* "When I was with her, I was someone else."

"Who you are is lovely," Cade's mother said.

Cade rubbed her temples.

"Who I am is your accountant."

"No!" her parents said in unison.

"You're our jewel," her mother said.

"Our Athena," her father said. "Our changeling."

"Because I got stolen from my boring parents."

"That's a joke, honey," her mother said. "We don't think that. You're not boring. You've never been boring."

"I wasn't enough for her." Cade looked down at the leaves floating at the bottom of her tea. They didn't tell her anything.

"And she didn't tell Selena how she felt," Amy added.

That would start a round of well-meaning advice Cade did not want.

Josiah saved her, strutting in the door in his usual three-piece suit and skinny hipster goatee.

"You faithless!" he said before he'd taken two steps in. "Cade Elgin, I am never going to play with you again."

Whatever this was about, *Thank you, Josiah.*

"Your daughter," he said to Cade's parents. "There are rules in love and war."

He clasped his hand to his heart. Cade had to smile.

"She has violated them all."

"What?" Cade said. "I'm not stealing your Senegalese painter. I thought about it. He's good, but you found him first."

Josiah pulled out his phone.

"If we were both on a quest for the Holy Grail, and I found it, I would keep it for myself." He adjusted his glasses. "Obviously. But I would not let you keep looking."

Cade furrowed her brow. The tea must be getting to her.

"What are you talking about?" she asked Josiah.

He held his phone out to her.

"At auction. Tonight. Online bidding allowed. You could not possibly buy all of them or show all of them. And yet, you harpy, you did not tell me."

Cade stared at the screen.

"What is it?" Amy asked.

It was Cade, sleepy, naked, wrapped in a quilt of Crown Royal bags.

The door opened, and a courier came in with a package. Obviously, a painting. Far too large to ship via regular mail. Unsolicited. Artists were always sending the gallery work like that. Hope was dumb.

Cade's father called to the intern in the back room. "Would you unwrap that for us and find some place to put it for now."

"Let me see?" Amy reached for Josiah's phone.

Cade was still staring at it. It was the Aviary website. She scrolled up and down. There was a photograph of Selena, a short bio, and dozens of her paintings. Maybe all of them. Up for auction that night. The portrait of Cade was the only one marked NFS. Not for sale.

Cade's parents and Amy all leaned in.

"What is it?" Amy asked again.

"Your friend and I," Josiah said, with exaggerated composure, "have a friendly competition to bring new talent to light, and we found an artist that we both liked. A mystery. Name scraped off the canvas. Skill of a grand master. Soul of an angel. All that stuff. But your friend, your daughter"—he pretended to scowl at Cade—"told me she was an unknown. No one has any idea who she is."

He gently took the phone from Cade and set it on the counter for the others to see.

"But she posed for them. You knew all along."

"Excuse me?" The intern appeared in the door, the painting in her hands, facing away from them. "Do you want to see this?"

"That's okay," Cade said.

The intern hesitated.

"It's you."

She turned the painting around so it faced them. It was the same portrait, like Cade was looking in a mirror to the past. Her heart filled with longing. *Selena*. It was exquisite work, even better than Selena's older paintings. It captured everything Cade had felt that night, love and tenderness and shy hope and happiness.

"It's called," the intern read off the back, "'My Heart Breaks When You Turn Away.'"

"Is that by your inamorata?" Cade's father asked.

Then everyone was talking at once. The intern set the painting against the wall. Cade's father moved it into better light. Her mother exclaimed over the brushwork. Josiah called Cade a ruthless woman. Amy said, "God, that's totally you!" Cade wasn't paying attention. She was just repeating the name over and over.

My Heart Breaks When You Turn Away.

Finally, they all turned around to stare at her. Cade gulped her tea.

"She's in love with you," Cade's mother said.

Cade started to say no, a painting wasn't proof of love no matter how good it was. But even Josiah was nodding.

"Her soul is on that canvas," he said.

"I didn't know she was selling her work," Cade whispered.

"Right," Josiah drawled.

"She didn't even want to show it."

What would it be like for Selena to auction everything she'd done, the work she'd thought she'd lost? Selena had just begun to paint again. Auctions could be fast, cruel affairs. She'd talked to artists who'd broken down after auctions where they made thousands of dollars. It wasn't the money. It was seeing their work whipped away like so many stocks and bonds. And they didn't put half as much soul in their work as Selena did. Selena had never been through that. Cade could see her in the Aviary. She'd be wearing something fabulous, fake fur and glittering pants. She'd be excited and nervous, smiling, gorgeous, but would she be ready? Cade wanted to be there with her, to stand behind her and wrap her arms around Selena as the auctioneer began, to whisper in Selena's ear, *Whatever you've made is beautiful because it's yours.*

"Oh," Cade gasped.

Cade had to be there, and there was no way.

"I told her I wanted to wait and see what happened," Cade said.

"What?" her mother asked.

"She said she didn't want to commit to anything, but I said it too. I said I was busy and long distance was hard. It never worked out."

And she loves me. Cade wasn't misreading the painting.

"I love her." So simple and so true. "And I fucked up." Also simple and also true. "She thinks I don't want anything serious. She thinks *I* just want to wait and see. I said we didn't have to be exclusive." Cade hung her head. "It's her first auction. Those things are terrible, and I can't be there with her."

"Ridiculous," her father said. "You're an Elgin. You can be wherever you want to be."

Optimistic and wrong.

"When has an Elgin stayed at work when love was at stake?" Her father gestured like a Shakespearean actor. "You *are* motorcycles. You are whiskey! You are a shooting star winging your way to your lover."

If only.

"I can call her."

"But why not a grand gesture?" her father asked.

"Because I'm in New York, and the auction starts at eight."

"And it's only 2:45," her mother said. "Don't worry. Calendria, that nice woman from the funeral, she said her nephew's ex-girlfriend works for Delta. If we ever needed a last-minute flight, the universe will provide."

"It's almost three," Cade said. "Can you even get across

the country that fast? I would literally have to get on a plane in ten minutes."

Maybe she could get a flight for tomorrow or the next day. Maybe if she flew standby.

"Everything works out the way it's supposed to," Cade's mother said. "Trust me. You get a cab to JFK. I'll call Calendria."

Cade looked at the painting, then at her parents.

"We'll keep it safe," her father said.

"Now go," her mother said.

There was no way Cade's mother's friend's nephew's ex-girlfriend was going to magically produce a direct— it had to be direct to make it on time—flight from JFK to Portland and get Cade on it in the next ten minutes. Cade must have been high. She grabbed her coat and ran for the door.

chapter 37

Selena leaned against the railing of the Aviary balcony. Becket stood beside her, holding one of Zen's cocktails.

"Not all bad," she remarked. "Kind of tastes like lemongrass that hates you."

Inside, the Aviary sparkled. Hundreds of folding chairs replaced the usual settees. Lights trimmed the auctioneer's stage. The auction attendees were dressed in gowns and suits. Selena wore the sweatshirt Cade had loaned her that first night on the patio. She watched the attendees move around the work set up around the perimeter of the space. Artists stood by their work, trying to have nonchalant but meaningful conversations with potential buyers. Selena had heard Beautiful Adrien talking about *the dominant paradigm of potentiality*. On any other night, she would have called bullshit. Tonight, she'd just nodded and given him the thumbs-up.

"We've never had so many people," Becket added. "I am

so glad I'm performing, not selling. Everyone in there is popping Ativan. How are you doing?"

"Fine."

"For real?"

Selena's work stood by itself in the far corner of the Aviary. It would sell or it wouldn't. She didn't feel like hovering over it, explaining the work to people who were looking for something to go with their green carpet.

She was fine when it came to selling her work.

"For real."

"You know if it doesn't sell, it's not because it's not good," Becket said.

"I'll make enough for first, last, and deposit," Selena said. "I'll get off your couch."

Selena didn't care if she slept on a couch or on a yoga mat or a flat in the Pearl District. But Becket deserved her privacy, and Selena kept losing her shoes in the sea of sequins and chiffon that covered Becket's floor. She would have lost her clothes too (Becket's floor was their birthplace; they'd be like salmon swimming home) except she'd been wearing Cade's sweatshirt for two weeks.

The lights in the Aviary dimmed and came back on, signaling the beginning of the evening's events. One of the Fierce Lovely troupe appeared in the doorway to the balcony holding Becket's signature gold tailcoat.

"Beck, are you ready?" he asked.

"I've got to go," Becket said apologetically.

"You're going to rock this," Selena said.

Selena moved to the doorway, standing half in, half out of the Aviary. The crowd took their seats. The lights dimmed again. At a cue from Zen, the DJ started Becket's music, and Becket descended from the ceiling, belayed by one of her troupe mates and shining in gold. She was fabulous as always, but nothing sparkled for Selena.

After Becket, a few more Fierce Lovely members performed. Then the auctioneer, a drag king with a perfectly coiffed pompadour, stepped up on stage.

"Welcome," the auctioneer boomed. "Ladies, gentlemen, gentlepersons, and all you wonderful creatures in between. I am here to stun you with artistic masterpieces. To help me are my lovely assistants who will be spotting those paddles as you bid. You will never regret the purchase of fine art." He introduced his assistants, four drag queens in full sequined gowns. One stood behind a computer at the side of the stage. "We'll be taking internet bids as well," the auctioneer went on. "So bid high and bid fast, friends. LA is on the line. New York is on the line. Milan is waiting to outbid you. Now shall we begin?"

Selena watched for an hour. At least she stood in the doorway facing the stage. She couldn't say whose art had auctioned or how much it made. Finally, she pushed off the doorframe and headed for the exit. Everyone was focused on the stage. There was no point in pretending she was too. Outside she walked to the end of the block and sat down on the curb. The motion-sensitive streetlight flickered to life.

Is this what you wanted me to learn, Ruth? Pay rent and get a new phone?

She saw Cade standing behind the counter at Satisfaction Guaranteed, looking like British royalty trying not to notice the paparazzi. And she saw Cade sprawled naked on her bed, her body flushed, hair damp with sweat.

I just needed another month. Selena looked up at the cloudy sky. *It just went too fast. We had something. I love her.*

The streetlight went off.

Selena wanted to lie on the damp sidewalk, but that was dramatic, and someone would probably see her and try to have an intervention. She'd have to explain that she hadn't drunk too much of Zen's liquor and she wasn't waiting to be run over by a skateboarder, she was just sad because she'd fucked up when she was trying so hard not to.

She stared at the gravel and little bits of litter that had collected along the curb. The sidewalk was cold beneath her.

She checked her phone again. There was only the one message from Cade. *Thank you for the painting. It's lovely.*

It was lovely. How could it not be? It was Cade. But *Thank you for the painting. It's lovely?* That's what people said when they got a nice birthday card. Selena's heart ached. Cade of all people could look at a painting and understand its meaning, not that you had to be Cadence Elgin to read the meaning in *My Heart Breaks When You Turn Away.* Selena had mixed her desperate yearning into that paint. Her love was in the paint. Her tears had streaked the oil. She'd signed her name, clear and legible. And Cade had texted, *Thank you for the painting. It's lovely.*

She cradled the phone in her hands, looking through Cade's texts. Their story in little bits. *What kind of coffee? Can't wait to see you. Last night was heaven.* Then *Thank you for the painting. It's lovely.* It was too hard. She selected all the messages, hesitated for a moment, then touched delete. Then she opened speed dial. Cade's number. It was midnight in New York, but what Selena had to say was short.

Whatever it was they were doing, this shadow of a relationship, this long, drawn-out goodbye: she couldn't bear it.

I love you, and I can't do this. She touched Cade's number.

"Selena." Cade picked up on the first ring, breathless.

Selena clutched the phone. There weren't a lot of reasons people were breathless at midnight. Cade might be exercising, but there were other possibilities. Selena hadn't even thought about Cade hooking up with someone else. She clutched her arms around her knees.

"I'm sorry," Selena said.

I love you, and I can't.

"Where are you?" Cade gasped.

Did Cade think Selena was outside her building? Had she become Alex, showing up where she wasn't wanted?

"It's okay. I'm in Portland." She rocked back and forth, curled in on herself as tightly as she could. "I just need to talk to you for a minute."

"Are you at the auction?" Cade's voice was full of urgency.

"Yes?" It came out as a question.

"Where?"

How could it matter?

"I'm outside," Selena said, hope rising in her chest, even while her brain told her no.

The street was quiet, but she heard someone running from the Aviary, their footsteps clanging on the metal staircase. Selena stood up.

She would have recognized that silhouette anywhere. Cade. Her overcoat flapping, running toward her.

"Am I too late?" Cade gasped, her eyes full of hope.

"For the auction?" Selena was so surprised, it came out sounding confused, not happy.

Cade's face fell.

"For you." Cade bit her lip, her face suddenly taut with worry. "The painting. It's beautiful. I thought…"

The surprise that had held Selena rooted in place for a second evaporated. She flung her arms around Cade, cradling Cade and falling into Cade's arms at the same time.

"Oh, Cade."

Cade clung to her.

"I was upstairs looking for you," Cade said breathlessly. "I didn't say what I meant to say when I left. I meant to say I love you. I'll move to Portland. You could live with me in New York. I know we've only known each other for a month, and you wanted to keep it casual, and you're probably thinking I'm a stalker, but I got the painting. And I knew I'd fucked it up. Even if you don't—" Cade caught her breath. "Even if you don't want what I want, I want you to know. I want you to know how amazing you are. Last month, being with you, that was the happiest I've ever been. I thought that kind of happiness was for other people." Cade wiped at her eyes. "Maybe it is, but when I saw your work, I thought maybe…"

"I love you," Selena whispered against Cade's cheek. Over and over. "I'll go with you wherever you want. That's what I wanted to say, but I didn't want to freak you out. Go big or go home, but I thought *be chill and don't fuck this up.*"

"We were already engaged," Cade said with a soft, teary laugh.

"I should have just set the date." Selena's heart expanded with love. "I wanted to tell you how I felt, but I thought... *this is too important to mess up*. You don't make crazy decisions, so I tried to be cool, but *that* was messing it up. That wasn't me."

"I was in New York this morning." Cade looked at Selena. Her eyes were moist but there was that spark of humor that Selena loved. "I got the painting, and I had to see you. My mom said her friend's nephew's ex-girlfriend could get me a flight to Portland if I got to the airport in ten minutes. Things don't work like that." A smile spread across Cade's face. "So, I ran for the airport. Crazy."

"And she got you a ticket?"

"First class. It was waiting for me at the counter. And once I got up into the air I realized, I was so massively high I didn't know my own name."

Selena squeezed Cade's waist and kissed her.

"I would have loved to see that," she said. "How did you get high?"

"My mother. I tried to text you, but I couldn't figure out how to turn on my phone, and then I was here, and not high, and if you want to choose the monogrammed napkins, I'll say yes."

With that, Cade pulled Selena into a kiss so deep the world disappeared. Selena's soul expanded. They were in love, and their love filled the street. It soared above the lampposts. It was brighter than the Aviary lights. It was bigger than the sky.

I love you. I love you. I love you.

When they finally drew apart, Cade stroked Selena's cheek, a worry crossing her face.

"You're auctioning your work."

She hadn't told Cade.

"How did you know?"

"Josiah saw the website."

"You didn't tell him?"

"I didn't know," Cade said. "Josiah said I was faithless because we'd both been trying to find the woman who painted Ruth's portrait, and I didn't tell him that I had. How did it go?"

"I don't think it's gone up yet," Selena said.

Cade stroked Selena's back. "It's yours to sell"—Cade frowned—"but why?"

They still had their arms around each other. Nothing else mattered.

"Rent money," Selena said. "Becket wants her couch back. I suppose I should go in and watch."

"Your work should sell for millions." Cade spoke slowly. "But good work doesn't always get traction. People buy what's trendy. People buy what they think their friends want."

"What goes with their carpet."

Cade rolled her eyes. "Sad but true." She stepped back, still holding Selena's hands. "If I go in there and tell them the Elgin Gallery is buying a piece, you'll go viral. It'll triple whatever you were going to make or more. You shouldn't need that, but it's true."

"I know."

Every artist in the Aviary would kill for a chance to be in the Elgin Gallery. They'd kill to be mentioned in an Elgin Gallery tweet. They'd kill to buy Cadence Elgin a drink from across the bar.

Selena cupped Cade's face and planted a soft kiss on her lips.

"But I want to do this on my own," she said, "And I don't want you because you're Cadence Elgin of the Elgin Gallery. I want you for you."

They kissed again. Then Selena took Cade's hand, and they climbed the stairs and stepped into the warmth of the Aviary.

"Our final artist," the auctioneer was saying, "Selena Mathis. We'll begin with *William with Sunflowers*. This is a three-by-five oil."

Becket caught sight of them. Her mouth dropped in surprise, then she grinned, pointed to Cade, and mouthed, *Fuck yeah!*

"We'll begin the bidding at five hundred," the auctioneer said.

Cade squeezed Selena's hand.

From where Selena stood, she caught strains of whispered conversation.

"That's beautiful."

"Five hundred," the auctioneer said again.

Another person whispered, "I've never heard of her."

"Do I hear four-fifty?" the auctioneer continued. "Four hundred and the big five O. This is a beautiful piece, folks. My assistants are placed around the room to take your bids."

The price dropped. Four hundred. Three-fifty. Three hundred. Less than the cost of materials. A man in the back waved his paddle. The auctioneer tried to bring the price up, but it stayed at three hundred.

"Going once. Going twice. Sold to bidder 103."

Selena thought she didn't care about the money, but her painting's failure stabbed at her heart.

"The money doesn't mean anything." Cade stood behind Selena with her arms around Selena's waist. "You are amazing." Cade made each word a sentence.

The auctioneer's assistants brought another painting to the stage.

"Do I hear four hundred?"

The assistant standing behind the computer called out, "Online bid. Four hundred from New York."

A man in the back raised to five.

"Online bid. Six hundred. Minneapolis," the assistant called out.

A few paddles went up.

A thousand.

Two thousand.

"What's happening?" Selena turned to look at Cade.

"What's supposed to happen," Cade said.

"Online bid. Six thousand. New York," the assistant called out. "Online bid. Eight thousand. Miami."

The room sang with excitement. The Portland bidders flung their paddles in the air, but they couldn't compete with the online bids.

"This is all you," Cade whispered.

As exciting as it was to hear the price rise, it was Cade's lips brushing her ear that made Selena tremble and her knees go weak.

The bidding closed. The auctioneer didn't count up the total sales for each person, but the artists did.

Becket flew across the room, holding her phone up, open to the calculator.

"One point two million! *Million!*" She grabbed Selena

and squeezed her so hard Selena's breath rushed out. Becket released her and looked at Cade. "Did you do this, Cade?"

"I would have, but no." Cade was beaming.

People swarmed around Selena, taking her picture, congratulating her, and asking about commissioning work. For a moment, the crowd separated her from Cade.

"It's your night," Cade called out. "Enjoy it."

But it wasn't her night without Cade in her arms.

"Come here." Selena reached through the crowd and pulled Cade to her. "This is our night."

It was after two when they finally stumbled into the boutique hotel room Cade had rented.

Selena wriggled out of her sweatshirt—Cade's sweatshirt—and handed it to her.

"I wore it every day."

"If I'd had one of your corsets, I would have worn it," Cade said.

"You would have looked lovely."

Selena switched off the overhead light, and they were bathed in the light of the city skyline. Cade looked gloriously happy, and the dark circles under her eyes made her look like a soulful Norwegian actor who had been in New York that morning and had flown across the country, high, on a first-class ticket from a woman she didn't know, so she could declare her love to a woman she wasn't quite sure would say yes.

"Are you tired?" Selena said.

"God, yes." Cade rested her forehead on Selena's shoulder.

Selena reached for the hem of Cade's shirt and lifted it over her head.

"How about," Selena said, "we get naked, fall asleep until noon, order champagne, and then I show you how much I missed you?" She trailed her fingernails up Cade's back. "And you show me how much you missed me too."

"Yes," Cade said. "Yes. Yes."

Naked together, Cade's body felt so good, Selena almost went back on her suggestion. The way Cade's hand trailed over Selena's body told her Cade wouldn't mind if Selena rolled her onto her back and ravished her. But the beautiful thing was they also had time. They could wake up together like a couple who always woke up together.

"I love you," Selena whispered.

"I love you."

Cade wriggled closer. Selena loved Cade's muscular back, her hard thighs, her strength, her vulnerability.

"You know," Cade said dreamily, "with the kind of money you made, you could probably still buy back the house, maybe even the store. There are deadlines, and then there're deadlines for rich people. That kind's easier."

Selena rested her cheek on Cade's chest.

"Yeah," Selena said thoughtfully. "Absolutely, we can keep it if you want to. And we should do that if it's a good investment. But I was thinking…what would you say if I said I wanted to do something else? Something new? Something we do together? I don't think Ruth wanted us to live her dream. I think she wanted us to live our dreams."

epilogue

Cade stood by a twelve-foot-tall, blown-glass clitoris illuminated from the bottom with an ever changing show of LED lights. Behind her, summer evening light spilled in through high windows. Selena stood on a platform in front of the crowd that packed the opening of the Artemisia Studio. Part gallery of art exploring female sexuality, part studio space for emerging artists: it was the Aviary in New York with giant clitorises and Selena's new collection of portraits. She had painted customers from Satisfaction Guaranteed. Selena had flown back to Portland for a few weeks to paint them, sleeping on Becket's couch because they'd rented Ruth's house to Zen and his new partner.

"Thank you for being here," Selena said.

She looked gorgeous in tuxedo slacks and a jeweled corset that Becket had made for the occasion.

"I am so excited to welcome you to the Artemisia Studio. As some of you know, I grew up in a trailer. A lovely trailer with a view of the desert. My father"—she gestured to her father, who stood near the front looking proud and uncomfortable—"taught me to love art. Thank you. And I made it to art school and through...recently. Diploma is in the mail."

The crowd clapped.

"But it was a long trip. School, materials, studio space; it's all expensive. And it's doubly hard for people who want to explore things that society tells us...maybe don't."

Selena looked up at the vulva mobile rotating slowly in the summer breeze. The crowd chuckled appreciatively.

"So, this will be a space where new artists doing groundbreaking work will find a home, mentors, and support."

Cade already had a long list of past Elgin Gallery artists ready to coach Selena's emerging artists.

"But before I let the first generation of Artemisia Studio artists speak for themselves, Cade..." Selena held out her hand.

Cade made her way to the front of the room.

Everyone knew who Cade was, but no one had given her their elevator speech that night. People had been too busy giving Selena their elevator speeches. Cade loved seeing Selena at the center of everyone's attention, like Selena deserved.

Selena took Cade's hand. Cade would never get tired of that. When they were a hundred and twenty-nine, she'd still be holding Selena's hand.

"I want to thank my partner, Cade, for everything she has done for me, with me, for being my everything."

She kissed Cade, then raised their clasped hands above

their heads in victory. The crowd applauded. People cheered. It felt like the whole world was smiling at them. Cade felt herself blush with happiness.

"Welcome," Selena said, "to this wonderful new adventure."

about the author

Karelia Stetz-Waters (she/her) writes happily-ever-afters for women who love women. Her novels include Lambda Literary Award and Golden Crown Literary Society finalist *Forgive Me If I've Told You This Before.*

She lives her own happily-ever-after in Oregon with her wife of over twenty years. Karelia has a BA in comparative literature from Smith College and an MA in English literature from the University of Oregon, and she currently teaches English at Linn-Benton Community College. Karelia loves to hear from readers. Be sure to stay in touch by signing up for Karelia's newsletter, available on her website.

You can learn more at:
kareliastetzwaters.com
Twitter @K_StetzWaters
Facebook.com/KareliaStetzWaters
Instagram @KareliaStetzWaters

reading group guide

When I teach creative writing, I teach my students the difference between plot and theme. Plot is what happens. Theme is what it means. The theme of *Satisfaction Guaranteed* can be summed up by one of my favorite quotes of all time:

> "To look at a thing is very different from seeing a thing. One does not see anything until one sees its beauty."
>
> —*Oscar Wilde*

I didn't start *Satisfaction Guaranteed* thinking I was going to write a story about the transformative power of being seen for your true self. I thought I'd write about a sex toy store because that would be funny. I got the idea while shopping at She Bop, my favorite sex toy store in Portland. My dog had eaten one of my best vibrators. (Don't worry. The dog's fine.) I had to explain this to the salesperson to stop them telling me about all the features of the vibrator I was holding.

"It's okay," I said. "I've had this one before. It's just that my dog ate it."

The salesperson nodded sympathetically. "My ex's rottweiler ate three of my dildos. That's probably why I broke up with her."

I had to write about a place where you could have this conversation with a stranger.

And so Satisfaction Guaranteed was born. Google She Bop and you'll see what it looks like after Selena cleans it up: colorful toys spread out on clean shelves. A bright, cheerful atmosphere that says *have fun* and *don't be nervous*. It's one of my happy places.

I always do research before I write, so I started reading up on female sexuality. I took pleasure education classes. I talked to sex educators. I read about the pleasure gap: the gap between how often men orgasm and how often women orgasm. Only fifty-seven percent of women report having an orgasm all or most of the time, while ninety-five percent of men report having an orgasm all or most of the time.[1] That's a big difference.

But the pleasure gap diminishes to almost nothing when women have sex with other women.[2]

When I learned this, I felt like you do when you read a great book or find some awesome life hack. (I'm still looking for a life hack for peeling mangos, so if you find one, let me know.) I wanted to run out and tell everyone. *Guess what I learned? Try having sex like a lesbian!*

---

1   Laurie Mintz. *Becoming Cliterate: Why Orgasm Equality Matters—and How to Get It.* HarperOne, 2017.

2   Malachi Willis, Kristen Jozkowski, Wen-Juo Lo, and Stephanie Sanders. "Are Women's Orgasms Hindered by Phallocentric Imperatives?" *Archives of Sexual Behavior* 47 (2018). 10.1007/s10508-018-1149-z.

Why is lesbian-esque sex so great for women? Because it's all about the clitoris. Of course, lots and lots and lots of women like penetration. Cade would have to rethink Satisfaction Guaranteed's inventory if they didn't. But the clitoris is where it's really at.

The clitoris, in case you didn't know, is shaped like a wishbone with two "bulbs" and two "legs" which flare out on either side of the vagina. It's about nine centimeters or 3.5 inches, give or take. Everyone is different. That's about the size of the non-erect penis. It becomes erect when aroused. And it's almost entirely inside the body. The little pearl on the outside is just the tip. Literally.

I didn't know that until I started writing *Satisfaction Guaranteed*. Now that I'm obsessed with collecting clitoris merch—clitoris models, clitoris-printed dresses, clitoris stencils—I can't believe that just a little while ago I didn't know what my own sexual organ looked like. (By the way, if you have a line on good clit stuff, tell me where I can find it.)

But we're not taught about the clitoris. Often little girls aren't even taught the words *vulva* or *clitoris*. We say boys have penises and girls have vaginas. But the clitoris is the woman's version of the penis, not the vagina. That's why Selena insists that people use the right words. It's important. Talking about women's sexuality without talking about the vulva or clitoris is like talking about men while pretending the penis doesn't exist. That's not just a metaphor. The clitoris and the penis develop from the same embryonic tissue. For the first eight weeks of life, they're the same thing.

Wow! I wanted to tell the world. And how better to tell

the world than to write a woman-loving-woman sex toy store romance? I was ready to be everyone's wise, lesbian sex Yoda.

But stories have a way of taking on a life of their own. The more I wrote, the more *Satisfaction Guaranteed* became a story about how we see ourselves and what can happen when someone sees our true gifts. Cade is worried about her lack of sexual experience, but it isn't just about sex. She's convinced that she's boring. People only like her for what she can do for them. Meanwhile, Selena can't see that she is an amazing painter, and she's not a fuck-up. She's just gone through a tough time.

I've been there. I think we all have. I used to think I couldn't stand up for myself. I wasn't adventuresome. People only liked me because I was unfailingly polite. Turns out, none of that was true. (Well, people don't mind that I'm polite, but it's not why I get invited to parties.)

Selena's ability to paint a person's true essence and Cade's ability to spot talented artists symbolize the book's theme. Wonderful things happen when we see people's beauty. The happy ending isn't just Cade and Selena falling in love with each other. It's each of them falling in love with themselves. They can do that because they've seen themselves reflected in each other's eyes.

Some of my favorite scenes to write are the ones in which one character is thinking how plain or dull they are. Then the chapter changes and we see that person through their lover's eyes. Of course, the lover sees all their great qualities.

And it turns out, that theme isn't at odds with my sudden desire to become everyone's sex coach. I've always said that I don't really know my characters until I've seen them have sex. Selena tells Cade that if she were a ghost, she'd watch people having sex because she wants to see the moment when they can't hide who they are.

We get a lot of messages telling us not to live our full sexuality. The media tells us we're too fat, too old, too prude, too promiscuous. We should wait until marriage and look like a porn star. Wax it all off! Don't have a disability. Oh, and don't forget, being queer is a sin.

Bullshit. All of it.

In fact, even though I was styling myself as a sexual expert, even though I'd been having great sex with my wife for twenty-plus years, I discovered I too had more to learn. I too had issues that kept me from reaching my full sexual potential. (If you go to my website, you can see me telling an audience of four hundred all about it at a Valentine's Day edition of the Mystery Box Show: True Stories All about Sex.)

There is no "wrong" sex between enthusiastically consenting adults, provided they safeguard their own and each other's mental and physical health. If you have a fetish for licking mashed potatoes off your lover's knees, you go for it! YOLO! When we acknowledge our desires, we see an important part of who we are. When we celebrate those desires, we celebrate our true selves.

When Selena embraces her true self, she realizes she doesn't want to live Ruth's dreams, she has her own. When Cade embraces her true self, she's finally able to see that her parents do love her and she is an Elgin and, for her, being an Elgin means both being responsible and running for the airport, high as a kite, so that she can declare her love to Selena.

As I put the final touches on the last chapter of *Satisfaction Guaranteed*, I want to see more of Cade and Selena. Cade still has much to discover about her sexuality. And Selena gets the privilege of being with Cade on that journey. How wonderful to initiate the woman you love into new heights of pleasure! I know I'll write those scenes and share them with my subscribers. If you aren't getting the HAPPILY newsletter, be sure to sign up on my website and stay tuned for the next chapters. I love Cade and Selena too much to let them go. I hope you do too. But more importantly, I want you to love YOU. You are a beautiful, perfect being, unlike anyone who has come before or anyone who will come after you. See that. Celebrate that. And treat yourself to something special from your favorite feminist sex toy store.

RECOMMENDED READING

Becoming Cliterate: Why Orgasm Equality Matters— and How to Get It, Laurie Mintz
Come as You Are: The Surprising New Science That Will Transform Your Sex Life, Emily Nagoski
She Comes First: The Thinking Man's Guide to Pleasuring a Woman, Ian Kerner

RECOMMENDED VIEWING

OMGyes video series: omgyes.com

discussion questions

1. Cade feels like her parents don't appreciate her and only love her because she runs their gallery. To what degree do you think that's true? Would Cade have been happier if she'd had accountants for parents?

2. Selena considers herself a "fuck-up." Is she? What things in her life symbolize the fact that she hasn't quite mastered adulting?

3. Cade is almost thirty and she's only had sex six times, and she feels bad about it. Would she feel the same way if there were no societal expectations about when and how often a person has sex? What pressures, expectations, and judgments does society place on women's sexuality? On young women? On older women? What pressures have you felt?

4. What roles do Selena's friends play in her life? Are they good friends?

5. Cade and Selena's ex-lover Professor Alex Sarta are both in the art world, but they play very different roles in Selena's journey as an artist. How are they different? How is Cade's appreciation for Selena's art different from Alex's appreciation?

6. Before Selena cleans up Satisfaction Guaranteed, Cade thinks the store would make a lot of people feel out of place. Why does she think this? Have you been to sex toy stores? What made you feel comfortable or uncomfortable?

7. Why can't Selena see that she's a great painter? Have you ever had the experience of being really good at something and not knowing it?

8. When Cade goes back to New York, she and Selena both play it cool, pretending they aren't *that* into each other and saying they'll just *see what happens*. Why is this so hard on them? After all, they didn't have a huge fight or breakup.

9. Throughout the book, Selena wants to save Satisfaction Guaranteed so that she can work there and live in Ruth's house, but at the end of the book she decides she wants something different. Why does she change her mind?

10. When Selena paints someone, she captures who they truly are and presents that image with love and acceptance. If Selena painted you, what would the portrait be like?